AFTERSHOCK

AFTERSHOCK

A QUAKE RUNNER: ALEX KAYNE THRILLER

J. KEVIN TUMLINSON

CHAPTER ONE

Being "Fugitive Number One" was sometimes a grueling sort of life to live.

The constant running and hiding, watching over her shoulder, obsessively observing everyone and everything around her, assessing threats—and then, if it came to it, either dealing with those threats or hitting the road all over again. It was a transient sort of life, and one that most fugitives couldn't sustain for more than a few months, at best. Those who lasted years had an edge.

Alex Kayne had an edge.

QuIEK—the Quantum Integrated Encryption Key, an artificial intelligence so advanced it operated like a skeleton key for any digital system she encountered—was the sort of tool that could keep a fugitive off of law enforcement radar indefinitely. And so far, she'd proven that to be true. For nearly three years now, Kayne had used her invention to keep ahead of the whole alphabet of Federal agencies in the US, plus those of foreign nations, all of whom seemed to want QuIEK for their own questionable purposes. She couldn't allow that. It was one of the reasons she'd taken her software and gone on the run.

The other reason was that she'd been framed for the murder of her business partner, Adrian Ballard, and accused of treason and espionage for a foreign government. She was entirely innocent of all of those charges. But she was guilty of a lot of other crimes, since going on the run.

It's impossible not to become a criminal when you're a fugitive in the wind.

Now, roaming the world under a digital cloak of invisibility, she *could* just find a spot to retire to, and let the world move on without her while she soaked up the sun on a beach, and lived a low-key life of relative luxury, forever outside the grasp of those who would lock her away and use her life's work for whatever evil purpose they had in mind.

But *nah*.

Instead, here she was shivering against the cold of a polar vortex, in *Texas* of all places, monitoring the comings and goings of a security team as they continued to keep anyone from entering a building with more than two-million-dollars worth of protective measures in place. Measures meant to keep out thieves, spies, and even the likes of Alex Kayne.

As she sipped coffee from an insulated mug, she tapped a gloved finger on her phone's screen, and cycled through everything QuIEK had discovered for her so far. She was shaking from the cold, despite the hot beverage and the coat, and the irony of doing so while using software she referred to as "quake" didn't escape her.

The facility she was planning to infiltrate had more and better security than most government buildings. It even topped casino security—which Kayne had long ago determined might be the epitome of technological paranoia. Casinos employed tech such as facial recognition, gait recognition, even predictive algorithms that essentially read body language and pupil dilation. Most militaries worldwide could take a page from the Vegas book of security.

But this place...

Curie Motors, Inc. was initially founded in Silicon Valley back in the early 2000s, as a pet project by billionaire Ross Eckhart. The company launched with the plan to build electric vehicles for the masses, to bring a new era of roadway tech that was sustainable, good for the environment, and affordable for all. This, of course, made Eckhart and Curie Motors a lot of political and industrial enemies. The company was plagued by a barrage of FTC and other filings for years. Ever-increasing taxes and intrusion on their business from state and local governments didn't help.

But the final straw was when Lee Coben—former tech industry entrepreneur turned domestic terrorist—attempt to literally nuke Silicon Valley out of existence. That sort of thing tended to put a bad taste in one's mouth.

And it tended to send one packing. Eckhart had his Palo Alto facility shuttered, and everything in it crated up and shipped to a new, multi-billion-dollar facility in Texas, practically within the month.

In reality, Eckhart had been funding the build for the new facility for more than two years, but had initially billed it to the press as an expansion, not a move. Industry insiders, as well as a healthy chunk of people on Twitter, had, of course, speculated that Eckhart would leverage the new facility to force California to shift away from trying to tax Curie Motors out of existence. But after taking a deep look into the company, including some of the files hidden on a private server, Kayne knew the plan had always been to move. Ross Eckhart wanted to give a middle finger to the people he saw as his enemies, and taking several billion dollars in tax revenue away from the state was a pretty good solid swipe. Moving Curie Motors from Silicon Valley to the Silicon Prairie was Eckhart's F-U to California, and to special interest groups.

All of that was interesting and intriguing, in its way. Kayne had been part of the Silicon Valley set herself, back when she and Adrian Ballard had been running Kayne's own tech company, Populus. She knew how rough things could get—the sense of entitlement that local, state, and federal governments seemed to feel toward the intellectual property (and the earnings) of a tech company. She couldn't blame Eckhart one bit for his move, and sort of admired him for the flair with which he'd done things. She was even kind of impressed that he'd chosen to name his company for famed chemist and physicist Marie Curie. It was kind of nice to see someone honor an often overlooked contributor to science. *Respect.*

But Ross Eckhart wasn't really the reason that Kayne was currently shivering to the point of potentially phasing through the rooftop under her feet.

It was her client, Shai Salide.

Kayne had found Shai the way she found a lot of clients these days—QuIEK alerted her after scanning through mountains of digitally stored news stories, federal case files, blog posts, and social media. Even for an AI as advanced as QuIEK, this was a monumental task. Sifting through billions of records and files to sniff out anyone who had ever been disenfranchised and ignored by law enforcement, or who had suffered injustice at the hands of corporations (or anyone else, for that matter), yielded a never-empty inbox of results. Sifting and sorting through that to find a prime candidate for Alex Kayne's mission required a lot of cycles of computing power.

To pull it off, and not take several million years of processing, QuIEk used an ever-expanding network of dedicated microcomputer modules, collectively known as "Smokescreen." These were devices that Kayne built and hid as she went, stashing them anywhere she found a WiFi hotspot, and linking them together in a virtual private network that collectively formed her own personal cloud.

Over the past few years, she'd built and stashed a *lot* of these devices. Practically every coffee shop in the US had one disguised as anything from an obscure part of the security system to an electric air freshener in the restroom. The modules, built with tiny microcomputers that could fit easily in the palm of her hand, could be camouflaged as almost anything, and Kayne had gotten very creative with them over the years. And using them, she could appear to anyone watching on line as if she were in any place in the country, at any given time.

A useful distraction—or *smokescreen*—when she needed the FBI to be looking for her in one place while she operated in another. But the whole system was also useful in expanding the size of QuIEK's virtual "brain," giving it more processing power than any other system on Earth. A virtual "body" for Kayne's artificially intelligent software.

She used QuIEK and Smokescreen in all sorts of creative ways, and usually on the fly. But lately she'd put it to work on what she considered her most important task: Finding her next client.

This had become necessary after she'd had an encounter with an International thief and criminal mastermind named Roger Bale. Using her own goodwill and loyalty to her clients against her, Bale had manipulated Kayne, endangering both her and her client. She vowed she'd never let that happen again, and that meant she had to come up with a new way to find and vet the people she would work with.

So when it came to finding her next client, QuIEK did the searching, and Smokescreen did the sifting. And the result was a regular report to Alex Kayne, delivered directly to whatever phone or device she was carrying, alerting her to the next best prospect, and generating a dossier on them and the problem they faced.

QuIEK was getting pretty good at pointing her in the right direction, too. It wasn't a perfect process yet, but the AI was learning. It was starting to understand her and her mission. It was starting to understand which cases would get Kayne's attention.

Shai Salide, her newest client, didn't even know she was a client. Not yet. Maybe not ever. Kayne liked to connect with the people she was helping, to give them some hope, and sometimes to get more context and insight into the job. But for the moment she felt that Shai might be better off not knowing about any of this. The players in this particular game had a lot of reach and a lot of influence, and it was better to keep Shai insulated from it, and out of sight for now.

Plus... well, Kayne had to admit she might just be a little gun shy after what happened with Bane.

But never mind. Here she was. And she had a job to do.

According to the profile that QuIEK had constructed, Shai Salide had started her career as a part-time technician, coming out of high school as part of a co-op technical program and then attending MIT and cruising through the engineering program with impressive success. By the time she'd graduated, she was already named as a co-creator on several small patents. She was also a prime candidate for recruitment by some of the big players in the Valley.

But Shai had a social conscience as well as a passion for engineering. She wanted to be a part of a tech startup that had more than profit as its goal. She was aiming to build something that would make the world a better place.

As a result, she became part of the engineering team at a

lowly electric vehicle startup, where she contributed an impressive catalog of designs. And unlike in her university days, these designs were all hers—concepts and creations that came directly out of her brilliant brain.

The startup had policies regarding patents, requirements Shai had to adhere to, or she'd find herself in violation of her contract. There was an internal process for filing a patent, with credit and ownership to be split between the company and the engineer. This meant that Shai had to file her patents via the company's own representatives and they would take care of the official filing with US and international patenting offices—a sort of double-filing process that was meant to ensure that the originator had some ownership alongside the company, and that no costly mistakes were made.

It wasn't that unusual for tech companies to require a split in ownership with their employees. The assumption was that the employee was utilizing company resources and proprietary information in the development of ideas, even if the ideas were happening in the employee's free time. So it was common practice for these businesses to have employees sign a stack of agreements governing the ownership of intellectual property. Nothing too alarming there.

Indeed, the policies and practice had worked fine for the first two years of the company's existence. Shai shared co-creator status on a handful of very promising patents. But with so many engineers and technicians filing patents internally, the process became cumbersome and slow, and the bulk of ideas sat waiting for the company's team to approve and file. Many of Shai's would-be provisional patents were languishing on pause, stalled by the glut of such patents within the company. The business simply didn't have enough resources to get every patent registered in a timely fashion.

In the third year, things changed.

Year three was when the company was quietly acquired by Curie Motors.

Upon the acquisition, all the engineers on staff were locked out of their own files, while Curie Motors assessed everything it had just purchased. This meant that Shai's pending work was all inaccessible, while the team from Curie Motors combed through it and picked what they wanted.

Before she knew it, Curie Motors had accelerated the internal patent process. And when it did so, it became clear that the previous regime had been a bit incompetent in their approach.

Curie Motors filed thousands of patents within the first year of taking over the company, several hundred of which were from Shai. But due to weak record-keeping practices, Shai's name was ultimately left off of each one.

Upon learning of this, she engaged an attorney, and through him she approached Curie Motors about providing partial ownership of the patents, as her contract outlined. The attorney she could afford, however, was no match for the entire law firm that Curie Motors had on retainer—Bertrand, Owens & Cromwell. Within months, BO&C had legally maneuvered around the patent disputes, and ultimately terminated employment for Shai and dozens of other engineers.

All of this was kept quiet by gag orders and NDAs, and in the end Shai found herself not only out of work but blacklisted in her own industry. Non-compete agreements kept her from taking a position with any other Silicon Valley firms or startups for a period of four years. But even after that contract lapsed, Shai was radioactive in the industry. Word had gotten out that she was trying to grab IP for herself, and no one in the Valley would hire her.

Now, five years later, Curie Motors was housed in a shiny new multi-billion-dollar facility near Austin, Texas, and Shai

Salide was working as a customer support operator for a cleaning supply company. She was financially destitute, thanks to the legal bills. And her dreams and career were ancient history, in technology years. Gauging by her social media posts, Shai had resigned herself to her fate, accepting it as inevitable. To Kayne she sounded sad, haunted. It was gut wrenching.

She was going to fix it.

QuIEK had run all of this down for Kayne in a mostly clinical and pragmatic way, but she could sense a sort of human-like reasoning under it. The AI wasn't intelligent in the way humans were—or even in the way science fiction liked to portray it. It didn't have any sort of emotional intelligence. But it did seem to have a grasp of how stories such as Shai's *should* have played out. As it ran searches and applied data sets, as it used comparative analysis between news stories and FBI case files and some of Kayne's previous clients, QuIEK could somehow see the injustice, and it flagged it as something Alex Kayne would want to see.

And it was almost *always* right. Often enough, at any rate, that Kayne could rely on it for leads, which she would further vet and choose whether to pursue.

But the work aside, the way things were unfolding, the results she was getting from her AI, all of it was leading Kayne to a pretty astonishing conclusion...

QuIEK was getting *smarter*.

When she'd first designed the AI, it had been a cobbled-together collection of code and applications, a kind of kluge of software and apps she'd tinkered with and designed over the years, stretching all the way back to high school. It had been a side project, a hobby, but had ultimately become her life's work. And when she'd partnered with Adrian Ballard and formed Populus, it was a rudimentary form of QuIEK that was at the heart of the company. Everything they built both radiated from her little personal project and added to it at the same time.

Of course, it all boiled over when Adrian got greedy, and cut a deal with the Russians. A deal that was in direct conflict with their US government contracts. A deal that got Adrian killed, and Kayne framed for his murder, and for the treason that Ballard, himself, had committed.

Bygones, Kayne thought, mentally waving away the nagging memory of it. She tried waving this away every time the topic came up. *Bygones*, because Adrian was dead. *Bygones* because Populus and all the dreams she'd had for the company and their software were burnt. *Bygones* because now that Kayne was the world's most wanted fugitive, she'd found a sort of purpose for her life—a reason to keep going. A purpose for her *and* for QuIEK.

Helping people like Shai Salide. Helping the disenfranchised, the forgotten, the people let down by law enforcement and the system of rules that governed the country and the world. Let down by everyone who was supposed to *stand* for them.

So *Kayne* would stand for them. Because she happened to know what that was like, to be abandoned and left to the injustice. And because, as PaPa Kayne had taught her, "You can be a victim or you can be a warrior."

Alex Kayne was a warrior.

She shook her head. Actually, her *whole body* was shaking. This cold was unbelievable, and unexpected. Weather reports had wildly underestimated how deep the chill would go, and so had she. The coat she was wearing was providing almost no real warmth. Too thin—a choice she'd made to keep herself more mobile and unencumbered. But she could hardly remain mobile and unencumbered if she was frozen solid on a Texas rooftop.

Wasn't this state supposed to be hot and humid all the time?

She'd gotten as much as she could here, anyway. She knelt and disassembled the small can antenna she'd built, tucking each component into the oversized purse she was carrying. Her disguise was a little on the posh side, this time around, but she might not have needed to bother. No one was out today, and instead most people were tucked into warm homes, drinking warm beverages, having warm interactions with their families.

She sighed as she turned and left the rooftop, bouncing down through the stairwell, welcoming the relative warmth of the building after shivering on its rooftop for the past hour or two. QuIEK was live-masking her out of CCTV footage as she moved through the building, and after a few minutes she finally bounded through the ground-level exit and out onto the street.

The data she'd managed to glean from the Curie Motors facility was a little on the thin side, but it might be enough. The can antenna had allowed QuIEK to sniff out and connect to the building's WiFi, and from there it was easy to infiltrate the rest of the systems and mirror a copy of all the company servers to Smokescreen. QuIEK was already sorting and categorizing that data for Kayne to review later.

But the real prize was sniffing out a vulnerability in the facility's air-gapped network—a series of computers purposefully kept off of the WiFi, to prevent someone like her from gaining access to them. It was a pretty effective security measure—unless someone screwed up and left a back door open.

Someone had.

The air-gapped network was where the real meaty stuff was being kept, the patents and notes on secret projects within the company. If there was anything to show that Curie Motors had intentionally swiped Shai Salide's patents, it would be there.

The trouble was, because it was air-gapped, that meant it had no WiFi or external connection to the internet or any other outside network. In fact, the only reason QuIEK had been able to detect it at all was because one of the research departments was working on a prototype for an always-on broadband for the next generation of Curie Motors vehicles. The company had a stated goal of creating a roving network, linked to a system of micro-satellites, that would effectively blanket the world in internet relays. In essence, it was similar to Kayne's own Smokescreen network—a roving collection of internet-connected computers that could work in unison, with the goal of "internet for everyone."

Ross Eckhart's public statements about the plan were hopeful and inspiring, and Kayne had found the whole thing charmingly altruistic.

Of course, now she suspected he was full of it, which was disappointing. The whole "billionaire technologist is secretly evil" thing was so cliché and trite, it made her want to gag. But if she found Shai's files on the Curie Motors servers, what other conclusion could Kayne come to? It was sad and disheartening, but she'd seen it a million times now.

Out on the street, Kayne huddled under a bus stop, barely protected from the wind. It took more time than she was used to, but an Uber driver finally pulled up.

"What are you doing out here, lady?" the guy asked. "It's below freezing!"

"Same as you, I guess," Kayne smiled as she hopped in the back seat. "Just doing the gig."

The guy laughed. "I'm a single father with three children and an accent," he said. "This is the only work I can get right now. But a lady like you, I would think you could do *anything!*"

He drove, and Kayne smiled at the thought. She liked him. She took out her phone and had QuIEK look him up, tracing him from his Uber profile to his deeper background.

A fairly recent immigrant to the US, and formerly a professor teaching engineering, before some unpleasantness in his home country sent him and his family running to the US. His wife was killed by a drone during an attack on his home city. As was his fourth and oldest child, and both of his parents. His request for asylum had been granted because he'd lent a hand with some US contract work.

But finding work in his field, here in the US, had proven challenging, since his records were either destroyed or mired in layers of bureaucracy. He couldn't show proof of his education, his work experience, even his own identity. And because of this, he'd been relegated to doing gig work for whatever scraps of income he could manage, while he and his three kids huddled together in a one-bedroom apartment on the northern outskirts of Austin.

That is until Alex Kayne nudged things a little.

Recreating his education and work records was a breeze. Some were actually available on various US government servers, though no one without the clearance would ever have been able to see them. She didn't have that limitation. Or, rather, QuIEK didn't.

She organized these into an email from a fake US official, sent directly to not only her driver but to all the prospective employers he'd interviewed with over the past year. She nudged these up in priority where she could, and included some letters of recommendation from some very prominent political figures, all of whom would show records of their emails in their own digital files.

That should help him find a job, she thought. But since it was nearly Christmas, Kayne did a little extra magic. Uber's accounting software suddenly discovered an error. Tipping had been under-reported on every ride he'd given since he'd started driving. Not by much—a nickel here, a quarter there. Nothing that would impact anyone's finances, just little sips. But it added up.

A credit would be applied within the next 24 hours, direct-deposited into the driver's account. Grand total, it came in around thirty-thousand dollars.

The car pulled up to Kayne's stop. "Merry Christmas," the man said to her over his shoulder, smiling. She could tell it was a rote greeting—given his cultural background, it seemed unlikely he would celebrate Christmas. But it was a kind gesture, a welcoming thing for him to say to someone, and to Kayne it spoke volumes about who he was. Given the way life had turned on him, his attitude was remarkable.

"Merry Christmas," Kayne replied, smiling, as she stepped out into the cold.

CHAPTER TWO

Round Rock, Texas

"Ok, Ross Eckhart... who are you, really?"

Kayne had set herself up in a rental in Round Rock, close enough that she could simply walk to restaurants and grocery stores as needed. The FBI and other agencies were currently scouring Brooklyn, New York, after several video clips of Kayne had been flagged. She'd had QuIEK plant all of those, of course—copies of videos she'd kept aside from a previous trip to Brooklyn.

For good measure, she also had QuIEK replicate digital records for the purchases she made at the various locations she'd visited months ago, and ping IP addresses at several local coffee shops, bars, and hotel lobbies. When the FBI looked into it, they'd see a trail that matched her activity on video. It would be pretty convincing, and it should be enough to keep their attention glued to the absolutely wrong place to find her for a couple of weeks. Maybe. The FBI didn't tend to employ idiots, and by now they knew her M.O. pretty well. This was a very "fool me three times" kind of tactic. But Kayne knew that they would follow up on any lead that came their way, regardless, and that meant she could keep them busy. Busy enough for her to focus on her current case without worrying too much about looking over her shoulder, at least.

This cold snap in Texas had been a bit unexpected, and was putting a couple of kinks into her plans. For one, her new Uber driver friend aside, most car services weren't running at the moment. The freeze had made conditions too dangerous. Ice on the roads in the middle of Texas was a much bigger deal than it would have been in the northern states. Texas just wasn't as equipped to deal with this sort of thing.

That was even more in evidence as she scanned the local news. Traffic accidents were at an all-time high for the area. Worse, the cold was having an impact on the local power grid. Some parts of the state were experiencing scheduled blackouts, with power cycling on and off throughout the state in an effort to keep resources stable. This meant that millions of people were freezing in their own homes, sometimes for days.

It was a mess. State and federal officials were making all sorts of wild comments and accusations. Few were offering any real solutions.

The potential for this to derail Kayne's plan was huge, too. Power was kind of essential to everything she did. QuIEK, for all its digital muscle, was vulnerable to all the same things any technology is vulnerable to. *No electricity, no worky.*

So far, the little rental she was using had maintained electricity. But given that she could find herself stuck here, she'd made sure to stock up on food, water, and lots of batteries. She'd also splurged and bought a ton of satellite equipment to help her stay connected and online even if the grid went down.

Kayne's background was more engineering than programming, when it really came down to it. She'd gotten into coding because it was becoming an essential skill, even as far back as her high school days. Her PaPa had drilled that into her, along with his own brand of jury-rigged, cobbled-together, makeshift engineering.

So building things like the microcomputers she used as part of Smokescreen, or the can antenna she'd used to sniff out the Curie Motors WiFi, that was all lightweight stuff. And so was building a satellite relay that would allow her to stay connected, even if the power grid failed. QuIEK was able to get her access to even the most secure satellites in orbit. A power she tried not to abuse—unless it was absolutely necessary.

One of the new toys she'd picked up was a very compact but powerful satellite smartphone. It was a little bulkier than her regular phone and had a knob-like protrusion on top that functioned as the antenna. If anyone looked closely, it wouldn't be hard to see that it was different from the standard smartphone. But a casual glance would probably gloss right over it. And having a device that could always be online, even in the most remote locations, was too handy to pass up. She should have done it sooner.

She installed her own operating system on the phone, effectively wiping out everything that came pre-programmed. Including, she was amused to see, the bevy of spyware that relayed everything from her location to the numbers she called or texted. Even her keystrokes and site visits were logged. She had QuIEK trace this back and found that the company was keeping these records as part of a secret contract with the NSA. They were exploiting a loophole in the privacy laws, which didn't adequately cover direct-to-satellite communications. Basically, they had a back door into any satellite mobile device. *Sneaky, sneaky.*

And probably unconstitutional, though anyone caught up in the web of an NSA investigation would likely never get the opportunity to protest in court.

She was suddenly very glad she'd taken the extra paranoid precaution of having the phone shipped to a service two counties over, at any rate. The extra time it had taken to get to the drop point and then take a circuitous route back to the rental all felt worth it.

With her internet and power needs met, Kayne settled in with a hot cup of noodles, bundled head to toe in warm clothes, and scanned through everything QuIEK had found of her on Ross Eckhart.

The son of German immigrants, Eckhart had become a US citizen when he was eight years old. His dual citizenship had been something of an advantage for him over the years, allowing him to first attend the Technical University of Munich, where he received a Master of Science with honors, with an emphasis on information technology, of all things. He entered a doctoral program at Berkeley, at the age of 22, but dropped out to build and launch his first company.

And that first startup was, obviously, a digital greeting card website.

It was an odd beginning for a man who would eventually become something of a legend in the tech industry, but it wasn't all that unusual. Silicon Valley was ripe with stories of entrepreneurs who started with one idea, then parlayed it into another. Elon Musk started Zip2, which provided city guide information to newspapers, of all things. And look how he turned out.

Eckhart's first business was something of a financial success, but it never quite took off for him. Eventually, he sold it to a similar company, which eventually sold to yet another. The ecosystem of Silicon Valley startups was omnivorous and veracious of appetite. Every fish at every other fish, eventually.

Eckhart applied what he'd learned from the venture, however, along with the money he'd gotten from selling it, to make into a much more stable business: Virtual landscape planning.

Kayne laughed out loud as she read through Eckhart's eclectic resume of business ventures. From landscape planning, he branched into home and office planning, then into a small startup that sold custom eyeglasses, then into an app that let users share selfies to a limited network of friends and family. And the list kept going like that, with each venture selling to someone else, merging with some other business, usually with a small but not insignificant profit for Eckhart.

These were all small potatoes, of course. Dinky, almost funny ventures that were never going to make someone a billion dollars. But the more Kayne dug into Eckhart's past, the more she started to see a pattern.

These little businesses weren't the point. They were *research*.

With each ridiculous, small-time business that Eckhart built, he took away lessons and data that would help him with the *next* venture. Greeting cards gave him a system for collecting user contact information, and even personal preferences for things like color, music, even clip art. Landscaping and interior planning allowed him to crowdsource data about spacial organization and manipulation, as users both created virtual spaces and organized objects within them. That data would later help him to perfect automated systems that guided the design of his cars, as well as other spaces, training a rudimentary AI to see each space the way humans see it.

The selfie app gave him data for perfecting digital security over a peer-to-peer network, again crowdsourcing key aspects of the software out to people who were voluntarily training his AI in facial recognition and location tracking.

These dinky, seemingly pointless little forays into technology looked like jokes to the outside world, but as QuIEK showed Kayne the whole picture, she saw it for what it really was. These apps and services weren't what made Eckhart a billionaire, but they *were* the foundation he used to make billions. He patented and leased his technology to other industries, and in turn captured more and more data that he could turn into an ever-expanding digital empire.

Even Curie Motors was part of a larger plan. Electric cars that also served as part of a roving network of internet relays.

That caught Kayne's attention. The idea was to provide high speed internet to even the most remote locations on the planet, by turning his cars into mobile hotspots, all designed to share their internet connections, as part of a wide, virtual cloud. It was smart. It was ambitious.

It was... familiar.

It was, in essence, Eckhart's version of Smokescreen.

For years now, Kayne had been planting her little discreet devices all over the place, using them to create an enormous virtual private network that QuIEK could use as an outsized memory. Each Smokescreen relay was part of a serious amount of redundancy, not only storing its own data and sharing it with the rest of the network, but routinely housing copies of that data, along with thousands of other units, for quick access. It was similar to RAID storage—a "Redundant Array of Independent Disks" that computers could use for data redundancy and improved performance.

Basically, QuIEK's "memory" was constantly in motion, never reliant on any one device, but always spread across thousands of devices.

And over time, Kayne had looped other computers into that

network as well. QuIEK's roving memory sometimes resided, at least in part, in systems maintained by huge corporations or even government, military, and law enforcement servers. Without knowing it, the FBI was often supplying the processing power QuIEK needed to keep them good and fooled about Kayne's actual location and activities.

All of that was part of Kayne's strategy for self preservation, of both her and QuIEK. But at its roots was something she'd originally intended to benefit the whole world—the idea of an ever-expanding network of devices that could relay data to wherever it was needed whenever it was needed. And in that, Ross Eckhart had created a nearly identical network in the form of his cars. Kayne's idea, realized through Eckhart's tech. Or, at least, it would *eventually* be realized. It stood a much better chance in Eckhart's hands, at least.

For the moment, Eckhart's network was depending on local broadband services, connecting to LTE and 5G networks across the US and the world. Satellite connectivity was already being implemented, however, with new models connecting directly to Eckhart's much-vaunted private network of micro-satellites. And in time, every car he manufactured would be tied directly to that network, while also operating as a connection point for it.

Basically, if a Curie Motors car was anywhere in an area, it would link to local mobile phone towers and other transmission devices, and share its internet connection. The more of those cars (or any other devices manufactured with this tech) that showed up in an area, the better the network would get.

Broadband for everyone. But also Ross Eckhart's network, *everywhere.*

It was Alex Kayne's plan for Smokescreen, gone large-scale and corporate.

And she had to admit, she was impressed.

But also suspicious. Because what Eckhart was building was a system entirely independent of any sort of oversight from the outside. Even if world governments decided to implement some sort of restrictions on this, it would be easy for Eckhart to ignore them. Or, more likely, placate them by pretending to do as he was told, while continuing to put more and more relays out in the world. There would definitely come a time when no one could stop him, or reverse what he was doing.

And that scared the hell out of Kayne. Because it was exactly the problem she was being hunted over.

Kayne had gone on the run precisely to keep QuIEK out of the hands of anyone who would abuse it. It was a digital master key—a way to empower someone to flat-out ignore any barrier to access, and to operate in a sort of God Mode among the communication networks of the world.

And while Ross Eckhart's network lacked QuIEK's ability to infiltrate systems as if their security didn't exist, it opened every network up to the vulnerability of being at least *visible* to Eckhart. And given the man's track record with iterative digital development, turning aspects of his various apps and services into pieces that added up to a greater whole, it was only a matter of time before Eckhart managed to build his own version of QuIEK. One that no one but he, and now Kayne, would know existed.

The "evil billionaire" cliché might have made her groan, but it just got serious.

T he cold started to fade after the fifth day.

Thank God, Kayne thought.

She'd spent three days with no power, which meant no means of heating the rental or keeping herself warm beyond a small kerosene camp heater and a pile of blankets. And while she'd managed to keep her laptop and other devices powered up and her internet connection active, it was so cold in her little space that her fingers ached as she tried to work. In the end, she resorted to giving QuIEK verbal commands through chattering teeth, letting the AI show her whatever she needed as she bundled up and sipped hot soup and coffee.

Now, as the world thawed, and it looked like there might just be a chance for things to start getting back to normal, she was preparing for a little excursion.

The polar vortex, and the impact it had on Texas, had yielded her an unexpected opportunity.

Ross Eckhart had announced in a press conference that he would be visiting the new Curie Motors facility, in Round Rock, and speaking with his employees. He would do a press conference from the grounds, and once there, he would give details regarding some of his plans for helping Curie Motors employees and their families.

Again, it was a heartwarming and inspiring speech, and Kayne found herself drawn to taking it at face value. But her continued research and profiling of Ross Eckhart had made her less sure, and more suspicious.

The troubling thing was, in many respects, Eckhart seemed to be everything he advertised about himself. Kayne had dug in on the guy for a week now, scanning every public interview and private email, scouring the files on his various laptops and tablets and mobile phones. There was plenty of "dirt." Kayne had long ago come to the conclusion that nobody becomes a billionaire without some sort of skeleton lurking in a closet somewhere. And Eckhart had his, for sure. There were hints of dirty dealings, leveraging his wealth and influence to get his way. But most of it was aimed at people in power—senators and governors and other government types who were blocking his progress. The few times one of his companies strong-armed an everyday citizen, there was inevitably some sort of compensation made, and usually a very public apology as well.

In other words, if Eckhart ever found out that one of his business dealings had a negative impact on someone who lacked power and agency, he made it right.

That discovery irked Kayne. Because if it was true, then her current case was off to a bad start. It was entirely possible that Shai Salide's work *wasn't* stolen by Curie Motors. At least, not intentionally. And if that was true, then she might be wasting a lot of time looking in the wrong direction.

Really, it all came down to whatever was on that air-gapped network tucked away inside Curie Motors. The one with limited access that might be hiding more than she could sniff out remotely. And Kayne was determined to get to it.

But first, she wanted to meet Ross Eckhart.

She spent an hour cleaning the rental, putting everything back in place. She gathered what few things she'd brought in with her, stuffing everything into a rolling suitcase that she'd drop into a dumpster later. The electronics she broke down and put into her backpack. She'd stash that in a locker she was renting. It might come in handy later.

The little kerosene heater was the only thing she'd leave in the rental, and she touched it with an almost fond gesture. Her gift, to the next miserable soul who might have to huddle here for warmth.

With that, she left the keys on the kitchen counter, just as she'd been told to do, and let the door lock closed behind her. This had been the longest stay she'd had in one place for almost three years, and only because of mitigating circumstances. She already had multiple other rentals and hotel rooms and AirBnBs lined up, all over the area. She'd pick one as she needed it.

For now, though, she had a press conference to attend.

CHAPTER THREE

Curie Motors Facility | Round Rock, Texas

The bitter cold had faded, but it was still chilly enough that Kayne was wearing a long coat and scarf as she mingled among a passel of reporters and civilians. The scarf was handy for obscuring her features—since this was going to be a nationally televised event, it was best to keep a low profile. But just in case, QuIEK was actively scanning live feeds and digitally altering her features as the video was transmitted. So that only left people here on the ground to worry about. It seemed unlikely anyone would recognize her, but unlikely things tended to happen more often than she'd like.

The crowd gathered on the grounds of the Curie Motors campus seemed cheerful enough. All the talk and chatter was along the lines of "How did *you* keep from freezing to death in your own home?" There were some grumblings about things like Texas' energy infrastructure, and what should be done about bolstering it. And there was lots of talk about who was to blame for everything, whether the Republicans should be ousted from office or the Democrats should be put in jail for this or that potential crime against common sense. People were raw at the moment, hurt and looking for someone to blame, but also glad to be past the worst of it.

Kayne avoided all the talk, engaging with no one and dodging among the gathered crowd until she managed to position herself close to the makeshift bullpen of reporters. They were all eagerly waiting to ping Ross Eckhart with questions. Some were doing live standups, talking to anchors in distant studios, speculating on what Eckhart would say.

There was a temporary stage and podium set up, with the giant logo of Curie Motors looming from the building in the background—a stylized "CM" that evoked a sort of bygone era of science and exploration. Ross Eckhart, Kayne knew, was fond of a more "vintage" era of engineering. He was a huge sci-fi nerd, and most of his goals for his businesses read like a kid plotting to make *Star Trek* into a reality.

She kind of liked that about him, honestly. She had similar sensibilities about technology and the future, a sort of hopeful longing for what *could* be, if only we could get out of our own way. Of course, Eckhart's public vision and persona might turn out to be all show, which would be a little disappointing, though not altogether unexpected.

Billionaires, Kayne thought, shaking her head.

She'd met and dealt with a lot of them, even before she went on the run and had become a source of justice for the disenfranchised. Silicon Valley bred billionaires, and almost all of them worked from a hustle-first ethic that, Kayne had decided, somehow warped their brains. It desensitized them to what it meant to be a normal human being, for a start. They often fell for their own press, believing the messianic levels of adoration they got from those who yearned to have their access to cash. But to Kayne, the truth about most billionaires was that they were some of the poorest people she'd met. They had all the money in the world, but tended to lack the vision to match it, to make it *useful* for something.

Conversely, some of the most financially destitute people Kayne had encountered had lives of absolute treasure—friends, family, a stable home, a community they belonged to. She'd give anything to have all of those things. She, who might actually be a notch above all the billionaires in the world, in terms of access to wealth and power, would give all of it up if she could just settle in with someone she loved, committing herself to building something with that person.

For now, and maybe forever, she'd have to settle on doing whatever good she could in the world, despite being hunted.

The gathered press were all greeted by the Curie Motor's PR rep, who first read a statement about the current state of the company. Most personnel had all been sent home, she stated, when it became clear that conditions were dangerous. Only a skeleton crew remained, and they were all given warm clothing and comfortable quarters, as well as ample compensation for their time.

It was only today, the PR rep stated, that the human presence within the facility had started to ramp back up. But that didn't mean that production had ground to a halt.

"Our automated systems continued to run throughout," she smiled. "As many of you are aware, we have numerous industrial generators on site, and of course, we have ample solar panels and stored power. That technology is proprietary, so I can't give you specifics. But I can say that we were able to keep operations going for the past five days despite the blackouts and even with the heavy cloud cover. As team members arrive and get back to work, we will be able to meet all of our projections. And before anyone asks," she said, smiling, "yes, employees were paid for the down time."

Reporters began firing off questions, but she held up a placating hand and waited for them to quiet down. "Mr. Eckhart has instructed me to let him answer all of your questions from this point forward."

There was a surprised rumble among the reporters. Eckhart wasn't shy about talking to the press, but everyone had just assumed he'd let his PR team handle the more mundane questions, while he offered his usual "profound soundbites at the finale," as one Washington Post columnist referred to them. Eckhart adhered to a sort of Steve-Jobsian "one more thing" approach to talking to the press, and it was unusual for him to take direct questions regarding operations.

Kayne was surprised as well. Eckhart was a chronically busy guy—as an itinerant CEO, he moved around a lot, and was personally and directly involved in dozens of projects across his entire catalog of companies around the globe. The fact that he'd even made a personal appearance here today was enough to keep the news cycle talking. But for him to be the sole person taking questions...

Something was up.

After a few more pat PR statements, the rep finally introduced Eckhart, and there was actually some applause from the civilians present (and even among the press) as he stepped out from behind a barrier beyond the stage. He smiled and waved as he walked forward to the podium, where he braced his hands on either side and leaned in toward the microphone.

"Good afternoon," he said, his voice the familiar quiet, paced tone everyone had come to recognize. There was a slight trace of a German accent, a holdover from his childhood, despite living as an American citizen most of his life. It had the effect of giving him an exotic air. "I first want to express how happy we are to report that all the Curie Motors employees and their families have been accounted for, and were able to get through this unusual weather event with relatively small issues. Some employees had pipes burst and flood their homes, among other troubling issues, and I've actually created a charitable fund to help them get things back together. I've also initiated a program to ensure that each Curie Motors employee receives a solar generator, provided by our sister company, Envolt."

There was an appreciative murmur from the crowd, and even Alex found herself impressed by the generosity of the move. Envolt was another of Eckhart's *Star Trek* dream companies, manufacturing next-level battery technology that could be charged from almost any source, but was particularly efficient with the company's proprietary solar panel tech. Like any smart tech billionaire, Eckhart had irons in a lot of fires, and all of those irons worked together. Eckhart's style of horizontal integration made it possible for him to own production for everything each of his companies needed, which meant advances and innovations could come at a more rapid clip. If he needed batteries for his cars, he had a company for that. And likewise, Curie Motors produced the trucks that delivered those batteries and other products to distributors—most of which were owned by Eckhart's retail division.

This wasn't a new approach, of course. It had been the method used by the likes of Henry Ford and Thomas Edison in their day. Supply chain issues weren't a problem when you owned the entirety of the supply chain. But for whatever reason, such integration was a rare event in the modern digital era. Eckhart was one of a few technologists on the planet using methods like these, and the results were nothing short of impressive. All of Eckhart's businesses were flexible and adaptive—and more importantly, *hugely* profitable.

"As our employees return to work," Eckhart continued, "we'll continue to provide any assistance they need. But we're also extending financial assistance to the local community. The fund is being managed by a non-profit, and is open to donations. The bigger the fund, the greater its reach. So, I call upon everyone who is able to donate any amount they can, from wherever you are in the world. All funds will go to helping families who have been impacted by the polar vortex, to repair damage caused by the freeze."

More approval, more goodwill, more applause. Eckhart was good at this. It was hard for Kayne to tell, though... was he truly altruistic? Or was this more of an opportunistic play? Goodwill from the public often had a positive impact on the bottom line.

She couldn't be sure. There was a part of her that *wanted* all of this to be genuine, but she did have some doubts. Life on the run tended to make one jaded and pessimistic.

"That is all very important," Eckhart said, waving as if clearing the air. "And it's been a great concern for all of us here at Curie Motors. But that isn't entirely why I wanted to speak with you today. Before the polar vortex interrupted our plans, I had intended to come here anyway, and announce something very important. I was already here in Round Rock when the freeze happened, lest anyone think I made a special trip just for the photo op." He grinned at this comment, and there was a smattering of appreciative laughter. But when it died down, he looked around and smiled lightly. He took a breath, and pulled back his shoulders, then nodded.

"Effective immediately," Eckhart said, scanning along the faces in the press pool, "I am stepping down as the CEO of Curie Motors."

. . .

O nce the initial shock of the announcement passed, there was an immediate explosion of questions from the press and protests from the people gathered. Eckhart had become something of a folk hero, especially here in Round Rock. In a time when so many were suffering from the impact of a natural disaster, and casting out for any hope they could find, it came as a kind of psychological blow to learn that there would be such a major change to Curie Motors.

Kayne was as shocked as anyone.

Absolutely *nothing* in the profile she'd amassed on Eckhart had hinted at a plan for him to step down. He was such an integral part of the operations of each of his businesses, the idea of him leaving leadership of even one of those companies to someone else was absurd.

The press asked most of the questions Kayne wanted answers to. Was Eckhart retiring altogether? Was he having any health issues? Who would take over as CEO? What did this move mean for his other companies? What was his end game?

Eckhart gave mostly fluff answers to the press. Vague responses that, Kayne knew, were meant to fuel more speculation in the media and the public, to keep the conversation going and to point it in a particular direction. To her, it felt like a move meant to create a smokescreen, a diversion to keep people from seeing what was really happening. Kayne suspected Eckhart was showing some of his cards, so that everyone ignored the deck.

And, of course, it was already working. Just within the short radius of where she stood, she heard hundreds of armchair theories about why he would make a move like this, even why he chose this particular time to make his announcement. Conspiracy theories, mostly. But some actually seemed to have a bit of merit, with people suggesting it was a move to pivot into something else. Something very different from everything Eckhart had done before.

Government, maybe? Would Eckhart run for office?

Or maybe he was engaged in some new business that would draw scrutiny from the SEC?

Military contracts? Space exploration? Was he moving his operations to a foreign country? He did still have ties to Germany, the home country of his parents.

It was all plausible speculation, but Kayne wasn't letting any of it influence her. She hadn't studied Ross Eckhart for long, but she felt she'd learned enough about him to know that his plans always fell firmly into the "unguessable" category. No one was likely to know what he was up to, or to even guess it, until he was ready to share it with the world.

Well... *almost* no one.

She glanced down at the sat phone and tapped a few commands for QuIEK. Maybe she could find some communication Eckhart had made, a text or email, anything, that would give her some clue as to what he was doing.

The real question she had to face, however, was simple and straightforward: *Is this relevant?*

Things had gotten a bit weird and off the rails since arriving in Round Rock, with the polar vortex hitting so hard and shutting things down. And with it turning out that Ross Eckhart was kind of a weirdly intriguing guy. That was unexpected.

But she couldn't let herself forget the real reason she was here. She had a client who needed her help. Even if that client didn't currently know Alex Kayne existed, she was still a client. She still needed help. And right now, Ross Eckhart and Curie Motors appeared to be the bad guys in that scenario.

Kayne still had a job to do.

Whether Eckhart's odd business move factored into that

job, she'd have to figure out later. For now, all of this weirdness had created an opportunity, and she needed to take.

For five days the Curie Motors facility had been locked down tight, with only a skeletal team of security personnel and essential workers present. Two million dollars worth of security measures made this place tough to crack at the best of times, but it was ironically much harder with fewer people on site.

QuIEK could get her past any digital security measures as if they weren't there. Cameras wouldn't see her, scanners and sensors wouldn't notice her. Door alarms would mysteriously disable themselves, and keycard and biometric access would be wide open to her. If it was connected to a network, and that network had any outward-facing access point, QuIEK owned it.

But with no *people* in the building, beyond the roving teams of security personnel and a worker skeleton crew, there was no one for her to blend in with. She'd stick out as *very* noticeable—an unfamiliar face who had no business being in the building. It was a fast pass to a prison cell.

Kayne could handle herself if things ever came down to a physical altercation. But even she couldn't take down an entire team of trained security guys, with orders to break the limbs and extremities of any intruders they found. And after a week of observing that security team in action, Kayne knew some of their patterns. They had the place sewn up pretty tight. There were no gaps wide enough for her to get in unseen.

Her original plan had been to go in disguised as a consultant, with clearances established ahead of time by QuIEK. Once she was on the inside, the security thinned a bit, and relied more on the digital gatekeepers. No need to police the halls of a building that almost no one could get into without being seen. She had a better chance of getting to that air gapped network without being spotted once she was past that first level security scrutiny.

But the polar vortex had turned that apple cart over. All nonessential personnel had been ordered to leave, the place was physically locked down, and the security team literally lived on site for five days. Kayne's plan had been rendered worthless.

But today...

The spectacle of Ross Eckhart's press conference, and the shocking announcement he'd just made, were practically custom-tailored to be the perfect distraction. And with personnel returning in droves, including consultants and contractors who were not necessarily regulars in the halls, there was now a shifting army of strange and new faces moving into the facility. Security was stretched a little thin, making sure all the people gathered to hear their boss speak were kept out of the facility. Fewer guards manned the doors and the scanners within the building, and they were at their limits dealing with checking and verifying identifications and credentials. As long as no one had a gun in their pocket or some other forbidden object, nearly everyone was being waved through with minimal scrutiny.

This was the time.

Kayne had dressed appropriately, wearing business clothing that made her look the part of a consultant, but wouldn't restrict her movements. She kept her gear light—the sat phone and her smart watch were her connection and backup connection to QuIEK, respectively. She had a couple of paperclips in her pocket to use as a makeshift pick and tension wrench, in case she needed to pick a physical lock. And she had on a stylish pair of sneakers instead of pumps or heels, because running was just something she inevitably had to do.

There was always running.

At least the sneakers were somewhat high fashion, and didn't look out of place among the health-conscious Austin crowd.

She would have loved to go in with more of an arsenal of tools and resources, but it was better to travel light. The first rule of illegally infiltrating a place was "carry only what you need."

The first barrier to entry was simply getting through the crowd and into the queue for the security checks. Everyone on site was eager to speak with Eckhart personally, it seemed. Everyone except Kayne. She managed to squeeze and dodge her way through the crowd and get into a line leading through the first set of X-ray and ATI scanners. No one raised an eyebrow over the items she put into the little tray—her phone, watch, and paperclips were innocuous enough. And she wasn't wearing anything unusual that might have caused her to be stopped and searched. She was the least interesting person in the queue.

Once on the other side of that set of security measures, she moved to the next. Here, the guards checked her credentials against their in-house systems. QuIEK had generated a full profile for her, including her photo, and she had created a driver's license to match her data. The guard checked all of this, scrutinizing it, and Kayne was glad to see her work passed muster. She was ushered through and into the facility.

From the front entrance, she checked in for a temporary badge, which gave her access to certain areas. She was informed that the badge had a RF tag that allowed the building's scanners to track everywhere she went. "So don't lose your badge," the woman behind the desk smiled. "Security holds people for twelve hours when they're found without a badge, or if they end up in an area where they have no clearance."

"Good to know," Kayne smiled. "Twelve hours is kind of a long time."

The woman shrugged. "They run a ton of background checks on anyone they detain, and it takes at least that long."

Kayne understood. This was part of the "reasonable time-frame" that Texas courts used as a standard for detainment. Though she knew that it took far less than twelve hours to run even the most extensive state and federal background check. The timeframe was meant to be intimidating, to deter anyone from breaking the rules, or from ever breaking the rules again.

Kayne had no intention of being detained. But she did plan to break a lot of rules.

Almost from the instant her RF badge was generated, QuIEK had reprogrammed her access levels, and established an echo of her badge in the system. No matter where she went in the facility, the internal systems would register as someone and some*where* else. If anyone stopped her and scanned her badge, they'd see she had access to wherever she happened to be. And if they checked it against the system, it would dutifully report that she was in that location.

Of course, her image was being live-masked out of all video footage. She was effectively a ghost in the system.

She moved away from the lobby and took the elevator to the third floor—the top floor for the facility. This was where a series of offices and work spaces had been set up, and it was where she would be expected to go, if she really were a consultant or contractor. But for her purposes, it was a good access point for her target.

The Curie Motors facility was *massive*—more than a mile long, with vast spaces dedicated to assembly line work. The office level stretched the entire length of the building, along the second and third floors, and was the easiest way for Kayne to get from one end of the facility to the other. She had a 3D rendering of the entire building on her phone, stitched together from a combination of public blueprints, city planning documents, and the building's own internal cameras and sensors. With this, QuIEK was guiding her through the maze of corridors and cubicles, to a stairwell that would get her close to the vault she was trying to access.

The air-gapped network was inside that vault—really a set of nested labs and dedicated office spaces on the first floor, set aside from the assembly line and segregated from the rest of the facility. To even have a shot at accessing it, she would need to get down to the first floor via a stairwell on the East end of the building. That particular stairwell was locked off from casual access—it required a special key card, along with biometric screening. Very secure.

Easy.

And there was a bonus.

The likelihood of encountering anyone in that stairwell would be slim. Only authorized personnel could even get in there, and most people in the building—even including security personnel—had no need. According to her surveillance, the people working in the air-gapped lab all came in through a dedicated entrance on the ground floor, and rarely required access to the levels above. The lab was its own space, its own ecosystem within the Curie Motors facility, and anyone coming and going was already scrutinized, vetted, and verified. So if you were there, the assumption was you *belonged* there.

QuIEK would make it so that Kayne belonged there. Or at least would appear to. Again, easy.

Still, it always paid to be extra paranoid, especially in confined spaces. She had QuIEK run through worst-case scenarios, finding her as many ways out of there as possible. Meanwhile, she concentrated on continuing through the gamut of office spaces on the third floor.

It took a very long time to get to the stairwell. Covering a mile through cubicles and corridors, dodging anyone who might look too closely and ask too many questions, meant it was slow going, end to end. At one point she stopped at a break room for a cup of coffee—which turned out to not be so bad. Curie Motors had a very hip atmosphere, for a corporate office space, and the "break room" was actually a faux coffee shop and café setting, with a fully functional espresso machine and even a selection of healthy meals, available for free to employees and visitors alike.

Kayne always avoided eating and drinking when she was on a job. It wasn't like she'd get a chance to stop and use the restroom if someone started chasing her. But she justified stopping and sipping a latte and nibbling on some fruit, in the name of stealth and camouflage. To anyone watching, she was just another consultant enjoying some surprisingly good coffee and a healthy nosh.

Noshing complete, however, it was time to get back to work.

She took the coffee with her.

The closer she got to the secure stairwell, the more the office crowd thinned out. The people she encountered now were typically working at the Director level—a notch above management, a notch below the executives. She was more cautious here, and began disguising her movements by snagging file folders and papers, studying them as she walked, nodding perfunctorily as she passed anyone who might notice her.

File folders were the clipboards of corporate life—carrying one was essentially a deer-tail signal to everyone who looked your way, flagging you as "someone who is supposed to be here and is also busy, and so should not be bothered." It didn't always work, but it helped her move without garnering all that much suspicion.

It went like this for more than an hour—much longer than she had hoped, but less time than she had feared. As she picked her way through the space, several times she had to sidetrack, or divert around people or obstacles in her way. The pace was slow, but she had time. It was better to creep along than to gain attention by appearing to be in a hurry, especially in a place where she wasn't a familiar face.

Finally, the door for the secured stairwell loomed ahead of her. She had the file folder and papers closed against her side, and her coffee cup in hand. She put the cup on the edge of an empty desk, then angled toward the door.

"Miss?" a woman's voice came from behind her.

Kayne felt her heart thump. *She was so close!* But she couldn't exactly make a break for it. Everyone in this end of the offices would know that the stairwell was secure access, and that not just anyone could go there. If she tried to ignore whoever this was and bee-line to the door, she'd inevitably alert security that something was up. She'd have to deal with this with tact.

She turned to see a middle-aged woman, well-dressed, holding the cup of coffee that Kayne had just set down. "You forgot your coffee."

Kayne smiled and shook her head. "I'm sorry, thank you! I guess I just have a lot on my mind," she held up the file folder, as if its contents were the source of all worry and concern.

The woman smiled and held up some file folders of her own. "Don't we all?"

Kayne laughed lightly and took the cup from her, then turned and moved toward the door. She wasn't sure what would happen if she just went to it and used her bogus keycard to get in. But... well... why not?

Without looking back, but knowing the woman was watching her the whole way, Kayne stepped up to the door and waved her keycard over the sensor. Then she placed her hand on the biometric sensor plate as she leaned forward and looked into the unblinking eye of a retinal scanner.

The moment of truth.

A blue light blinked brighter, along with a charming little sound, like tiny harp strings. The all-go signs that access was granted.

Kayne opened the door and stepped through, glancing back to see that the woman had, in fact, been watching her every move, likely waiting to see if she actually did have access to this, the most sacred and secure of doors.

Kayne waved with her coffee cup, smiling, and the woman smiled and waved back, before turning to walk away. Apparently she was appeased by the fact that no alarms or sirens went off, and that Kayne had actually been able to enter the forbidden zone. Trust in the system was complete.

As the stairwell door closed, Kayne leaned against it briefly, and let out a breath. Then, file folder and lucky coffee cup still in hand, she made her way down the three flights of steps that would deposit her near the air-gapped lab.

So far, so good.

Though, somehow, she hardly thought this had been the toughest part.

CHAPTER FOUR

Ross Eckhart Private Office | Curie Motors Facility

"Sir," one of the security detail said. "There's something you should see."

Ross Eckhart still didn't like being called "sir." It had felt weird to him for nearly all of his adult life. No matter how much money he made, no matter how many businesses he built, no matter how many times his face appeared on the news or his voice echoed back to him from an interview, Eckhart always felt like people who called him *sir* were either addressing someone else or being contemptuous.

Sometimes the latter was true.

It had been about an hour since he'd managed to escape the press and the public, and to duck into his private office in the Curie Motors facility. And this really was his *private* office—not the Executive Suite he used when he was entertaining investors or other CEOs or even just the media. This little space, tucked into a corner of the ground floor of the Curie Motors building, was a replica of others he had scattered among all of his various businesses. It was a largely utilitarian space, with a drafting table and a workbench dominating one whole wall, and research materials adorning all the others. If anything, this looked more like the space he'd started in—a tiny garage apartment in San Francisco, where his landlord had forever been threatening to kick him out for being late with rent or, sometimes, for setting the place on fire.

These little offices were replicas of the very space where all of this had started for Eckhart. A humble space, too small for much more than him and his obsessions. It was comforting to be in such a humble setting. It was a reminder that billions of dollars shouldn't change who he was at the core, if he was determined enough to keep his values in check.

It was kind of an indulgence, otherwise. And a private haven to retreat to, when he'd extroverted enough for one day.

Usually, no one bothered him when he was in here. And he would have preferred to have a couple of hours alone, to come down after the press conference. But security always had a pass on interruptions. Eckhart had learned years ago that in this business, in any tech industry business, the key to keeping things from going sideways too fast to handle was to let security types have their say and their way. Paranoia could be very useful.

He waved for the man to enter and took the digital tablet when it was handed to him. He watched the footage, then looked up in surprise. "Who is she?"

The man shook his head. "We're not sure yet. We're trying to run facials, but it's like there's a glitch. She looked dead into the retinal scanner, but we show no record of it. Every interaction with those scanners is usually recorded, but there's nothing."

"Which camera is this?" Eckhart asked, pointing to the tablet. The footage was weird—like a recording of a security monitor, taken from a handheld camera.

"The stairwells have three sets of cameras at each landing. One is networked, connecting to the general system. The other is infrared, also networked. The third is direct, connected to a DVR and monitors from inside the air-gapped lab. No network. Your rules."

Eckhart nodded. "I see. And let me guess... the networked camera and the infrared camera aren't seeing anything?"

The guard nodded. "It's like she's invisible. To the networked cameras, at least."

"She's using some kind of live masking," Eckhart said, awed. He studied the woman on the screen. She looked familiar, but he hadn't quite clicked to who she was yet. The footage hadn't given him a clear image of her face, just quick profiles as she moved past. "This is the second floor. Did she come down from the third?"

"Yes sir," the man replied, nodding.

"And she had a badge?"

"Yes sir, and she passed the biometric scans."

"The stairwell camera on the third floor is hard wired, isn't it? Direct line to the DVR?"

The security agent thought for a moment, "Yes sir, I believe that's correct." He immediately took out his phone and made a call. After a few short moments there was another knock on the door, and the agent answered, taking a tablet from the guard outside.

He handed it to Eckhart. "Every time they try to send any video of her over the network, it vanishes."

Eckhart nodded. "I don't know how she's doing it, but it's impressive. She's live-masking herself out of any footage, and whatever she's using is doing it in real time, across the network. We're never going to see her that way."

"This was shot on a tablet that isn't on the network," the agent said, handing it over. "Handheld, but it should be clear enough."

Eckhart took the tablet and opened another video clip. This one was a shot of the third floor doorway. Sure enough, the door opened, and the woman stepped through, holding a file folder and a cup of coffee. She must have been nervous, because she paused and leaned against the door. And in that moment, she tilted her head back, giving the camera an unobscured view of her face.

"Alex Kayne," Eckhart whispered.

"Sir?"

He looked up at the security agent. "Tell security to start quietly locking down the building, especially the first floor. Get someone on every exit and stairwell. She's headed for the air-gapped lab. Let her. But once she's in, surround it. No one gets in or out without my say so."

The guard nodded. "Do you want us to call the police? FBI?"

Eckhart considered, then shook his head. "No." He looked back at the footage. "I want to talk to her."

Air-Gapped Lab | Curie Motors Facility

Something was wrong.

Kayne checked her phone. QuIEK wasn't indicating anything, and as far as she could tell there hadn't been any alarms or other signals. In fact, she had nothing to go by, as far as why she was suddenly feeling her guts twist. It was just... instinct.

PaPa Kayne had always taught her to listen to that instinct. *Your body and your mind know more about the world than you do,* he'd say. He was a man who had lived by his gut instinct and intuition all his life.

Kayne had, too. In fact, gut instinct and intuition were sort of the secret sauce of how she'd invented QuIEK in the first place. Because while it was true that she had mad coding skills, she would be the first to admit that she was not the world's best programmer. She wasn't the super-hacker that the FBI and other federal agencies made her out to be, either. She was just someone who had a decent level of skill, who also listened to her gut and made intuitive leaps.

And though she wouldn't exactly say that QuIEK was just an example of "lucky guesses," she knew that it *had* come about as a sort of synthesis of ideas—most of which were based on her intuition and instincts.

So Kayne trusted her gut. Instinct had saved her a million times since becoming *Fugitive Number One* among the nations alphabet agencies and law enforcement the world over. She listens, when she got that nudge. And now, as she made her way closer to her target, instinct was telling her that something was up.

The door to the air-gapped lab was ahead of her. She still had half a dozen ways to escape, right now, if she needed to. All of them involved *running*, but at least she'd brought the right shoes for that.

The trouble was, if she ran now she'd blow this opportunity. And given the level of security in this place, there was no way to know when the next opportunity might come, if ever. If she was going to get whatever records were inside that vault, and find a way to help Shai Salide, *this* was the time. It had to be now, instinct or no instinct.

She dropped the file folder and coffee cup and tucked her phone into her pocket. Time to keep her hands free.

The door to the lab had the same biometric security measures that she'd encountered at the third-floor stairwell. She scanned her card, palm print, and retinas, and got the same blue glow and tiny-harp welcome. She opened the door and slipped inside.

There was a loud thunk from the door, when it closed behind her. It coincided with a thunk in her chest.

Something was definitely wrong.

Moving cautiously, Kayne stepped deeper into the lab, watching for any sign of doom approaching. Her *paranoia sense* was tingling, big time, and she knew that ignoring it was a bad idea. But she was in it now. No turning back.

Oh hell, let's just turn back, she thought.

She turned and pushed the bar on the door.

Nothing happened.

She pushed again, harder, but it wouldn't budge.

She took out her phone and accessed QuIEK, looking for any sort of release for the door. No good. The lock appeared to be on a direct connection to some switch within the facility, and there didn't appear to be a network linked to it. It was effectively deadlocked.

She cursed herself for being stupid and tried the door a few more times. When it still wouldn't give, she turned back to the room she'd worked so hard to get into. She took a few deep breaths, made herself calm down, let the adrenaline flow through her until it began to fade, at least a little.

Nothing to do now but face whatever came next, she decided. She stepped forward and began moving cautiously down the corridor and out into the lab itself.

One of the reasons Kayne had chosen to infiltrate on this

particular day was the fact that most personnel were still off site. Those who were returning were primarily out on the assembly and manufacturing floor. There were people in the offices on the levels above, but not many. Enough to provide her with the camouflage she needed to get in without standing out as an intruder. And the air-gapped lab had limited personnel most of the time anyway, so she'd gambled that it would be the last space to "fill up" as people returned to business.

She'd apparently been more right about that than she'd realized. As she made her way deeper into the lab, the space began to feel eery and creepy. The lights were dimmed, with only a few overhead panels lit for security and safety. The few offices and cubicles she passed were all darkened and empty. The only sounds were from various machines and devices running throughout.

According to her 3D map, the server room was up ahead and on the left. That was where she had determined she'd find the data that could link the stolen patents to Shai Salide, and possibly others as well.

Since Kayne had alarms going in her head anyway, and she was pretty sure she was on the verge of being caught, she might as well try to complete the mission—some good should come from all of this effort. And if she was about to lose her freedom, she'd go out doing the job.

No sense being sneaky when no one's around, so she moved at a brisk pace now. She made a rapid circuit through the labs and offices, and in a moment she stood before the door she was looking for.

She hesitated.

There was no sign of locks or scanners or *anything* preventing her from opening that door. There were no windows, either. And, scanning through QuIEK, there were no cameras inside. At least, none that were networked. No eyes for her to see what lay on the other side.

She was about to go in blind.

Her *paranoia sense* shifted from a tingle to an impending migraine.

She took a deep breath, let it out slowly, and opened the door.

The room was empty.

Not *literally* empty. The room was filled with dozens of server racks, each containing rack-mounted CPUs and hard drives, and thousands of twinkling lights that pulsed on and off in an indecipherable rhythm. It was like seeing a time lapse of a city skyline at night, a digital urban landscape populated by beings made of pure data.

Her favorite kind of room, traditionally.

She stepped inside and closed the door behind her, then got to work. If she was caught, she was at least going to complete her mission. Because the data she needed was here, and QuIEK could copy and offload it and follow through on her directives, even if she was chained to a wall somewhere in a federal prison.

There was no WiFi network associated with these servers, and she had no way to physically plug her phone into any of the systems. But she'd thought ahead on this.

Though the servers were not accessible via an external network, they *were* networked to *each other*. So, accessing one would give her access to all. *Handy.*

The next bit was a little more complicated.

When most people think of wireless data transmission, they're usually thinking about either WiFi or Bluetooth. These are the two most common names for referring to wireless data, and from a public perception the two are unique and distinct. But the reality is that both are simply forms of radio transmis-

sion. And just as with FM or AM radio, there is a transmitter
and a receiver, and if both are tuned to the same frequency,
communication is possible.

What many people do not realize, however, is that the
physics behind radio also apply to smaller systems. In digital
electronics, there are millions of tiny "antennas" at work all the
time, in the form of circuitry and components. There's a certain
amount of "bleed" that happens as data moves within a
network. IC chips, like all things that use electricity, have an
electromagnetic signature. And that signature pulses and
changes as the various gates open and close—virtually speaking.

QuIEK was built as a quantum-based artificial intelligence.
Effectively, rather than relying solely on the binary states that
most computers used—ones and zeros, switches that go from on
to off and back again—QuIEK used four quantum states, or
what was known as a "qubit." And though it might seem that
with four states, instead of two, you'd basically just get twice
the computing power, there was a concept known as "superpo-
sition" that made it possible to stack operations, and get far
more out of a processor than one might expect.

It could get complicated—the understatement of the
millennium—but in general for every 1 or 0 in a standard operation, QuIEK could apply hundreds of additional states beyond
"on or off." And those increased states added up to giving
QuIEK the ability to process far faster than a standard
computer.

All of that was the heady, *sciency*, brain-melty stuff. But
what it meant, in this exact moment, was that by placing her
phone close to one of the CPUs, and allowing QuIEK to use
the phone's various built-in radio antennas and sensors, it could
mirror the flow of ones and zeros, and interpret those millions
of binary states as raw data.

Basically, QuIEK could read the server's mind, if it was in close proximity. And not only that, it could interrupt and insert itself in that flow of data by transmitting its own signal via EMF, and effectively *take over* the system.

Digital mind control.

It took a beat, but Kayne had worked ahead on this, setting QuIEK up with parameters for what she needed so that it would already know how to prioritize the data stream. Rather than burning time having to interpret the data from the servers, she had QuIEK simply *copy* all the data into Smokescreen. There, in her own private cloud space, thousands of microcomputers all networked together and running QuIEK could make short work of deciphering and translating all of those files and searching for what was relevant.

Ideally, Kayne would return to one of her rentals now, and bundle up in a warm blanket while she sipped hot chocolate and sifted through the files and the results that emerged with the highest relevancy scores. And, if she were so inclined, she might use anything she found to help nail Curie Motors and Ross Eckhart for corporate espionage and other nasty stuff.

But as the door behind her clicked and opened, and the negative pressure of the server room definitely shifted, first her ears popped, and second she realized there would be no blanket, no data-sifting, and no hot chocolate.

Surprisingly, now that the data she was here for was safely copied into Smokescreen, her *paranoia sense* settled down a bit, and the alarm bells from her gut went quiet. She felt a serene sort of calm come over her. Reservation and resolve regarding her fate.

She'd been running for a very long time. It was inevitable that she'd eventually run too far to stay lucky.

She turned to face what would surely be a well-armed

group of security personnel or police officers or even FBI agents. She wondered, briefly, if Eric Symon would show up.

But instead of a gaggle of armed personnel, there was only one man standing in the doorway.

Ross Eckhart.

"Hello, Alex," he smiled. "You have no idea how long I've wanted to meet you."

CHAPTER FIVE

Air-Gapped Lab | Curie Motors Facility

They were alone in one of the small offices within the air-gapped lab. Kayne had taken Eckhart up on his offer to let him lead her to some place where they could chat comfortably. She was under no illusions, though. He was being courteous to the point of making her feel nauseated, but she knew that if she tried to run, she'd find herself trapped. The deadlocked door had been her first and final clue.

She sat in a chair on one side of a round table, and Eckhart took a seat opposite. He was still smiling and occasionally shaking his head. "I can hardly believe it," he said.

"Same here," Kayne replied.

Eckhart laughed. "Yeah... Ok, I'm sorry for the circumstances. But it's just... it's hard to believe this is happening right now. I've kind of pictured this for the past couple of years."

Kayne made a skeptical expression. "This?"

"Meeting you," he replied. "And, honestly, I kind of pictured it a little like this." He nodded to their surroundings.

The office was utilitarian. There were no photos or decorations, no art on the walls, not even on one of those employee motivation posters. It was just a desk, a meeting table, and a video screen mounted on one wall. It was the kind of place someone would use for an impromptu meeting, to discuss a project or some findings from an experiment, or to duck into when they needed to make a quick, private call. Not exactly an interrogation room, but not far from it. "You certainly have low expectations," Kayne said.

"I'm sorry, did you want anything to drink? I saw you had coffee, earlier."

"You... saw?"

Eckhart smiled and nodded. "Yeah, though I admit, that wasn't easy."

"It..." she started, but stopped. She still wasn't sure how much she should be saying to this guy.

"It shouldn't have been possible?" Eckhart asked, echoing exactly what she'd been thinking.

"Mind reading now? Are you, like, a wizard or something?"

Eckhart laughed. "Well, no. Ok, sort of. But... listen, I know you have some wizardly powers of your own. You have a way to live-mask yourself out of security footage, and walk through scanners and security like none of it is there. I have some theories about that, mostly based on rumors I've heard. But you do sort of have an obvious weakness."

She thought about it, about the deadlocked door and the server room with no WiFi. She got it. No point hiding it now. "If it isn't on a network, I can't do anything with it."

Eckhart smiled and nodded.

It was more than she'd really wanted to admit or confirm,

but he was right. It was obvious. At least, in this setting. She might come to regret the confession, but seeing as how she was probably headed for a dark hole buried at the very bottom of a maximum security prison somewhere for the rest of her life anyway, she couldn't quite see the harm in giving a bit of intel to the guy who caught her.

All those federal agents, all those police and foreign security people, and I'm caught by the guy who makes electric cars. I wonder what Eric will think?

Agent Eric Symon, she knew, would play the stoic card. But she secretly hoped it burned his soul to see her caught, much less by someone like Ross Eckhart.

"We have cameras in that stairwell that link directly to a DVR," Eckhart said. "No network. When someone noticed you were in the stairwell, but weren't showing up on the networked cameras or on the infrared system, they shot video of you on one of the monitors using a smart tablet. Gotta give you credit, though. Every time they tried to send me a copy of the footage, you disappeared from it. So they got clever and took video of the playback from the DVR, recording the monitor."

Kayne was impressed. "That... really is clever."

"I pay a lot of money for clever," Eckhart smiled.

"Ok, then," she said, leaning back. "No, to the drink, thank you. I kind of regret the coffee, now that I have a full bladder and I'm probably going to prison. But I'm curious why that isn't already happening. You have a *lot* of security people on site here. I'm trying to figure out why you didn't bring any of them with you. Not to brag, but I'm kind of a big deal. At least, I'm on top of all the most-wanted lists. *Dangerous fugitive.* I guess you have a team of people waiting outside?"

"Well, there really isn't any way in or out of here that we can't cover. So yeah, in a way, I do have people waiting for you out there," he admitted.

"And they just let their CEO come in here with a known fugitive?"

"I'm not the CEO anymore," he said, a slight smirk on his face.

"Oh yeah, that's right... I was at the press conference."

There was a brief pause.

"You're dying to ask," he said.

That irritated her. "What makes you think so?"

"Because *everyone* is dying to know why I stepped down. I spent most of an hour avoiding the question, giving all kinds of vague and pithy responses that make better soundbites than answers."

"So there's very little chance you'll answer me if I ask, then," Kayne said.

"A better chance than you think," Eckhart said, and there was something in his voice. A dare, maybe. A hope.

She blinked, then shrugged. "Ok, why did you step down?"

He smiled. "Instead of answering you, how about I show you?"

E ckhart led her deeper into the lab, and she followed without a word. This wasn't the first time she'd been trapped by a guy who was all smiles, with every exit covered. It hadn't been so long ago that she'd been lured into a trap, set by a guy calling himself Reed Harltan. Harltan had actually turned out to be a thief named Roger Bale, who was working for a massive man-mountain named Victor Stanley, who was hiding himself in plain sight, posing as Harltan's bodyguard. The two of them had set her up, kidnapping her client to use as leverage, so that she would steal a rare book for them. Which, of course, she did. And brilliantly, she might add.

It was the sort of thing thriller novels were made of, but

Kayne couldn't say she'd been all that thrilled with the experience, while it was happening. Or once it was done, for that matter. She didn't like being manipulated, and she certainly didn't like her clients being put into jeopardy.

And now, as Ross Eckhart, the famous billionaire industrialist, smiled and led her deeper into his web, she was feeling a profound sense of *déjà vu*. She pictured Reed Harltan—née *Roger Bale*—glancing back at her smugly as he walked her through a suite of offices, just to show her he'd outsmarted her. Or that Victor Stanley had, as it turned out.

It was too similar. Too close. She felt her pulse speed up and adrenaline start revving. She calmed herself, or tried to. Right now she had nowhere to run. Though she did have QuIEK working on it.

Eckhart stepped through a secure door and held it open for her. As she entered he said, "Lights."

The lights came on, revealing a workspace brimming with the detritus of hands-on engineering. Equipment lined every wall and covered most flat surfaces. A large, steel table dominated the center floor space. And on it was an entire chassis for one of Curie Motors' electric vehicles.

Kayne didn't recognize the model, though that may have been due to the fact that the car had no side panels, doors, hood, or trunk. It did have an engine and a significant amount of cabling and technology woven through it, however. With its barebones, skeletal frame and a weave of thick cabling that resembled entrails a little too closely, the whole thing looked sort of "tech-macabre." It was as if a carcass had been picked nearly clean by some carrion creature, leaving only a jumble of nerves and sinews clinging to a skeleton. Though in reality, Kayne realized, it was sort of the exact opposite of that. This was new assembly. They were building it, not picking it apart.

"This will be the next model to roll off the line," Eckhart

said, gesturing toward it with what Kayne thought was affection. "The most advanced electric vehicle ever built. And a real game changer."

"Why's that?" Kayne asked. She really was curious. She loved technology, and particularly tech that fell into the "game changer" category. She wasn't yet sure what game Eckhart was playing, though, much less which game he was trying to change.

"The short version? This model will have a proprietary set of features that won't exist anywhere else, or with any other manufacturer. Not until other companies start leasing the patents from us, anyway. For a start, it will have an always-on internet connection, linked directly to the network of micro-satellites that Orbit X has been putting into orbit for the past few years."

Orbit X, Kayne knew, was Eckhart's satellite communications division. It was the key component in his publicly stated goal to provide high-speed broadband internet worldwide, to even the most remote areas of the planet.

"You're going to use the cars as relays for the Orbit X internet," Kayne said, nodding. "That's... well, it's pretty much public knowledge. Sorry."

He laughed, nodding. "I never made a secret of it, so that's ok. But there's more happening than you think. This model is a proof of concept. We'll offer to retrofit the Orbit X network to all of our previous models. And as we go forward, we'll do the same for vehicles from other manufacturers. The big innovation there is that we're going to make the whole network free."

Kayne was nodding along, but stopped, blinking. "Free? You're not going to charge for broadband access?"

He grinned and shook his head. "Not one penny. We're also not going to charge for the upgrade."

Kayne considered this, her expression shifting from skeptical to surprised. "I'm impressed. That's gotta be a few billion dollars in revenue your shareholders won't see. *That's a bold strategy, Cotton.*"

Eckhart laughed. "Is that a movie reference?"

"It's from *Dodge Ball.*"

Eckhart nodded. "Nice. I've never seen it. But yes, shareholders aren't thrilled with this plan. Which is one of the reasons I resigned as CEO. I'll be making the same announcement for Orbit X in a few weeks."

"Why?" Kayne asked. "Wouldn't you have more power to push this through if you stayed in charge?"

"I'd have more of an obligation to shareholders," he said. "That doesn't always equate to decision making power. But stepping back lets our biggest shareholder have more say."

She blinked. "And... who is that?"

Eckhart held out his hands. "That would be me. I own at least 51% of both companies. Of *all* my companies, actually. Through various holdings, of course. I masked my ownership through dummy corporations and other corporate sleight of hand. I needed to gain a majority hold over it all before anyone knew it was me. It helped keep anyone from rushing out to buy out stock, or to try blocking me. Kept the costs down, of course. But mostly it kept me from dealing with the headache of having someone working against me the whole time."

Kayne whistled. "I'm betting that still was a chunk of money."

"*Most* of my money," he smiled. "I'm in the 'billionaire on paper only' club now." He laughed and shrugged. "I have a lot of liquidity, but rebuilding reserves of cash will take a minute. Worth it, I think."

She shook her head. "Why? *Why* is it worth it? What's the part you haven't told me?"

He looked at her, a little surprised himself now. "Well, part of it is that I want everyone on Earth to have access to data and information. The internet is the great equalizer."

She laughed. "Is it? I mean... lately it seems like it's just opened up a path for the rise of new overlords."

"Social media, and traditional media, and all the partisan BS," he nodded. "You're right. They all seem like they're invested in creating more division, and scraping profit from the ruins they create. And there's the whole World Economic Forum, and their ridiculous 'Great Reset' idea. Mostly they seem to want to reset the world to the point where only the wealthy elite had any say in how things worked. Not exactly the world any of us envisioned. But no, the internet really *is* the great equalizer, as long as you have access to it. And as long as that access is... unrestricted."

She thought about this for a moment. "What do you mean?"

He studied her, then sighed and leaned against the edge of the steel table. "I saw you give a talk once, at Berkley. It was several years ago. You had founded Populus, and you were talking about some of the goals of the company. *Your* goals, I think."

"So are you trying to tell me that I'm so much older than you that you saw me speak at your college?"

He laughed. "No, I was a graduate. I sat in as an Alumni. I was looking for any inspiration I could find, on what I should focus on. Where I should start. I hadn't yet hit my stride with some of my businesses, but I was getting there. And I had been following Populus. I followed all the Silicon Valley crowd, trying to learn everything I could, to apply it all to what I was trying to do. But... well, I'm sure you've noticed, there's a lot of altruistic talk from Silicon Valley. But they tend to drop it all when the money starts rolling in. They cut deals with the wrong people."

Kayne thought back to the deals that Adrian Ballard had cut—deals with the Russians and possibly others, that ultimately resulted in her being framed for Ballard's murder and accused of betraying her country. Deals that turned her life over like a car crash on a mountain highway, and made her a fugitive for the past three years.

"But you were different," Eckhart said.

"Maybe you haven't been following my career so closely since then," she said.

He laughed. "Oh, I don't believe a word of what they've been saying about you," he replied. "I mean, it doesn't really make any sense, in the end. Why would you murder your business partner? You gained absolutely nothing from it. And the whole espionage thing, trading secrets and dirty dealing with foreign governments—unlikely. Again, what do you gain? Money? I'd been following Populus almost since it was founded. You guys had money, and could have made billions more based on some of your patents. But instead, you *gave things away*. Which I'm guessing didn't sit well with everyone at the company. I didn't know Adrian Ballard, but every time I saw him in an interview his jaw was clenched so tight I thought his head might pop off."

Kayne actually smiled at this. "He hated the public benefit programs," she said. "He really did want to make those billions. So did our shareholders. It was kind of a thing—a fight we always had."

"A fight you kept winning," Eckhart replied.

She nodded. "But only because I was the only one who controlled..." she stopped herself.

It was clear that Eckhart knew at least a little about QuIEK, but she wasn't clear on how much. And she wasn't sure how much she should share. Federal law enforcement knew, at least to some extent, some of the more choice details about her quantum-based AI and what it could do. There were plenty of foreign governments that also knew about it. But they would all keep mum on the particulars. Letting a secret like that out into the wild meant inviting more scrutiny and, frankly, more competition for getting their hands on it.

Some billionaires in the world were powerful enough to be their own nations, however. And if keeping foreign governments, especially the enemies of the US, from getting their hands on QuIEK was a priority, it would be no less so for keeping it from the private sector. Imagine Apple or Google or Microsoft having the power to breeze past any and all digital security measures, any time they wanted. Fair trade, fair competition, personal privacy, even government sovereignty would be a thing of the past.

This was why Kayne had been running all these years. Her freedom was top of mind, of course. She didn't like the thought of being locked in a cell. But it was about more than that. She had the freedom of every soul on Earth in mind. She ran so that no one could enslave humanity, using QuIEK. A lofty-sounding mission, but it was the truth.

"... controlled our patents," she finished. And if Eckhart thought there was anything odd about her answer, he simply nodded and accepted it without question.

"So, my big plan is to be one of the first tech industry powerhouses to *actually* do something for the good of humanity. *Ta-da!* And I'm not entirely alone. I'm working with Ethan Patterson on the launches for Orbit X, and he's not even charging me. Well... he's not charging me *money*. He's basically just asking for access to some of the tech for his own big, super-secret project that no one thinks is all that secret."

"Ethan Patterson... Athena Astronautics?"

Eckhart nodded.

"The guy who wants to start colonizing Mars?"

"Among other planets," Eckhart shrugged. "And other goals. I've set him up with licenses for our solar and battery tech, as well as the communications network I'm building. He's... well, this will seem kind of crazy, I know, but the whole relay plan I'm putting into cars, here on Earth? He's going to do the same thing with spaceships. And satellites. Relays, really, between here and Mars, and then on into the rest of the solar system. And then on into the galaxy. The guy's got some big plans. You should see the work some of his people are doing on this cool light-beam propulsion thing..."

"Wait," Kayne said, shaking her head and holding up a hand. "Wait... what... what does *any* of this have to do with me?"

Eckhart inhaled and blew out the breath, shrugging. "Well, nothing, really. I had no idea you would be here, so it's not like I planned for us to meet."

"So why are you telling me all of this?" Kayne asked. "Why aren't I in jail right now?"

"How long would a jail hold you?" he asked, curious.

"Plenty long if they know they need to deadlock me in place," she said. *And keep me away from cameras*, she thought but did not say. No need to give Eckhart any *more* details to work with.

He shrugged again. "So... maybe they don't find out."

She studied him, shaking her head. "What is it?"

"What is what?" he asked.

"What is it you've decided you want from me, in exchange for not sending me to prison?"

"That depends," he replied.

"On what?"

"On what it was you came here for, and why."

She studied him.

He studied her.

"My client," she said, deciding. She was going to trust him, at least this far. She wasn't sure why. Gut instinct again. If she had listened to it before, she might not be in this situation. So it could be the only way out. "Shai Salide."

"The engineer?" Eckhart asked.

Kayne was surprised. "You know her?"

"We bought her patents," he said.

"You *stole* her patents," Kayne corrected.

He made a curious face. "No... I..." he paused, then fished in his pocket to take out his phone. He swiped for a moment, searching, then showed her the screen. "We bought the company she worked for, and all the patents they owned. She was a named patent holder, so I had my people cut her a deal for her ownership. She accepted. Pretty lucrative deal, too. About thirty-million."

"She's currently working as a customer support operator because she's been blacklisted from the industry, and she can't get work in her field. She's broke."

Eckhart looked surprised. "That's... that isn't what I was told."

Kayne studied him for a moment, trying to figure his game. But the more she looked, the more convinced she became that he wasn't playing at anything. "You didn't know."

He shook his head, then made a face, his features going a bit dark. "You're saying we cheated her out of her IP, and then left her to rot? Blacklisted her from the industry?"

Kayne nodded, unsure what to think of this. She'd been working this one with the assumption that Eckhart knew everything.

Eckhart shook his head and stood. "I'll figure this out," he said. "I think I know where to start."

He walked away, slipping through the door of the lab and moving at a brisk pace toward the exit.

"Wait!" Kayne said, rushing to catch up. "Are... are you going to have me arrested?"

"You came here for this?" he asked. "You came here to find a way to get her IP back?"

"Yes," Kayne said. "I've already copied the files from your server, so that... so that a friend outside can find anything related to her. It's done."

"What about the rest of the files? Did you take anything else?"

"All of it," Kayne confessed. "Everything." There was no sense in hiding it.

"Ok," he said, nodding and considering as he kept up his pace. "Are you planning to use those files against us? You're going to take down the company? Sell secrets to our competitors?"

"No, I'd never do that," Kayne said. "Unless..."

"Unless you discover that we're exactly as crooked as you assumed we were," he said.

"Yes," she said. Again, no sense denying it.

He stopped and squared off with her. "We're not. At least, *I'm* not. And if someone here *did* do this, they've probably done it before. I want to find them, and I want to hold them responsible. So to answer your question, no. I'm not going to have you arrested."

He turned and strode toward the door. There was another loud *clunk* as he approached, the lock disengaged as he pushed through to the outside.

"I'm going to hire you to help me find them and make this right," he said. "I'm your new client."

CHAPTER SIX

Conners Ranch & Exotic Animal Safari | Near Lone Wolf, Oklahoma

Agent Eric Symon wanted to shoot Agent Roland Denzel.

Not literally.

Not... *entirely* literally.

He was a big enough man to admit that a lot of his irritation and frustration with his new boss was spinning out of their history. And he was further willing to admit that a lot of that history, particularly the parts Symon resented most, wasn't actually Denzel's fault. Symon knew he was shooting the messenger.

Still...

When Denzel and his partner, Dr. Dan Kotler, brought down Director Crispen on charges of espionage and domestic terrorism, it had the side effect of derailing Symon's very promising career trajectory. And for a few years, Symon had to work in abject drudgery and misery just to clear his name and shake off some of the reputation that had been unfairly heaped on him.

That whole thing wasn't entirely a bygone. Not yet. There were aftereffects that lingered to this day, despite all of his very best efforts and hard-won victories. And though Symon was determined to be professional and pragmatic, and even more important, "do the job" despite any resentment on his part, it still chapped him to have to take orders from Denzel.

At least Dan Kotler wasn't around.

That guy came off like he knew absolutely *everything*, and it wasn't exactly comforting to know that he sort of actually *did* know everything. Symon wasn't a fool—he gave credit where it was due. And he could see that Dr. Kotler was every bit as brilliant as he seemed. No pretense. No airs. From the most practical and objective point of view possible, Kotler was a real, certifiable genius. And that was really, truly annoying.

At the moment, Symon was following an order from Denzel to look into a lead on a potential art theft. Possibly an entire ring of art thefts. It could be big.

This should have been something that fell into the laps of the FBI's White-Collar Crimes division, but there was a special twist that brought it to Historic Crimes—the new inter-agency task force that was designed to deep-dive into threats that emerged from the quirks of history. The team was established to look into the stuff that was specifically labeled "weird," which lumped in everything from the lost city of Atlantis to Sir Isaac Newton's hidden laboratory. And, somewhere in that spectrum, stolen documents and artwork that could potentially indicate a bigger threat to the world.

That's what this particular case was about. The artwork in question had a questionable provenance, and one that might be indicative of some deeper trouble. It was outside the typical purview of the FBI, for one reason or another, and so it became part of Denzel's new pet project, known internally as "Outsiders." Which, at the moment, mostly consisted of Denzel, Kotler, Symon and his partner, Agent Mayher, and, of course, Alex Kayne—Symon's confidential informant, and fugitive *extraordinaire.* He had some suspicions about just how much of his landing the Historic Crimes gig came down to his own skills and reputation, and how much came down to being Kayne's handler. Either way, his job was to run down leads, and a lot of those leads were going to come from Agent Denzel. That was the job.

The current lead in question was an exotic animal safari in Oklahoma. There was an insane amount of money funneling through these things, and at present there were all sorts of criminal investigations happening. A lot of these places were being shut down for some pretty awful practices. The animals weren't being well cared for in some of them, to say the least.

But there were other, darker secrets at play in places like this. Murders were common. People were taking out hits on each other, trying to eliminate the competition or keep witnesses from testifying. There were also hints of illicit trafficking in everything from drugs to weapons to people, and of course in the animals themselves.

It was a dangerous and hidden business. It reminded Symon of the Wild West days of the casinos in Vegas. Criminal empires, hinting at a seedy underworld that operated by its own rules, with a public face that was all lights and smiles and entertainment. A scrim of legitimacy and innocent fun, thinly stretched over a bulging, bloated empire of evil.

Symon wasn't alone on this job. His partner, Agent Julia Mayher, was with him, of course. And backing them up was one team of suited FBI agents and another team of SWAT-gear-clad operatives sporting the polished black steel of the Historic

Crimes badge. The FBI agents were there to fan out and start collecting evidence, once the federal warrant was served. The SWAT team was already taking up strategic positions all over the property, ready to pounce if things went sideways.

Symon didn't mind being the front man on any of this. Again, that was the job. And in this capacity, at least he was acting on his training and skills.

What he resented, however, was that Denzel had given him a script, and to make sure he followed it to the letter, everything Symon said was being monitored and recorded from a van parked a few miles away. Symon had Denzel's voice in his ear the whole time. Like a Jiminy Cricket who had once derailed Pinocchio's whole life.

"Teams are reporting that things look calm," Denzel said over the channel.

"Roger that," Symon said.

"You're clear to approach," Denzel said.

No kidding. Thanks for the pointers. I would never have known that I could do the job I was trained for and have done for more than a decade if I didn't have you whispering permission in my ear. "Roger that," he said again.

As Symon and Mayher stepped onto the front porch of the home, both wearing protective vests emblazoned with the FBI logo, and each with their own black-enameled Historic Crimes badges dangling from chains around their necks, Symon hit the button on the door camera, and waited.

"Well, hello, FBI," a man's voice said. This would be Derrick Conners, the owner of the ranch, and a real interesting character, according to his profile.

His tone was pleasant and knowing, and that gave Symon a sinking feeling.

Symon held his badge up to the lens. "My name is Agent Symon, with the FBI," he said.

"Don't forget to tell them your affiliation," Denzel prompted.

Symon fought the urge to roll his eyes. "Historic Crimes task force," he said, his teeth aching to grit.

"Never heard of it," the man's voice said. "And I'm not home."

Symon looked to Mayher, and both blinked.

"You're... not in the house?" Symon asked.

"No. So go away. This is private property."

Symon shook his head and held up the paper in his hand. "Federal warrant. We're here to search the property, including this house and all structures."

"Feds come through once a month," the guy replied. "They never find nothin'. All my animals are registered and cared for. No abuse. No guns or drugs on the property. You got no reason to be here. This is harassment."

"We're looking for a painting that we have evidence is in your possession," Symon said. "Let us in, or we'll force entry."

"Force whatever you want," Conners said. "I ain't there. But I'm sending all of this to my attorney, so smile and wave, Agent Simmons."

"It's Agent Symon," he replied. "And have them reach out directly to Agent Roland Denzel." He read off Denzel's personal cell phone number and email address.

"Thanks for that," Denzel replied dryly in Symon's ear.

"Last chance, Mr. Conners," Symon said.

Conners' reply was a series of expletives and directions for where Symon and his team should go, and what they should do to themselves when they got there.

"Give the order," Denzel said.

Symon sighed. He reached up to his vest and spoke into a radio, giving the order for a breech. "Extreme caution," he said. "We're not sure who's here or whether they're armed."

He stood aside as the team went to work.

It didn't take long, and there were no major incidents. Though Derrick Conners hadn't been lying when he said he wasn't inside the home, a handful of his staff were onsite. Symon presented the warrant to a panicked-looking man claiming to be Conners' assistant.

They scoured the property, and eventually found not only the specific painting they were looking for, but a hidden room in the basement that contained hundreds of other pilfered pieces of art and antiquities. It was a trove of stolen goods—the sort of thing guys like Conners kept around as both insurance and currency. Art was an easy way to pay for something that shouldn't be traced back to either the seller or the buyer.

"Looks like we can add art thief to Conner's resume," Mayher said. She was scanning through her phone, looking over the list of identified art pieces as the experts began cataloging the collection. "So far, there isn't a legitimately clear piece in the place."

Symon nodded. That was what they'd expected. And he had a hunch that before the day was done, they'd find a lot more. Their warrant gave them more access to the house than federal agents could justify, previously. Conners had made a huge mistake—appearing in that Netflix special.

By this time, Denzel and the agents accompanying him had arrived on the scene, and he was entering as Symon gave orders to start boxing things up. They'd made several arrests among the personnel on the property, and found enough evidence to move forward with charges on Conners, and to shut down his operation here. Symon was talking to some of his team members about arranging for the exotic cats on the property to be moved.

"Good work," Denzel said, as he approached.

Symon turned from the team, and exercised a respectable restraint in controlling his expression. "Thanks," he said flatly.

"I need to talk to you," Denzel said. "I didn't want to broadcast it over the radios.

Symon felt a slight anxiety rise in him, tinged with anger. He'd been going out of his way to keep his attitude in check, regarding Denzel. He was irritated by what he saw as micromanaging, but he hadn't been openly hostile about it. He actually planned to chat with Denzel man-to-man, to ask if he could have a little more breathing room and autonomy on his operations. He was a well-trained FBI agent, after all, and experienced in running his own ops...

"It's about Alex Kayne," Denzel said quietly, leaning in.

"Kayne?" Symon asked. "Is she... has she been apprehended?" The thought sent a thrill of dread through Simon, though he was constantly prepared for the news. She couldn't run forever, despite all evidence to the contrary.

"No. Not... exactly." Denzel nodded to the open door. "We might want to step outside. I'm guessing there are cameras and mics all over the place in here."

Symon nodded, and the two of them stepped out and moved to the other side of the van that Denzel had brought to the site.

"We got a call from the head of security at Curie Motors, in Round Rock, Texas," Denzel said. "They identified Kayne as an intruder at the facility. But they were told not to apprehend her, or to call the police or FBI."

"Who told them that?" Symon asked.

"Ross Eckhart," Denzel said.

"The billionaire?" Symon asked, confused.

Denzel nodded. "They said Eckhart met with her in private, and then the two of them left the facility."

"So, Eckhart is aiding and abetting a fugitive? What's their connection?"

Denzel shrugged. "They're both Silicon Valley alumni. Maybe they were friends."

Symon inhaled and let out a slow breath. "Not according to my files. I've studied everything there is on Kayne. I know everyone she knows. Or knew, anyway, in her prior life. As far as I'm aware, the two never met."

"Can't know everything," Denzel said, shaking his head. "Regardless, he's helped her escape. We need to look into it. And since she's a Historic Crimes asset, and you're her handler..."

"Got it," Symon nodded. "I'll get on a plane."

Denzel also nodded, then turned to leave.

"Agent Denzel," Symon said, stepping forward.

Denzel turned.

"I... listen, this isn't the time, but I'd like to have a chat. About my... my role with Historic Crimes."

Denzel studied him for a moment. "I know you're not exactly thrilled to be working under me. Is it going to be a problem?"

Symon's first impulse was to say no, to smooth it out, to assure his boss that there was no issue. But that wasn't his way. "Yes," Symon said, nodding. "I think it will be. It *is*. I can handle that, though. It's my problem to deal with. But I... I'm hoping you can do me a favor, that might help."

Denzel looked at him, curious. "Ok, ask."

"Like I said, this isn't really the time..."

"Ask, Agent Symon," Denzel said.

Symon sighed. "Back off."

Denzel arched an eyebrow.

"Respectfully... sir. Look, I've been an agent for a long time. I've run operations from end to end, more times than I can count. And with a high success rate. I know what it takes to do... *this*," he said, motioning toward the house they were currently searching. "I don't need a chaperone. Or a nanny."

Denzel considered this. Symon saw what he thought might be a flash of annoyance cross the man's features, but it faded fast, and after a moment Denzel nodded. "You're right. I apologize. I'm not actually trying to be your... *nanny*," he said this last with a slight smirk. "I'm actually trying to work out how this whole 'Outsiders' thing is supposed to work. Cases like this one, they aren't even the reason Ludlum designed this thing. We're supposed to be a sort of breakout team, a group that can take on... bigger stuff. *Unusual* stuff."

"I get that," Symon said. "So why have me on a mission like this one? Why me and Mayher here?"

"Because if we're going to be that breakout team, we need to start with the *team* part," Denzel said.

Symon considered this, an idea and realization occurring to him for the first time. "You're trying to do some team building?"

Denzel nodded. "Look, I know you, Eric. The same way you've studied Kayne, I've studied you. Looked at every file, dug into your history. You're one of the best Profilers the FBI ever had. And I know that the thing with Crispen set you offtrack. You've done a hell of a lot to get back, and I see it. But you've been... independent. Probably because everyone in the Bureau lost trust in you. Through no fault of your own," he added quickly, holding up his hands. "But it forced you to work alone, work at the edges. Become... well, like I said, independent."

"Not actually a bad trait," Symon said.

"No," Denzel admitted. "Not really. Not entirely. Believe me, I've worked with Kotler long enough to know that some independent and out of the box thinking can be a good thing. Annoying, but good."

"So is this whole babysitting thing meant to break me of some bad habits?" Symon asked.

Denzel studied him. "See, it's comments like that. You're being a little insubordinate. Passive aggressive. That's the independent streak in you. And I do agree that it's useful. But what I need to know is whether you can actually be a team player. I know you're the best Profiler there is, and that's part of why you're here. Another part is your connection to Alex Kayne. But Ludlum thinks you have more potential than you've been allowed to put on show."

Symon considered this. "And what about you? What do you think?"

"I think you're a good agent," Denzel said. "I think you've shown, over and over, that you don't let personal feelings interfere with your work. But I haven't seen you really work as part of a team yet. Not really. Not when you're not the one calling all the shots."

Symon felt like raging at this. Of *course* he'd worked in teams. He had to. That *was* the job, sometimes. And he'd even worked as part of teams that Denzel himself was commanding.

What more could Denzel want from him?

"I'd better get going on this Eckhart thing," Symon said, after a moment. "Maybe we can circle up when we're both back at Historic Crimes HQ?"

Denzel nodded. "I look forward to it."

Symon returned the nod, then went to find Mayher.

Curie Motors Facility | Round Rock, Texas

The first thing Kayne had to clear up was her client policy.

"Nobody 'hires' me. I pick my clients based on whether they've been disenfranchised by law enforcement or screwed over by corporations or kidnapped by international thieves with secret agendas."

They were sitting in Eckhart's private office, and Eckhart himself was already pouring over a copy of the files from the air-gapped lab. He looked up, studying Kayne. "Ok... but you have a client right now, right? Shai Salide? You're here to help her?"

Kayne nodded. "Exactly."

"So help me help her," he said.

She wanted to respond, but she couldn't think of anything to say that would make any real sense. After all, Eckhart could have had her held by security until the FBI arrived. She'd more or less be cooked. But he hadn't. And his reasons for *not* having her arrested coincided with her reasons for being there in the first place. She wanted to help Shai, and so did he. Among other things.

There really was no reason why they shouldn't be working together.

"You're the CEO..."

"Not anymo—"

"Got it, *not anymore*. But you *were* the CEO of the company that shafted Shai. You still have pull. And you own a majority share in the company. Why not just give the patents back to Shai and be done with it?"

"When you do this," he said, waving vaguely toward the

data he was reviewing, "is it enough to just give someone their property back, or whatever?"

She hesitated.

"Sometimes," she said.

"Really?"

She sighed. "Ok, no. Hardly ever. *If* ever. Most of the time I'm helping someone who's... who has suffered some kind of injustice. So... I make it right."

"You bring justice?"

"Yes," she said.

"You..." he held up his index finger and thumb in the shape of a pistol and made a little *bang* sound.

"No! I mean... that's happened, sure. But no, it's not like that, I promise. I don't want to kill people, I'm here to *help* people."

He observed her for a moment. "But you have, right?"

"Have what?"

"Killed people."

She watched his face, and he watched hers. She wasn't sure why she always felt the compulsion, but she couldn't keep herself from admitting the truth to Ross Eckhart, for whatever reason.

"Yes," she said quietly. "When I didn't have any other choice."

He considered that for a moment. "Did you kill Adrian Ballard?"

She shook her head, her expression sad. "No. That was the Russians."

"Who did you kill?"

"Well... the Russians. That was self defense. But I've also had to deal with others. Usually it was them or my client. Sometimes... them or me." She was thinking specifically of Jason Hawthorn, the son of a corrupt Congressman who was keeping his son's human trafficking business off the radar. Jason had brought Kayne to his own private warehouse, where he was running everything from guns to drugs to bootlegged booze, and after making it impossible for her to escape he had tried to rape her. She had killed him in self defense. But the weight of that was no lighter for having a reason.

She thought about trying to explain this to Ross Eckhart, but balked. It would sound like she was fishing for justification, maybe validation, or maybe some kind of sympathy. Maybe. But part of her just felt no need to explain herself or her actions to anyone. She was doing something no one else in history had ever done, and though she did not consider herself above the rules, or above the law, she did think of herself as fitting in a sort of unique category of justice. Like a CIA agent or a member of Special Forces—there were rules, but there were also gray areas. All of this would be impossible to explain to anyone without sounding like a sociopath.

So she settled on a simple statement that Eckhart could take or leave.

"I've had to deal with some very bad people, to help my clients. And I've had to do some very bad things, sometimes. And I don't regret the decisions I was forced to make, even if I regret some of the consequences."

He was watching her, quiet. She watched him back. And then, after a long moment, he simply nodded and turned back to the laptop.

"So it looks like we've done this patent thing to a lot of people," he said. He shook his head. "I had no idea. I thought we were getting all of this on the up and up, but I see at least a hundred patents on this list that have a pretty dubious pedigree."

"That's one way to put it," Kayne said, leaning in to look

over his shoulder. "So how does that happen without you knowing?"

He shrugged. "I hate to say it, but it's just too small of a thing to come to my attention. I own a dozen large businesses, Alex. A few of them take up more of my time and energy than the others. And I have this grand master plan I told you about. So I let my people deal with a lot of this stuff."

"Sounds like some of your people are dealing dirty," she replied.

"Sounds like it," he agreed. He sighed and rubbed his eyes. "This is going to take a month, sorting through all of these to find the trail. Whoever did this knows how to hide themselves. There are hundreds of these so far, and there are probably more I haven't found yet. I'll have to trace each one back to whoever was handling the accounts, see if there's anyone in common, vet everyone. Sorry, Alex. It looks like your client may be out in the cold for longer than you'd like."

Kayne glanced at him then back to the laptop and sighed. She'd been hemming and hawing about this decision since Eckhart had caught her in the server room, but now seemed the time to address it. The compulsion to open up to him, wherever that was coming from, would win this round. "I have another way," she said.

He looked up, hopeful.

"I have... some software, we'll say. Something that can sift through this quicker."

He smirked. "Is it the sort of software that would cause your business partner to try to cut a deal with the Russians and sell state secrets while under a US government contract?"

"Something like that," she frowned.

He nodded. "Ok. No need to give me all the details. I suspect this is what's had you on the run for the past few years, right?" He stood and stepped aside, gesturing to the laptop. "Be my guest."

Kayne sighed again and stepped forward. Instead of taking the seat offered to her, however, she took out her phone and tapped a few commands. QuIEK picked up on what she wanted, and went to work immediately.

Unlike the air-gapped laboratory, Eckhart's little office space had its own dedicated WiFi network. It was fire walled in all directions, preventing anyone from accessing any data within his sphere, unless he specifically authorized it.

Or unless QuIEK walked right through those firewalls and security measures like they weren't there.

On Eckhart's laptop screen, data danced, moving in a *Matrix*-style march from top to bottom as QuIEK sorted through every file, getting the scoop on context and history. After just a moment, a series of company names appeared on the screen.

One by one those names got cross-referenced against a convoluted trail of public records until finally they boiled down to only one name.

"Well, I guess that isn't all that surprising," Eckhart said, leaning forward to see the results.

"Bertrand, Owens & Cromwell," Kayne read aloud. "Is that a law firm?"

Eckhart nodded. "The same firm I've worked with for years. They helped me structure all of these companies, almost from the beginning. I... I've always trusted them."

"So, why isn't it surprising that they handled the patents?"

"It's one of the primary things I pay them for," Eckhart shrugged. "It was always easier to let them handle every acquisition." He looked up, "I tend to delegate details."

"Gotcha," Kayne said. "No judgment." Though, as she

considered it, details were kind of her jam. Keeping on top of every detail was how she stayed alive, stayed out of prison, stayed ahead of the bad guys and good guys alike. She couldn't imagine what sort of disaster her own life would be, if she just put things on cruise control. She even double-checked on QuEIK's work, most of the time.

But how much simpler would her life be, if she *could* let someone else handle it all?

Of course, she had let Adrian handle the details of Populus, and that had resulted in her being wanted as a fugitive by every government on Earth. A pretty solid argument in the "cons" column.

"I made the mistake of trusting they were doing things right," Eckhart said, standing up straight and frowning. "And that's resulted in people getting hurt."

She could hear the self-recrimination in his voice, and her instinct was to give him some kind of out, some kind of avenue for grace.

"It's possible someone within the firm just screwed up," Kayne offered. "That it wasn't anything intentional."

Eckhart looked at her, surprised. "You believe that?"

She shrugged. "I said it was *possible*." She sighed, shaking her head. "But no, I don't think it's likely."

"Well, either way, it needs to be cleared up. But there are two things I need to sort out first."

"What's that?" Kayne asked.

"First, I want to know what possible reason they would have for stealing patents I've authorized us to pay for and obtain legally."

"And second?"

"Second," Eckhart said, "I *really* want to know more about this software you're using."

CHAPTER SEVEN

Law Offices of Bertrand, Owens & Cromwell | San Francisco, California

Bertrand, Owens & Cromwell did not have a Texas office, but Ross Eckhart did have a private jet. And in less than five hours after leaving the Curie Motors facility, Kayne found herself standing next to Eckhart as they rode an elevator to the top floor of the law offices.

The elevator doors opened to an expanse of rich wood paneling and leather cushioned chairs. A waiting area, funneling arrivals to a large, oak desk where a receptionist stood to greet them, all smiles.

"Mr. Eckhart!" she said, a pronounced French accent coloring even these two, short words. "We were not expecting you!"

"A tale that has hounded me all the way back to my conception," Eckhart said, smiling in return.

The receptionist laughed, then stepped around from behind the desk. "I have already spoken with Madame Bertrand," she said. "I have been instructed to show you and your guest to her offices."

Eckhart nodded, and Kayne followed along as they were led through the upscale suite. As they went, Kayne noted that the décor of the place was extravagant, expensive, and mostly European. She leaned in to whisper to Eckhart. "*Madame Bertrand?*"

"Her husband was a French attorney and businessman. Very wealthy. And when he passed, he left all of his holdings to Adele. She has dual citizenship, but prefers the US these days. After her husband died, she stayed in Paris for a time, taking over his firm, until she relocated to Silicon Valley and opened offices here. When I met her, it was just Bertrand & Owens, and it was a much more modest set of offices." He looked around as they went. "Most of this was paid for by billing me and my businesses."

"When did the third partner come into the business?" Kayne asked.

"Four years ago," Eckhart said. "Why?"

She shook her head. "I like to know things."

"I sensed that about you," Eckhart smiled.

They were led into a large suite of offices, just as lavish as the rest of the space. Adele Bertrand was already standing and moving to greet them when they entered.

"Ross," she smiled, extending a hand. "What a pleasant surprise."

Eckhart took her hand and nodded, then indicated Kayne. "This is Alex Kayne."

Kayne's eyes threatened to widen, probably from the pressure of her heartbeat racing up by at least a hundred beats per minute. But she managed to keep herself in check and shook Bertrand's hand when the attorney offered it.

"*The* Alex Kayne?" Bertrand asked.

"Apparently," Kayne replied, giving Eckhart a look.

Bertrand also looked to Eckhart. "Ross... you've put yourself in a very precarious situation."

"I do that," he replied, smiling. "Which is why I pay you so much money."

"There are some things that even we can't fix," she replied.

"I haven't found one yet," Eckhart replied.

She studied him, then smiled, laughing lightly. "Well, I'll make sure this isn't the first. Come in, have a seat. Julia," she said, looking past them to the receptionist, "please bring coffee."

"Yes, Madame," Julia replied, and she was off.

They all took their seats at a ring of comfortable furniture occupying a corner of the suite. Kayne and Eckhart sat on a loveseat as Bertrand lowered herself elegantly into a plush chair. "Things certainly seem intriguing already," she said, looking at each of them. "How may I help?"

"It's come to my attention that some of the patents I thought we had purchased legally were actually stolen from their IP owners," Eckhart said.

Bertrand looked surprised. "Ross... I assure you, that isn't the case."

"No?" He took out his phone, opened the file that QuIEK had built, and showed it to her.

Bertrand looked it over, bringing up a pair of reading glasses that had hung by a pearl necklace from her neck. She examined the phone, shook her head, and handed it back to him. "I'll have our people look into this immediately."

"So you're saying you had no idea about any of it?" Kayne asked.

Bertrand looked at her with an expression that seemed more like amusement than irritation. "Certainly not. But it does appear that something is wrong. And I intend to find out what happened."

Kayne nodded, though she was not content to simply trust that Bertrand was on the up and up.

She hadn't told Eckhart this, but from the moment they entered the building, Kayne had QuIEK peeking into every open network it could find. She couldn't spare a glance at her phone, at the moment, but the AI should be gathering intel on everyone they encountered, and from there it would start looking into public and private records. An invasion of privacy, for sure. The exact sort of thing Kayne wanted to prevent world governments from doing. But this was how she'd not only helped her clients get the justice that was their due but also made sure that she, herself, stayed out of the worst kind of trouble.

Probably faulty and hypocritical logic there, she knew. But her life was strange. And sometimes you had to do the wrong thing to do the right thing.

They chatted for a time as Julia brought the coffee. Bertrand used a large display—revealed when a painting on her wall shifted to become a monitor—to bring up the files on all the patents and acquisitions QuIEK had uncovered. "These were not all handled by one individual in the firm," she declared. "Do you see the case numbers? The first three digits indicate the attorney assigned to oversee the acquisition."

Kayne quickly scanned through the file names, knowing that QuIEK was also snagging copies of these for later review. Bertrand was right, of course. There were hundreds of case files on the display, and rarely did any two of them share the same first three digits. "How many attorneys work here?" she asked.

"In this building? Fourteen-hundred are onsite, at any

given time. Worldwide, we have more than three thousand associates."

Kayne's eyes widened. "That's a lot of suits."

"And designer pumps," Bertrand smiled, nodding. "We're nearly 80% female."

"Go girl power," Kayne replied. Again, Bertrand smiled.

"With so many attorneys," Eckhart said, "how do you keep track of them all? To make sure they're doing everything on the up and up?"

"Oh, Ross," Bertrand said, shaking her head. "You always cut right to it. You've been our biggest client for at least a decade. Can't you trust me to look into this?"

"Of course," Eckhart said. "But you know the rule... 'trust but verify.'"

Bertrand sighed and nodded. "We have a system of checks and balances. We employ an entire department of security analysts. Each file is not only numbered but encrypted using the lead attorney's personal encryption key. No one can access the files without that attorney specifically opening it to them. Each remote access is logged and reviewed by the security analysts, and they, along with an in-house AI, flag literally anything that seems off. Flags trigger audits, audits require the lead attorney and a senior partner to review."

"What if a senior partner is the one breaking bad?" Kayne asked.

Bertrand laughed, shaking her head. "Well, there has to be a line somewhere. There are only three of us, so we are each other's checks and balance. But we have a pact of trust. Of course, trust can be broken. As the founder, I insisted on a breakaway clause in each partner's contract. If I ever discovered one of the partners was doing something illegal, I have the sole authority to expel them. It's my nuclear option."

"And if *you* are the one doing something illegal?" Kayne asked.

This time she could read a hint of annoyance in Bertrand's expression. "Then everything I built, everything I worked for, and the jobs of three-thousand good and hard-working people will all go away. That's not something I take lightly."

Kayne studied her. She wasn't sure if Bertrand was actually as sincere about her own culpability as she implied. But for the moment, there was no reason to doubt her. Because, in the end, she was right—if she was the corrupt one, she was risking every-thing. And for what? More money?

Kayne knew money could be a very powerful motivator. But looking around at Bertrand's offices, she couldn't imagine this woman feeling compelled to amass more than she was due. Everything in this space screamed "self-made woman." Kayne had a certain amount of appreciation for that.

And for what it was worth, she found herself liking Adele Bertrand, and secretly hoping she was *not* the one behind this.

They continued talking for another half hour, and then Eckhart asked if he could speak to the other two senior partners.

"Both are out of the country, I'm afraid," she replied. "I can arrange to have them conference with you over a video chat, if you like."

Eckhart nodded. "Thank you. I'd appreciate that." Then he paused, looked at Kayne and then back to Bertrand, and said, "I'm also going to need a little help with Alex, here."

Kayne's eyebrows shot up. "Help with me, how?"

"He's asking me to ensure he doesn't get into any legal trouble for aiding and abetting a fugitive," Bertrand replied, smiling lightly.

Kayne took this in, and nodded. "I see."

"Not just that," Eckhart said. "I want you to look into what it would take to clear her name."

Kayne hadn't had a sip of coffee in several minutes, but still found herself choking as if it had gone down the wrong pipe. "I'm sorry... what now?"

"That's going to be a challenge," Bertrand said. "These aren't light charges, Ross."

"I'm aware," Eckhart replied.

"And... forgive me, but how do you know she's not guilty?"

"Hey!" Kayne replied. "I'm kind of sitting right here."

"I don't," Eckhart admitted. "But I think she's innocent." He turned to Kayne. "Are you?"

"Innocent?" Kayne asked. "Of murdering Adrian and committing treason? Yes, I'm innocent."

"Is there more?" Bertrand asked. "Things for which you are not innocent?"

Kayne laughed. "Of course. I've been on a fugitive for the past three years. The crimes keep stacking up."

"But you're working for the FBI now," Eckhart said, prompting.

They'd had time to swap stories on the flight in. She'd told him about Agent Symon, and about Historic Crimes. "I'm just a confidential informant," she said. "They've already told me they can't get the charges dropped. Even your guy... Ethan Patterson... he's the head of the Historic Crimes Oversight Committee, and even he can't get them to reconsider."

"Even billionaires have their limits," Eckhart said, smiling lightly.

"But your work with law enforcement, and the support of both Ross and Mr. Patterson, might be a useful place to start," Bertrand mused.

Kayne looked to each of them. "I'm... not asking either of you for this..."

"There are no guarantees, of course," Bertrand said.

Kayne nodded. "I... was not expecting this. So I don't know what to say. But whatever you can do... if anything... thank you."

She wasn't used to being the one on the receiving end of this kind of help. It felt weird, and scary. And surreal. Like it might be yanked away from her at any minute.

Was this how her clients felt?

"I'm surprised you haven't been able to just clear things up with that magic software of yours," Eckhart said.

Alex shrugged. "I guess that's something I have in common with billionaires," she said. "We both have our limits."

CHAPTER EIGHT

Curie Motors Facility | Round Rock, Texas

"So... they just... *left?*" Mayher asked.

Symon and Mayher had finally arrived at the Curie Motors facility, after high-tailing to Oklahoma City to catch a flight into Austin, then rushing to Round Rock in a rental car. Agents from the local FBI offices had already scoured the facility, top to bottom, with the help of the Curie Motors security team.

"Yes, ma'am," one of the local agents said with a slight drawl. A native Texan, Symon figured. Though, he knew, a "Texas accent" was more of a spectrum than an objective phenomenon. Locals in the Austin area didn't typically sound any different from the general public in LA or New York or almost anywhere else in the country, in his experience.

Studying accents was a part of Symon's training as a profiler, and one thing he had learned over the years was that accents were not always an indicator of region. Some people adapted an accent as an affect, as a way to sort of hide in plain sight. A laid back, country-boy accent could do a lot to diffuse both tension and suspicion, under certain circumstances, merely by encouraging the listener to fall back on stereotypes and assumptions. If you sounded simple and harmless, people assumed you *were* simple and harmless. Verbal camouflage.

"Once we arrived on the scene," the agent continued, "security gave us full access. We have video of Ms. Kayne, after she entered a stairwell on the East end of the building. It was shot with a camera aimed at a live monitor. For some reason, she's missing from all the other footage."

Symon glanced at Mayher. "QuIEK," he said.

"Isn't that the same trick she used in Boston?"

Symon nodded. "Live masking. A new trick." He turned to the agent. "She has... software. The official name for it is the Quantum Integrated Encryption Key. She calls it 'quake,' and it's very powerful."

"Sounds like it," the agent said, nodding.

"I'm sorry, I didn't catch your name," Mayher said.

"Daniels," the agent replied, reaching out a hand and smiling. "Agent Christian Daniels."

Symon watched as Mayher shook his hand and noticed a slight blush in his partner's cheeks.

It surprised him.

Not because she might find Daniels attractive—he was a pretty clean-cut and fit guy, with classic good looks. Even *Symon* thought the guy was attractive. But it was more because he felt a kind of annoyance over seeing her preen for the guy, and that was unexpected.

Mayher had been Symon's partner for a few years now. There was nothing romantic between them. But spending so much time together, facing so many challenges, including nearly dying numerous times, it did tend to bond people.

Maybe, subconsciously, he'd started thinking of her in a more...
possessive way.

Well, if that was the case, he needed to watch it. And shake
it off. As his partner, Mayher was off limits. Whatever shadow
of a feeling he might have for her, his own personal ethics
wouldn't let it go anywhere.

"Do we have any footage of Kayne and Eckhart together?"
Symon asked.

Daniels shook his head. "Nothing. We have shots of
Eckhart leaving the building by himself."

"Show me," Symon said.

Daniels brought up a tablet and ran through a series of
clips. Sure enough, each shot showed Eckhart walking along by
himself, through the facility and out into a parking garage.

"Run that back," Symon said, leaning in. "There," he said,
motioning to the video.

"What is it?" Mayher asked.

"He's talking to himself," Symon said. He looked up to
Daniels. "Any audio?"

Daniels shook his head. "Video only on most of the security
feeds. The company has a strict privacy policy."

Symon nodded, returning his attention to the video. "He's
not talking to himself," he finally said. "He's talking to Kayne.
See? He looks over to her. Then here, he holds the door for her.
QuIEk is making her out, but leaving him in the shot."

Daniels whistled. "That's some software. If it weren't for
Mr. Eckhart's movements, you'd never guess anyone else was
there."

"That's the kind of thing you come to expect from Alex
Kayne," Mayher said.

Symon looked up to see the exchange of smiles between
them.

"Send me this footage," Symon said, a little more abruptly

than he'd intended. "And anything else you have. Do we know where they went, when they left?"

"San Francisco," Daniels said. "I've already reached out to the local Bureau offices there, and they're posting agents at the private airport where Eckhart's plane landed."

"No word on where they went, from the airport?" Symon asked.

Daniels shook his head. "We didn't have eyes on them when they left. Eckhart had a car waiting, and the service doesn't keep records of destinations. Client privilege. But if they come back to the airport, we'll have them."

Symon nodded. He wasn't quite as confident as Daniels, regarding how firm their grasp on Kayne could get. She had a history of being slippery, even when the noose was already around her neck. They couldn't count on her stepping into a trap as obvious as going back to the airport.

He *could* reach out to her.

Since she'd been working as a CI for Historic Crimes, she'd given him a means of reaching her if he ever needed her. It was untraceable—routing and rerouting through networks and systems all over the planet. There was no chance of back-tracking to find out where she was. But if any of the Historic Crimes caseload could use her particular skills, she was usually responsive and helpful.

It was part of a plan, on the direction of Director Ludlum, to create some grace for Kayne, and potentially remove her from the Most Wanted list. So far, the goodwill Kayne was generating hadn't amounted to much leeway among the decision makers in Washington. But it was still early days. As her numbers grew, and she helped close more cases and take down more bad guys, she was getting a growing, positive reputation. The hope was that it would be enough to bring her in out of the cold, maybe with a full pardon.

The standing directive, though, was that Kayne was still a fugitive, and she would still be apprehended on sight. And for three years now, Symon had been determined to do exactly that, regardless of her status as a CI, or any goodwill he or anyone else felt toward her.

He liked Kayne. He was convinced she was innocent of the crimes she was accused of—but he would do his job. He would do everything he could to put her in cuffs and lock her away, because those were the orders. Like them or not.

So far, though, he hadn't leveraged the relationship he had with her, as her handler, to lure her into a trap. Mostly because he'd always assumed it would never work. She was too clever, too paranoid, to fall for it. And trying it would only damage their relationship, make her less likely to trust him, and possibly result in losing her as an asset. Too much risk for too small of a shot at arresting her.

But maybe there was an opportunity here.

"Tell your people at the airport to pull back, stay out of sight," Symon said.

"Sir?" Daniels asked.

"What?" Mayher added.

"I want to know if they get back on that plane. I want the flight plan. And any transport they arrange for when they land. I want one of our people in the driver's seat."

Mayher caught on. "You're setting a trap," she said.

He thought he caught a tone in her voice—surprise, maybe. She knew him. And she knew Kayne. She was not exactly Kayne's biggest fan, and had always found the CI arrangement to be questionable at best. But it was clear to Symon that Mayher must have always assumed he was only *pretending* to be after Kayne. She must have assumed he was deliberately throwing the race, every time Kayne had slipped through his fingers.

He was not.

He did like Kayne. He did believe she was innocent. He sincerely hoped they could find a way to clear her name, and bring her in out of the cold.

But he would put the cuffs on her himself, and drag her into a cell, if he was able. Because that was the job.

The trouble was, Mayher was wrong.

He wasn't setting a trap for Kayne, because he knew she'd see right through it. And knowing that, the opportunity was something different.

He wasn't setting a trap. He was sending a message.

Kayne wouldn't set foot in that airport. She wouldn't board that plane. And they'd never be able to catch her on the other side, with an agent planted as Eckhart's driver. Kayne would see all of that.

What was important was that Symon where Kayne was *right now*. In general terms, maybe. But they'd get specifics somehow.

Symon assumed Kayne would know immediately that the FBI was on to her location. That would put her on high alert. She'd be monitoring for everything.

What he wanted was for her to see the plan. He wanted her to see that they were counting on her getting on that plane and stepping off into custody. She'd avoid that like a nuclear hotspot.

But she might just stay put, for now. She might relax, just enough, that he could catch up to her.

He might just have her this time.

CHAPTER NINE

Law Offices of Bertrand, Owens & Cromwell | Palo Alto,
California

Kayne wasn't used to this.

In fact, she was so unaccustomed to it, she barely had the words
to describe it.

Sitting beside Ross Eckhart, billionaire technologist, while
the two of them reviewed not only the files from Bertrand,
Owens & Cromwell but also the deep analysis of those files
offered up by QuIEK, the feeling that had settled on her was
one she hadn't felt in years. At least three years, by her
reckoning.

Trust.

Somehow, through a means she couldn't backtrack or trace,
and in a timeline so rapid she couldn't piece it together, Ross
Eckhart had managed to earn her trust.

It felt weird.

Paranoia and distrust had become default behaviors for her, over the past three years. She didn't fully trust *anyone*, except maybe to the level that she was certain they would inevitably betray her or turn on her. She knew she could always trust *that*.

Admittedly, that was a cynical sort of mindset. She tried not to linger on it.

Trust wasn't entirely foreign to her, of course. She had a certain level of trust in Agent Eric Symon. She liked him, and she believed he liked her. She even believed him when he said he thought she was innocent. So, she did trust him, at least a little.

But she also *knew* him. No matter what he said, no matter whether he believed her or not, he would arrest her, if he had the chance. She would never give him that chance. She would always keep him at a distance, always have an escape route ready for when he was around.

She trusted Eric to do exactly what he thought was right, at least. And that had to count for something, didn't it?

She had come to trust another fellow Historic Crimes "asset," too. Dr. Dan Kotler, archaeologist and FBI consultant— and inveterate troublemaker, from what she'd seen of him. Or maybe just "trouble magnet."

He was a charming guy—brilliant, personable, relatable. He'd even been a fugitive for a while. A *short* while, anyway. But being hunted had a way of sharpening your perspective, and it was a club that only had a scant few members worth knowing.

Kayne felt like Kotler was a kindred spirit, at least. Someone who could relate to her life in a few different ways. And someone she could talk to about it, if she ever felt the need. But did she really *trust* him?

Sort of.

Although she had no concerns that Kotler would try to get

her arrested, she also knew that if it came down to it, he wouldn't directly intervene to prevent her capture. He wouldn't interfere to prevent his FBI partner, Agent Denzel, from putting her in a cell. Though he *had* been known to give her some heads up, and to keep some of her secrets, there'd been no jeopardy in it for him at the time. It was more like an opportunistic kind of assistance—no harm in looking the other way, no danger in letting this fact or that observation slip.

It was possible, though, that she trusted Kotler more than any other human being on Earth. In a way, at least. After all, in her current social sphere, he was the most like her—an outsider with something to offer, with talents or skills or knowledge that could be useful, and with a willingness to actually help. It was an odd form of common ground, but it was enough to give them a bond.

Everyone else on Earth seemed to be gunning for her, though, so it was kind of a low bar.

Despite feeling a certain level of trust in Kotler, however, she didn't feel like she could *depend* on him. His loyalty to her could only go so far. And she couldn't really demand that he put his own freedom or his own life on the line for her. Trust was fragile. It had its lines that couldn't be crossed. And she wasn't willing to push those lines with Kotler, or with Eric.

Ross Eckhart, however...

She wasn't sure *why* she felt she could trust or depend on Eckhart. She just... *did*.

Again, it came down to gut instinct. And again, maybe it was because they shared a certain sort of background. Maybe he just felt like a kindred spirt as well, though one from a different aspect of her soul than Kotler or Eric. Less "kindred spirit," and more "complementary spirit." Maybe.

Eckhart had already shown her that he was willing to risk going to prison right alongside her, if it meant he was doing the right thing. It was a level of altruism she hadn't yet seen from anyone else—though she knew many good people who'd be willing to sacrifice themselves for the greater good. This was different, though. This was more akin to her own perspective, her own way of thinking. This was the most *like her* commitment to "doing the right thing" that she'd encountered, since going on the run. And it was possible she was letting it color her impression of him.

But she thought there might be something else lending an aura of trust to their newly formed relationship: Ross Eckhart was one of the most candid and pragmatic people she'd ever met.

This wasn't necessarily a revelation. Nor was it unique to his relationship with her. In his interactions with the media, Eckhart had always been a bottom-line guy. He didn't pull punches, and wasn't all that well guarded with his words. He was famous for tiffs with other influencers in the technology sphere, and with high-profile government officials. Public opinion of him tended to be "softly galvanized," with some of his biggest detractors frequently flipping to become his biggest defenders, and vice versa.

He was a hard guy to figure. But he was genuine, and he was authentic.

Kayne hadn't exactly followed him closely over the years, but he was impossible to miss, if you spent any time monitoring traditional or social media. His rise to the status of billionaire was always of interest, obviously, but it was the work he was doing in his various silos of business that seemed most fascinating. He appeared to be something unique in the current class of Silicon Valley billionaires: A futurist with a plan, and no concern about doing what was expected of him.

In other words, Eckhart was building an empire of technological advancement that was so far outside the box of profit-driven development, he sometimes came across as insane. His predictions about the future were bizarre and wildly off in the weeds at times. The focus of each of his businesses seemed ludicrous to even the most progressive financial analysts. On paper, Ross Eckhart seemed like a crackpot, destined for financial ruin and historical obscurity.

And yet...

All his predictions had a tendency to come true. All the tech he was developing had a tendency to attract a rabid following. All of his plans tended to inspire the public and ultimately set trends for other influencers in his sphere.

Ross Eckhart would be considered an eccentric crackpot, except for the fact that he always seemed to be *right*. Which meant other people in his orbit ended up following while he led. He set the pace, and they had to race to keep up. It was the sort of thing certain Silicon Valley egos eventually began to resent. It made enemies.

It made him an outsider.

It made Eckhart someone Kayne could relate to.

"What about Alishondra Cromwell?" Eckhart asked, startling Kayne out of her reverie. "You seemed to kind of flag on her."

Kayne blinked and shook her head. "No," she said. "I don't think so. I know she's relatively new to the firm, but she's a named partner. She's making a ton of money already without the need to get her hands dirty. I'm not saying attorneys would be above doing something illegal for money," she smiled, "but having one of the richest people on the planet practically giving them a money printing machine seems like it would keep the greed fires contained. Also..." She hesitated.

"Also?" Eckhart asked.

"My gut says no," Kayne replied.

She wasn't sure what she had expected from him, as a reaction. Maybe he'd burst out laughing? *Gut instinct* wasn't entirely absurd to someone like Eckhart, but he might laugh over the idea of using it to eliminate suspects.

Instead of laughing, or even smirking, he simply nodded, shrugged, and turned back to the work as if she'd just shown him proof that it couldn't be refuted.

"That's it?" Kayne asked.

"What's what?" Eckhart replied.

"I say, 'it's gut instinct,' and you're just... ok with it?"

He studied her, then shrugged again. "Most of my decisions in life are gut instinct. I'm not going to start questioning it now."

Kayne considered this. "Ok. So... does *your* gut say anything?"

Eckhart shook his head. "Not yet. But I'll admit, this kind of thing isn't my strong suit. I tend to default to trusting people until they burn me, and I don't spend much time trying to hunt down traitors in my midsts. That's one of the reasons I have lawyers in the first place. And a personal security team."

Kayne smiled, shaking her head slightly. *Defaulting to trusting people* was nearly the exact opposite of how she'd lived for the past three years, and she couldn't even imagine how she might do it and still survive. Trust was like a foreign language to her right now—or a language she hadn't spoken in a long while. It felt weird. Maybe even wrong. But it had certainly worked for Eckhart. And she imagined it must be a...

Well... it must be a *peaceful* sort of life.

Kayne envied him for it.

She settled back. The two of them were in a spare conference room in the Bertrand, Owens & Cromwell offices. They'd been given *carte blanche* access to anything they needed, with the exception of the firm's case files. They had agreed to Adele Bertrand's very strict conditions regarding access to internal files, and then almost immediately had QuIEK scour the entire network.

Someone here was dealing dirty, and Eckhart had agreed with Kayne that these were exigent circumstances. He seemed unperturbed by any moral or ethical qualms over it, as long as they stayed on their objective.

The data they were getting was limited, at any rate. Kayne wasn't interested in digging up dirt on anyone. She was looking for threads that they could tie together to lead them to whoever was behind all of this. And as they looked, it was becoming increasingly evident that things went deeper than they had imagined.

It wasn't just patents controlled by Curie Motors. The corruption extended to *all* of Eckhart's businesses, everything he had any ownership in.

"Someone here is definitely playing a game," Eckhart said. "But there's no common thread between all of these." He leaned forward, bracing his hands on the table, shaking his head as he considered all the dead ends.

Kayne was studying the files QuIEK had pulled together, looking for any hint of a common denominator. So far, the only facts these files had in common were that they were owned by Ross Eckhart, and they were managed by BO&C.

It was hard to conclude anything other than BO&C— possibly the entire firm—was dirty. That implied a pretty big conspiracy, which would have to be managed and kept secret among not only the senior partners but every attorney on staff, as well as every clerk, every intern, every contractor. It was corruption on a monumental and, frankly, unmanageable scale. But by all evidence, it *had* to be the firm itself. *All* of it. Or...

Or it was *Eckhart*.

Kayne felt the familiar pang. Trust, eroding. Suspicion, rising.

She glanced sideways at Eckhart, who was engrossed in reading through a group of patents and holdings, subconsciously shaking his head as he silently scanned, line by line.

He certainly *seemed* sincere in his desire to track this down, to ferret out whoever was responsible and help Kayne bring justice for her client. Could that all be an act?

Again, Kayne's gut said no. But how much could she really trust that? Instinct wasn't evidence. But she hadn't kept ahead of those who pursued her for the past three years by ignoring either evidence *or* instinct.

It was just that those two pillars of her life hadn't really come into such conflict before.

She was feeling a sort of cognitive dissonance, and a growing uncertainty. And *that* made her more basic instincts kick in. Something felt *off*, even if she couldn't quite define what it was.

Trust was a dangerous game. Trust was how fugitives got caught. Kayne had avoided capture all these years precisely *because* she didn't trust anyone, and she always remained paranoid, standing apart from everyone so they never had a chance to put their hands on her.

She could feel it happen, as she dug in to more of the files. The erosion of trust. Or, maybe, the *dampening* of it. Eckhart hadn't done anything to actually erode that trust so far, so this was Kayne tamping it down, keeping it in check. The longer she sat there, the more that gut feeling nagged at her. She tried to rationalize it away, but it kept coming back, kept whispering *something is wrong.*

Better to be paranoid than to be imprisoned. Or worse.

"I... need a restroom," Kayne said.

Eckhart looked up, and she thought she saw something strange pass over his features. But he said nothing as she left the conference room, moving through the richly decorated halls of the BO&C offices, past the receptionist's desk. Julia looked up as Kayne passed and smiled lightly as she tracked her movement toward the restroom. The receptionist's desk squarely faced the waiting area and the elevators, as well as the entrance to the main stairway.

No chance of getting out that way, Kayne thought.

In a moment she was in the restroom, and she quickly closed herself in one of the stalls. She took out the sat phone. She had QuIEK tap into public records for the building and turn it into a 3D model, highlighting any potential exits.

Her options were limited.

This was not like her.

How had she let herself fall into such a huge lapse of judgement? For the past three years, she didn't even go to the bathroom in her own *hotel room* without at least three exit strategies. And now, here she was, her guard down and her exit routes narrowed to practically nothing.

Was she really so desperate to trust someone that she'd fold at the first sign of a good man?

Maybe, she thought.

Because she couldn't help it—even now—believing that Ross Eckhart really *was* a good man. Even with things feeling off with this patent thing, and in the practices of his business. Even with the potential that not only was *he* the secret, real villain of the story, but that he'd managed to fool her and lure her into a snare so completely, to get past her meticulously arranged web of paranoia and self-preservation, and effectively trap her in this place. He somehow got her to let her guard down, and now...

She was back to being paranoid. She knew that. Maybe it was gut instinct again. Maybe it was just habit. Self preservation was a hard one to kick, particularly when you didn't want to.

She turned her attention back to the 3D model on screen and had QuIEK overlay it with a WiFi map.

By accessing all the various devices in the building, from mobile phones to tablets to laptops, even smart watches and set-top steaming devices, QuIEK could gauge WiFi signal strength throughout the entire structure. And by overlaying that with the 3D model of the building, it could effectively recreate details and features in the layout, the placement of furniture, even people moving around in the various spaces. It was, in effect, like using sonar—pinging a signal off of objects so that QuIEk could "see."

Doing this allowed QuIEK to use its predictive algorithms to determine a potential exit, and a strategy for getting there.

Kayne looked it over, made a few educated guesses about things that QuIEK could *not* see, and then made her plan.

She left the restroom, but instead of turning to pass back by Julia Faure's desk, she went the opposite direction. Moving quickly through the lavishly decorated suite of offices, she came to a door that led into a back stairwell. She pushed her way through, and quickly made her way down, swiping and typing on her phone as she went.

The bottom floor had an exit to the outside, as well as one to the lobby. The outside exit would trigger a fire alarm.

She pushed through and heard the siren spin up as she rushed away. A car would be waiting for her about three blocks East of the building. From there, QuIEK had randomized a set of arrangements, including decoys meant to throw off anyone who might be watching.

Her lapse in paranoia had meant that she had to do this all rough and ugly. She rarely relied on QuIEK to make her exit strategies. But strange times called for unusual methods. And if she was going to trust anyone or anything, QuIEK was her best choice.

But despite that, whether this exit worked out or not, she came to a decision. A commitment, really.

She would not make a mistake like this again.

Even if it turned out to be baseless paranoia, even if Ross Eckhart turned out to be exactly who he seemed to be, trust wasn't something she could afford.

From here on out, it was *trust no one.*

CHAPTER TEN

Curie Motors Facility | Round Rock, Texas

Symon cursed as he hung up and slipped his phone back into his pocket.

"Let me guess," Mayher said, "Kayne got away. Again."

"About ten minutes before local FBI showed up," Symon said.

"How'd she get wind of them?" Mayher asked.

Symon shook his head. "Maybe she had QuIEK looking for any calls to that area. I tried to keep it secure. Maybe she's monitoring phone calls now?"

Mayher shook her head, an annoyed expression darkening her features. "What about Eckhart?"

"He's in custody," Symon said. "But given the fact that he was literally in the offices of his attorney, he was lawyered up before we even got there. They're already hinting that he was coerced by Kayne."

"Was he?" Mayher asked.

Symon considered, then shrugged. "Who can really say? I wouldn't put it past Kayne to kidnap someone, if she thought it would help one of her clients."

"That video didn't look much like coercion," Mayher said.

"Coercion doesn't have to be physical," Symon replied. "Maybe she had some dirt on him. That seems likely, given her M.O. She would have come here to find some way to help her client. And he *is* the CEO, after all."

"*Was*," Mayher corrected.

"Was what?"

"*Was* the CEO. He stepped down, as of this morning. It's all over the news."

Symon considered this. "Eckhart stepped down as CEO of Curie Motors? Did he say why?"

Mayher shrugged. "News is full of speculation. He didn't really give a solid answer in the press conference. A lot of fluff."

"Is he sick?"

Again, Mayher shrugged. "Maybe?"

Symon thought about this, in light of Kayne's most recent activities. Did her appearance here have anything to do with Eckhart's announcement? Had she forced him into it? That would make a certain amount of sense, if he was her target. She might have planned to get justice for her client by making the CEO step down and lose power and control, maybe even a lot of money.

Except even a news-agnostic like Symon had heard of the business and technological empire of Ross Eckhart. Curie Motors wasn't the only business he ran. It wasn't even the biggest part of his revenue. Making him step down wouldn't serve much purpose. At least, Symon didn't think so.

"See what you can dig up on this," he said to Mayher. "It may be linked."

She nodded. "What are you going to do?"

"I'm going to talk to people here," he replied. "See if I can figure out what it was that brought Kayne here in the first place, and why she left with Eckhart."

They separated, with Mayher stepping back into the office that Curie Motors had loaned them. Symon left to find his way back to the security offices on the first floor, on the far end of the building, near the lab where Kayne and Eckhart had met for a chat.

There was something here that didn't feel right, but Symon was having a hell of a time putting his finger on it.

When he finally arrived at the suite of security offices, after walking half a mile through the Curie Motors complex, he held up his FBI and Historic Crimes credentials for the guard on duty, and was let into the overall suite without hesitation. The Historic Crimes Unit was still too new, and essentially unknown, for the fancy black badge alone to gain him access, so he was still in the habit of presenting his FBI creds. But that was fine—the point of the task force was that it was a *cooperative* effort between law enforcement agencies and civilian operations. Both Symon and Mayher were still FBI agents, effectively "on loan" full-time to Historic Crimes. They still operated under the authority of the Bureau. Symon suspected this was all intentional, on the part of the authors of the Historic Crimes charter. It was a way to sort of "borrow authority," along with government and civilian resources, in the name of a unified goal and purpose.

Since joining HCU, Symon had slowly started to get past his initial hesitation about the task force, embracing its mission as his own. In part, this might have been due to the struggle he'd been through in the Bureau, after Crispen's arrest. But he had also started to see the possibilities the HCU represented.

There was a lot of potential there. A lot of room for upward momentum, but also a lot of opportunities to do some very real *good* in the world.

And all he had to do was swallow his pride and follow Agent Denzel's lead.

He shook his head, involuntarily. That last was a jagged pill, for sure. As reasonable and rational as he tried to be about Denzel, it was hard to let go of the grudge he'd had for the past six years.

And then there was Denzel's concern about Symon as a "team player." The very accusation made Symon angry enough to punch someone. How could anyone say he wasn't a team player? He'd spent his career as part of a team, and then as a leader of others, even after years of being a pariah in the Bureau, after having his career derailed. Now he was going to have to prove himself all over again, because he was *too independent?* What was it going to take to show he was in it for the long term?

But that was a problem for later. For now, he had a job to do.

He was given directions by some of the security personnel, and eventually found his way to a large office in the back of the suite. He knocked, and was welcomed in by Stephen Spencer, Eckhart's head of security.

Spencer wasn't permanently officing out of Curie Motors, Symon had learned. He was head of *all* security for Ross Eckhart, and had journeyed to Round Rock with his employer for the big announcement. In his debriefing with Symon and Mayher, Spencer had told them that it was he who ordered his people to call in the FBI, once he knew who Alex Kayne was.

"Agent Symon," Spencer said, standing and smiling as he offered Symon a hand.

Symon shook it, and the two sat once again, on either side of Spencer's desk.

Symon looked around at the office, which was spacious compared to others in the suite, but had far fewer personal touches.

"I have work spaces like these at every business Mr. Eckhart owns," Spencer said. "All I have to do is enter the room and everything is waiting for me." He indicated his laptop. "The glories of the tech industry."

Symon nodded. "Remote work has its advantages," he said.

Spencer smiled. "What can I do for you?"

Symon sighed, shaking his head, shrugging a little. "I'm not entirely sure yet, honestly. I'm casting nets, looking for answers to questions I may not know I should be asking. You understand."

Spencer nodded. "I do. Of course, I've given you full access to everything, and I've told you all that I know. But we're here at the service of the FBI."

Symon considered for a moment, then asked, "How long have you worked for Ross Eckhart?"

Spencer thought for a moment, then replied, "I started with him not long after he started building his portfolio of businesses. About fifteen years, I believe."

"Long time," Symon remarked. "In all those years, did you ever notice anything that might indicate that Mr. Eckhart was into anything illegal?"

Spencer frowned. "Not exactly. I mean... there's always something going on that pushes the line. It's the nature of businesses like these."

"Did anything ever *cross* that line?" Symon asked.

Spencer shook his head. "No, not really. And anytime something illegal did happen in one of Mr. Eckhart's businesses, he was usually the first one to condemn it. I know what kind of reputation he has, but don't believe everything you hear. He's a good and honorable man."

"And yet, you called us to tell us that he was aiding and abetting a fugitive."

Spencer studied Symon for a moment and gave a brief nod. "That's the way I interpreted it. But maybe he didn't have much choice in it all."

"That's what his attorneys are hinting at," Symon nodded. "Have you been in contact with them?"

"I have," Spencer replied.

"And what did they tell you?"

"They advised me not to speak with law enforcement without one of them present."

Symon again nodded. "And yet, here you are. Are you concerned at all?"

"Should I be?"

Symon smiled, shaking his head lightly. "I appreciate you talking to me openly. I'm just wondering, what was it that Alex Kayne was after, in that lab?"

Spencer sighed. "Well, at this point I do have to decline to answer specific questions without my attorney present, under their advisement. The matter involves certain trade secrets, that I am legally prevented from revealing."

Symon considered this. "I could obtain a federal warrant, if it would help."

"It might be the only way," Spencer replied.

Calling my bluff, Symon thought. Though it wasn't entirely a bluff, at that. If he decided he needed that information, he felt like he had enough to get the warrant. He might even have exigent circumstances, in the right light. But pushing that could get messy.

So far, Spencer had been cooperative. And Symon could hardly fault him for deferring to the advice of his attorney.

There were big tech secrets here. Things that might even be covered by governmental secrecy and protection. Symon would have to look into that, which meant time spent on red tape and bureaucracy, rather than on his investigation. That was more "last resort" territory.

Pushing Spencer wasn't going to get Symon anywhere, he realized. Instead, he fell back on his expertise, constructing a mental profile of Spencer, trying to find the man's motives.

"Why exactly did you report Kayne's presence to the FBI? As I understand it, Eckhart had told you to let him handle the encounter."

Spencer shrugged. "That was my legal obligation, I believe. Once I realized who Alex Kayne was, and learned she was a fugitive, I thought it was my duty to call it in. She represented a danger to the company, and to Mr. Eckhart."

"But you told us that he left with her of his own free will."

"It's what I believed at the time."

"And now?"

Spencer again shrugged. "Now, I'm not so sure."

"Because you talked to the attorneys?" Symon probed.

"Is that a problem?" Spencer asked.

Symon shook his head. "It's what I'd expect. But it just feels a little strange to me, that your instinct about all of this changed so suddenly."

"I worked in law enforcement myself, for a time," Spencer said, spreading his arms and smiling. "You know as well as I do, sometimes your instincts shift when you have more information."

"True," Symon agreed. Though, in his own experience, the "more information" that fueled law enforcement instinct rarely came as advice from an attorney.

"Well," Symon said after a moment, "I only have one last

question. Can you tell me why Eckhart resigned as CEO of Curie Motors?"

Spencer gave a light laugh. "Is that relevant to your investigation?"

Symon returned a slight smile and shrugged. "Who can really say, at this point? It might be, so I have to inquire."

Spencer considered this. "In all honestly, I'm not allowed to say anything on that topic. Not to the press, and not to anyone else. Our attorneys have been very clear on that."

"It could be pertinent to my investigation," Symon replied.

Spencer shrugged. "It may be. But you and I both know that I have no legal obligation to assist law enforcement in an investigation. I've been very forthcoming, and since I'm not under criminal investigation myself... I'm not, am I?"

Symon shook his head. "No, you're not."

"Then I can't be compelled to present anything incriminating, anyway. I have no evidence that would prove the innocence of either Mr. Eckhart or Alex Kayne, so that also can't be compelled."

Symon listened to this, sighed, then stood, smiling. "Well, it certainly does sound as if you've been thoroughly briefed by your attorneys."

"They're really the attorneys for the business," Spencer said, also standing. "But... yes, I have."

He reached across his desk, and Symon returned the gesture, accepting Spencer's firm handshake.

"Agent Symon, I promise you, I'm not withholding anything relevant to the case."

Symon didn't believe a word of this, but nodded. "I'm sure that's true. And if anything comes up?"

"I'll contact you directly," Spencer said. "As I said, we're here at the service of the FBI."

Symon left the office and made his way out of the suite and

back to the space that Curie Motors had generally offered for their use, while they were here.

Chatting with Spencer had been a bust. There was nothing new there. But it had been fruitful in other ways.

It was time to talk to Eckhart. And it was a sure bet that meant talking to Eckhart's attorneys.

CHAPTER ELEVEN

Palo Alto Jail | Palo Alto, California

It wasn't Ross Eckhart's first time in a jail cell, but his previous stays had been over far more petty criminal activities.

When he was twelve years old, he'd been picked up for shoplifting, and because he refused to identify himself he'd been "given the treatment," as his father had later put it. Cuffed, carried away in a squad car, and put in a holding cell. He'd spent only a couple of hours there, and was by himself the entire time. His parents had been furious, both at him and at the officers for "locking a child up like a criminal."

The officers, for their part, had been congenial about it. "He *is* a criminal. And since he wouldn't tell us who he was or even how old he was, we couldn't know he was twelve."

Eckhart's father, a practical and pragmatic man, decided at some point that the officers were right, and that having young Ross sit in a cell for a bit might actually do some good.

It did, though not the way his father might have intended.

What the experience taught Eckhart was that, as scary as

going to jail was, it was something he could deal with. If it happened, he'd get through it.

Years later, he was picked up for racing on a public street. His car was impounded, and Eckhart was arrested and charged with reckless endangerment. Once again, he had refused to identify himself, which led to further charges. And once again, he found himself in a cell. This time for fifteen days.

Being charged and jailed hadn't scared him much, but it was something his father told him that did shake him up.

"There are going to be many laws and rules you'll want to ignore," his father said. "And for some of those, maybe you're right. But if you build a reputation for being a criminal, you'll always be under scrutiny. They will always be watching. And that will make it more difficult for you, no matter what it is you try to do." He forced his son to look him in the eye. "I can't make you do anything, and I won't even try. I just want you to know this. Pushing the rules, without breaking them, can give you many advantages. When you break the rules, and you get caught, it becomes that much harder to work in the gray areas of life. And the gray areas are where all the opportunities are."

It was a lesson Eckhart had taken to heart, because it was the first time anyone had given him a *philosophy* to live by.

Eckhart's own father had worked in "gray areas" all of his life. He'd never broken any laws, as far as Eckhart knew. He'd faced scrutiny, had been sued a few times, had been threatened. But he'd always managed to come away not only free but somehow *advanced.*

His father was a good man. Not a criminal. He was successful, because he was willing to take risks. What he wasn't willing to do was create a rebellious reputation for himself, because that would stack things against him from the start. Breaking the rules was only effective if no one expected you to do it.

Eckhart stopped doing things that crossed the line, from

that point forward. He nurtured a reputation as someone who pushed the line, who flirted with breaking the rules, who nudged things right to the edge, but never quite crossed over.

Until now.

He'd known that Alex Kayne was a fugitive. Talking to her didn't necessarily break any laws. His mistake, he realized, was flying her to San Francisco, after openly identifying her to his security team. Stephen Spencer—his security chief, and a man who had worked with Eckhart for years—had absolutely done the right thing by calling the FBI. It smarted a little, that someone Eckhart considered a friend would turn on him that way. But Eckhart, like his father, was practical and pragmatic. If Spencer *hadn't* called it in, he wouldn't be the man Eckhart hired.

So it was settled. Eckhart crossed the line, and here he was. Sitting in a cell might be just the first of several consequences, and he would face and deal with them as they came. That was that.

Now what?

Now, he waited.

Adele Bertrand herself had accompanied him to the police station, where he was being held and interrogated. She'd advised him the whole way, had immediately ordered him to say nothing, and had done all the talking with both the police and the FBI. She began hinting that Alex Kayne had coerced Eckhart into flying her to California. She had reminded them all that Kayne was listed as a very dangerous and capable fugitive. "My client had no way of knowing whether his life, or the lives of his employees, might be in danger, if he refused to do as she asked."

It was a pretty elegant defense, when it came down to it. And Eckhart figured that it would ultimately work. Though he felt a bit of shame about throwing Alex under the bus.

He wondered about her, even *worried* over her. It was weird.

How did she know?

How did she know that law enforcement was approaching, when she ducked out and made her escape?

It wasn't just Eckhart's question. Bertrand had asked him the instant they were alone together.

"How did she know the FBI were approaching?"

"She has ways," Eckhart said. "She must have been tipped off."

"So she excused herself, went to the restroom, then... disappeared." Bertrand was just outlining the facts, not asking for verification. So Eckhart simply nodded and said nothing.

The thing was, even though Eckhart knew that Kayne had her mythically powerful AI software doing her bidding, he couldn't quite figure out *when* she'd realized there was a problem. They'd been in the middle of scouring BO&C's files when Kayne had sort of... well, *stiffened* was the only way he could think of it. He'd noticed her getting tense, but hadn't asked her about it, figuring she'd tell him if she wanted him to know. And when she'd excused herself to go find a restroom, he didn't pry. He felt they'd established a rapport. *Trust.*

But then the fire alarm went off. And shortly after, the whole building was locked down as FBI and police raided the place, floor by floor, eventually storming in to put Eckhart in cuffs, with Adele Bertrand right on their heels.

And Alex Kayne was already gone.

Again, as a practical and pragmatic man, Eckhart didn't entirely hold it against her, that she disappeared and left him effectively "holding the bag." This was what she'd been doing for the past three years, by all accounts. She had instincts forged to protect her, to push her to run, to escape danger and avoid capture. That must have been what kicked in.

Or, he was forced to admit, maybe she'd seen *him* as a threat.

He had sort of "captured" her, after all. He'd confronted her in the lab, and had arranged it so that escape would have been impossible, even for her and her magic software. In fact, it was those arrangements which had ultimately snared Eckhart himself. When he'd led Kayne out of the building and straight to his private jet, it was really a given that Spencer would report it. That was his job. And at that point, for all Spencer or the rest of the security team knew, Eckhart really was in some sort of danger.

Though it was curious that what the FBI initially said about Spencer's report was that it was about Eckhart "aiding and abetting a fugitive."

Why would he jump to that conclusion, instead of assuming that Eckhart might have been abducted?

And why had he changed his story to coincide with Bertrand's strategy, after the fact?

An officer arrived at Eckhart's cell, opening it and telling him to follow. Eckhart followed.

He was ushered into yet another interrogation room, and introduced to the FBI agent who would be asking questions—Agent Eric Symon.

Also present was Adele Bertrand, who quickly whispered to Eckhart to let her do all the talking, at least initially.

With introductions complete, Bertrand talked to Agent Symon at length, as Eckhart sat silently. She deflected his questions and doubled down on the assertion that Eckhart had been coerced. Eckhart was tempted to interrupt many times, to make assertions and correct the record. But silence was the order he'd been given, and it was a good one. He would learn more and stay out of trouble, if he remained silent and let Bertrand do her job.

After a while, however, Bertrand looked to him and said, "You can answer Agent Symon's questions."

Eckhart nodded. He had been prepared for this. Inevitably, it would never satisfy the FBI for him to keep silent. He'd have to give his testimony eventually, if only to try to clear his own name. "Alright, Agent Symon. Fire away."

"Thank you," Symon said. "It was a long flight, getting here from Austin, and I'd hate to waste the trip. Five hours in coach has done a number on my back."

He smiled, and Eckhart smiled back.

This was a tactic, of course. *Camaraderie*. Common ground. But also, a little jab. *Some of us don't have private jets*, Symon was saying. It was a way to put Eckhart on the defensive, to alienate him. In the presence of Eckhart's attorney, Agent Symon was doing anything he could to tip the scales in his favor, to try to make Eckhart slip.

"I can recommend several very good chiropractors and massage therapists," Eckhart smiled.

"Ah," Symon waved, "my health insurance probably wouldn't cover any of it. Government policies, right?"

"Right," Eckhart said. "So, what can I do for you?"

"Well," Symon said, "since you were arrested for aiding and abetting..."

"Allegedly," Bertrand interjected.

"Right, *allegedly* aiding and abetting," Symon nodded. "And since your attorney is claiming you were abducted and coerced, I was hoping you'd be willing to cooperate, to help me track down Alex Kayne."

"And if he does so," Bertrand asked, "will there be an offer of immunity?"

Symon shrugged. "I can always ask about it."

"How about doing so, and then coming back with a guarantee?" Bertrand remarked.

Symon looked directly at Eckhart. "Well, it's hard for me to take that to my superiors when I haven't gotten much cooperation yet."

Eckhart knew the play. *Give me something, and maybe I'll see about getting you immunity.*

It was a sucker's bet, Eckhart knew, and one that the FBI was in no way obligated to honor.

Bertrand knew that, too, and she was about to say something when Eckhart put a hand on her arm. "Adele," he said, "It's ok."

"Ross..." Bertrand started.

He shook his head, then leaned forward a little, looking at Agent Symon.

"The truth is, I have no idea where Alex Kayne went, after leaving that conference room. We didn't discuss anything outside of what she was looking into."

"And what was she looking into?" Symon asked.

"She has a client," Eckhart replied. "A young engineer who was cheated out of some patents, when Curie Motors acquired the company she works for."

"Do you have the name of this engineer?"

"He's under no obligation to share that with you," Bertrand said.

"It's pertinent to my investigation," Symon said.

"Which Mr. Eckhart is under no legal obligation to assist you with," Bertrand replied.

"If he's withholding evidence, any chance of immunity is gone. I'll make sure we prosecute him for aiding and abetting, obstruction of justice, transporting a known fugitive over state lines, and anything else we can come up with."

"That's your right," Bertrand nodded. "But since we've already established that Mr. Eckhart was coerced, I'm more than certain your case will fall apart before it even reaches the bench."

"I wouldn't be so sure," Symon replied. Then he turned back to Eckhart. "But we can skip all of that, if you'll consider something."

Eckhart, curious, glanced at Bertrand, then back to Symon. "What would you like me to consider?"

Symon locked eyes with him for a moment, then held up a finger, rose from his chair, and left the room.

Eckhart blinked and exchanged another look with Bertrand. "Is he asking me to consider that he's weird?"

"Don't agree to anything," Bertrand said firmly. "And be very guarded about what you say. They're recording everything."

"Not anymore," Symon said as he re-entered the room. He pointed to the camera mounted near the ceiling, and Eckhart saw that the red recording light was off.

For good measure, the agent slid his chair to that corner of the room, and tilted the camera so that it aimed at the wall. He then unplugged the cable from the rear of the camera, letting it dangle.

He returned the chair to the table and took a seat.

"Off the record," Symon said.

"Agent Symon," Bertrand said, rolling her eyes. "We know better than to believe that *anything* could be off the record in this investigation."

Symon nodded. "You could be right. But I'm asking you to trust me, at least for the moment." He looked back to Eckhart. "For Alex Kayne's sake."

Eckhart was studying him. There was something in the man's demeanor. A tone. Eventually he nodded. "Ok. I'll take the risk."

Bertrand was alarmed. "Ross, I can't allow you..."

"I'll take the risk," Eckhart said, locking eyes with her.

She shook her head, sighed, and then shrugged. "Ask away," she told Agent Symon.

Symon nodded. "I know that Alex didn't coerce you into anything. I can't prove it, of course. But... I know her. I've been chasing her for years now. I've been in direct contact with her, more than once. She's one of my confidential informants."

"The most wanted person on the planet is your CI?" Bertrand asked.

"And an asset to the task force I work with, the Historic Crimes Unit."

"Historic Crimes?" Eckhart asked, smiling. "Sounds like the name of a CBS police procedural."

Symon smirked and nodded. "I didn't name it. But I do work for the HCU, as an FBI contingent. Basically, I'm on loan. But the point is, Kayne is an asset to the unit, and I'm her contact. I probably know her better than anyone else on Earth. And I know she would not kidnap you and force you to bring her here. Not unless you were into some pretty bad stuff. And if that was the case, she wouldn't just leave you to the FBI, to be picked up on charges that might not stick. Not without making sure there was plenty of evidence to shut this case tight. She's... more *thorough* than that."

Eckhart was listening. Everything Symon was saying sounded so absurd, but also intriguing.

And it lined up with what he'd experienced.

He had sensed a few things about Kayne, as they traveled to San Francisco, and as they worked side-by-side, poring over the patent files. He felt a kinship with her, in a way. They had a shared ideal—to use the technology they created for the betterment of humanity. And they had a similar attitude toward the "rules" of life and society. The fact that she was a fugitive didn't faze him and didn't change his impression of her.

He believed her, when she said she was innocent.

"You believe her, too," Eckhart said suddenly, the realization dawning on him. "That she's innocent. That she was framed for those crimes."

Symon hesitated, as if considering the ramifications of a confession, then nodded. "I do."

"But you're still planning to arrest her?" Bertrand asked.

Again Symon nodded. "I am."

"Why?" Bertrand asked.

Symon looked at her. "*Because* she's innocent. Because it's my job to bring her in. And I believe that's the only way I can really help her get out of this. But the thing is, she's good. Very good. She has a... resource..."

"QuIEK," Eckhart said.

Symon looked at them. "She told you."

Eckhart nodded.

"That means she trusts you. As much as she trusts anybody."

Eckhart felt a sort of thrill at this, for reasons he couldn't explain. It was as if, on some level, he and Agent Symon were agreeing on a somewhat abstract reality—the trust of Alex Kayne did not come easily, and only came to those who were worthy. It was something to... well, to covet, in a way. Her trust was a signal, of sorts. *I'm on the inside. I'm part of the inner circle.*

"Agent Symon," Eckhart said, leaning forward. "Alex came to Curie Motors to track down a series of patents, and to bring justice for her client. A woman named Shai Salide. She's a brilliant engineer. And when my company acquired the company she worked for, someone orchestrated the theft of her intellectual property. I was..." he hesitated, knowing that what he said next would completely destroy the coercion defense that Adele

Bertrand had constructed. He glanced at her, apologetic. "I was helping her track down the people responsible."

Bertrand stiffened slightly, but let it pass.

"And how did that bring the two of you here?" Symon asked.

Again Eckhart watched Bertrand's face as he spoke. "We believe someone at BO&C is behind this. Not just stealing Ms. Salide's patents, but doing it over and over with every acquisition made by all of my companies."

Bertrand said nothing.

Symon turned to her. "Do you know anything about this?"

"I knew that's what they were looking into," she replied. "I don't know who could be responsible. I assure both of you, I have no knowledge of any such activity within my firm."

Symon nodded. "Ok," he said. "At least we're getting somewhere." He thought for a moment, then said, "Mr. Eckhart, I'm inclined to drop the charges against you, in exchange for a favor."

Eckhart's eyebrows rose. "What favor?"

Symon leaned forward, "Help me find her," he said. "Help me find Alex Kayne. And help me to help her."

Eckhart studied Symon, then nodded. "Alright," he said. "I'm in."

CHAPTER TWELVE

Kayne was well away from the BO&C offices when she learned about the FBI raid. She was still too close to all the action to feel comfortable laying low in public, and so she had QuIEK arrange for a place to stay. For good measure, she rented numerous places all over the city, booked half a dozen hotel rooms, and bought airline and bus tickets, all using various pseudonyms, some of which had been linked to her already. This was, in itself, one big smoke screen, to keep anyone looking for her bogged down in tracing each and every lead, while she stayed put for the moment.

The place where she was staying, however, was found in a more low key, less traceable way. She had QuIEK scan listings on sites like Craigslist and elsewhere, reaching out on her behalf, usually via text message or email, arranging payments by prepaid credit card numbers, and eventually booking a small, single-room apartment in a seedier part of town. All of this happened behind layers of encryption and anonymity, so no one looking would ever be able to link the activity to her. And the parties she dealt with were unlikely to cooperate with law enforcement. Especially since these were under-the-table transactions.

When she arrived, the place already had occupants, in the form of cockroaches and, gauging by the droppings, a rat or two. Not exactly resort living.

It would do, though. For now. She didn't plan to stay long. And her M.O. tended to be much fancier, cleaner places, so this was almost like camouflage. It was less likely that anyone would look for her in a place like this.

Still, she'd play this as if someone might come kicking in the door at any time.

Locking the door behind her, she also moved a heavy dresser against it. The room had two windows—one in the living/sleeping space, and one in the very tiny kitchenette, tucked into one corner. Both led to the same brick-lined shaft outside, which rose from the ground to the roofline. The shaft was an odd feature, probably the remnant of some tiny court-yard from when the place was built, and more or less sealed off when it was remodeled some time in the 80s. If she dropped to the ground from her second-floor rental, she'd basically be trapped until she could scale her way out, or she'd have to bust through the window of a ground-floor apartment. Too risky.

But near the kitchen window was a pipe that she thought she could use to reach the roof. And the satellite photos of the building showed that she had a few options for escape from there, including a short leap to the building next door. If she was forced to improvise, she at least had a shot.

Not her finest escape plan, by a vast stretch. But it would have to do for now until she could set up better options.

She was off her game.

Eckhart had put her off her game.

No, that wasn't fair. The truth was, she'd put *herself* off her game, because of how things had gone with Eckhart. She'd opened herself up to greater risk, and it had come around to bite her in the butt.

She pulled a chair close to the kitchen window and tethered a laptop to her sat phone, propping the phone on the windowsill. She had picked up the laptop on the fly, ducking into a pawn shop and using her phone to pay for the first working unit she could find. In terms of specifications, it was kind of a dud. It was slow to start up, and sluggish to operate, bogged down as it was with bloatware and porn. But it could tether to the phone, and from there QuIEK could essentially wipe out its hard drive and rewrite its operating system to Kayne's preferences, essentially offloading processing power to QuIEK, which would then relay everything to the laptop as if it were just a dummy terminal.

The whole setup took around three minutes. And when it was done, QuIEK was already feeding her everything she needed.

She started by catching up on events since she'd left BO&C.

Eckhart had been arrested. That wasn't surprising, given that he had actually helped her escape from Curie Motors. She looked and saw that he was being charged with aiding and abetting a fugitive. That would be her.

Bertrand had gone with him, though. And a quick snoop into the captured video and audio from the precinct's interrogation rooms showed that the lawyer was in her element. Kayne felt herself relax a little. She knew how tense it could be, to find yourself in handcuffs and being interrogated. With Bertrand at his side from the start, though, Eckhart had an excellent chance of being absolved.

Especially since the defense seemed to be "blame Alex Kayne."

"Thanks, guys," Kayne groused, shaking her head. "Love being the scapegoat."

That was alright, though, despite being a little annoying. Kayne really was the reason Eckhart was in this mess. And though she didn't really appreciate the insinuation that she had "coerced" him, what better defense could Bertrand offer, under the circumstances? Kayne was already a fugitive, already wanted for a litany of crimes going right up the scale to treason. A little coercion in the mix didn't matter much, and it might actually allow Eckhart to go free. Something Kayne really did want.

More to the point, it might justify Kayne's instinct to flee the BO&C offices, leaving Eckhart behind. It might justify her doubt in the trust that was growing between them.

She had QuIEK set up to flag her as things progressed. She needed to step back and see what could be done to pull together the pieces of this whole thing. She still had a client out there, even if that client had no idea who Kayne was. And she could hardly help Shai Salide or anyone else if she found herself locked in a cell.

It was time to get her head back in the game.

First, she pulled together all the data and files that she and Eckhart had been scanning through at the BO&C offices. She added to this the files she'd lifted from the air-gapped lab at Curie Motors. QuIEK began running interpretive scans, looking for patterns that Kayne might have missed. It would flag and alert her to anything it came across, and she'd apply her good ol' gray matter to it a little later.

That served to keep the case moving. Now she needed to get her own situation sorted.

She engaged *Hyper Paranoia Mode*—her funny, not-so-funny term for obsessively plotting and planning as many possible scenarios and routes for escape as she could think of. QuIEK could add potential threats to the list, but even her astonishingly powerful quantum AI software didn't yet have the capacity to see all angles and consider all contingencies. Neither did she, for that matter. But between the two of them, they could cover most bases, and at least give her an advantage, regardless of the specific scenario.

It took nearly four hours, but in that time she had her plans, routes, and resources in place. And in a way that even she thought was more clever than usual.

Since leaving this roach and rat infested dump wasn't wise at the moment, Kayne used services like TaskRabbit and several other freelance labor sites and apps to arrange for a few things to be done IRL—*in real life*. She purchased materials and supplies from numerous retailers in the area, and engaged freelancers to pick up and deliver those things as needed. She rented storage lockers all over the city, using a web of false identities and fake bank accounts, and had the freelancers hide the keys in innocuous locations that she would visit as needed, or when the opportunity arose.

She tipped very well, and five-star ratings abounded. And given that no given freelancer was privy to more than a single aspect of her plans and preparations, there was very little opportunity for one of them to figure things out, or become a liability and talk to the police. If anything, the only real risk was that they might loop back to get a key they'd dropped off, and use it to steal whatever she'd had them stash for her.

Since most of what she had them pick up was mundane— rope, clothing, small tools, etc.—it wasn't likely any of them would care about taking any of it. And if they did, so be it. She had stashes like this appearing all over the city. Redundancy was fundamental.

Working this way, she eventually had an elaborate network of contingency plans in place. And much of what she set up was a sort of randomized stack of solutions and resources she could put into play as needed, depending on either her current location in the city or her shifting needs.

It was time intensive, and without QuIEK she'd never have been able to do it so quickly, nor could she have kept track of it all. But by the end, she was actually kind of impressed with the result. So much so that she had QuIEK replicate the process and start setting up similar stockpiles and contingency resources in just about every major metropolitan area across the US, and even in some foreign countries. QuIEK could easily multi-task the identities and requests and payments, and track them on Kayne's behalf. And anywhere she found herself, going forward, QuIEK could guide her to any resources she needed. She wished she'd thought of this years ago.

QuIEK got to work, and within a few hours Kayne would have a vast network of resources just waiting for her.

She felt clever and a little full of herself, which she took as a good sign. It wasn't every day that a temporary fix became, potentially at least, the best permanent solution. And now, with resources literally mapped out for her if she needed them, she could return her attention to the sort of bleak here and mildly stressful now of this drab, depressing, hopeless little apartment.

Temporary discomfort only, she reminded herself. She'd tough it out in the rat-hole for tonight, but she already had additional safe houses lined up, including a few locations that weren't technically residences. No reason not to use industrial spaces, from time to time. They could come in very handy.

She would transition away from San Francisco as quickly as she could, over the next few days. She wasn't sure where she'd go next—she only knew it would be *away from here*. And that was good—because if *she* didn't know where she was going, no one else would be able to guess, either.

She got a ping from her phone and used the laptop to check in on what QuIEK had found.

Agent Symon and Agent Mayher were looking into her appearance at Curie Motors. That was to be expected. Any time there was even the slightest chance that Kayne had finally slipped up, she could count on Eric to pounce. So seeing the two of them investigating at the Curie Motors facility was no real surprise.

What she hadn't really anticipated was that Symon would book a flight to San Francisco quite so quickly.

Something about his conversation with Stephen Spencer must have set off his Spidey-sense.

She scanned through video and audio surveillance, and QuIEK pieced together angles from several vantage points. Spencers office, itself, had no recording devices active, and since she hadn't been monitoring live, she couldn't tap into anyone's computer or mobile device to hear what was happening.

But there was a camera in the corridor that had a view of Spencer, via a reflection from the glass of an office across from his own. His blinds were open, and though his face was partially obscured, Kayne could see his lips moving.

She called up a few pieces of software she'd procured over the past few years and had QuIEK start scanning and extrapolating from the footage. It only took a moment, and QuIEK began reading Spencer's lips and translating his words to speech.

Kayne listened to Spencer's side of the conversation, translated into a lilting sort of AI voice. She couldn't hear Symon's side, but she could figure out his questions by context, mostly. It was a one-sided snooping, but she felt she had enough to get the gist, since Spencer was the one providing most of the answers anyway.

For the most part, he confirmed Kayne's guess, that Bertrand was advising Eckhart to go with coercion as a defense. That made sense.

What didn't make sense was the timing.

When had Spencer talked with Bertrand?

Kayne flipped back to the footage of Eckhart and Bertrand chatting with local FBI. She compared the timestamps to the chat between Agent Symon and Stephen Spencer. There was a gap—Eckhart and Bertrand had actually wrapped up their conversation before Symon had approached Spencer. But it was a gap of *minutes*.

She scanned back through security footage, looking at an hour or so of footage prior to Symon entering the security suite at Curie Motors. Spencer had been in his office the entire time, working at a laptop. His features were still obscured in the window's reflection. But at one point he stood, exited the office, and went for a cup of coffee.

Kayne froze the shot of Spenser, as he left the office.

He was wearing a pair of wireless earbuds.

He was *listening* to something.

She opened a new window and started picking her way through the Curie Motors network until she finally found the IP address for Spencer's laptop. He was set up with a roaming IP that would sync his computer with the local network of any business owned by Ross Eckhart. It was a bit like having a cloud-based central storage, with secure access that picked up as he sat in one of several offices worldwide. A virtual presence that allowed him to pick up exactly where he'd left off, as he followed Eckhart from business to business.

Kayne pilfered that virtual space, looking for anything useful. It didn't take long to find something.

Spencer had several streams of data being recorded to the cloud, from remote locations. One of those was coming from a smartwatch, owned and worn by Adele Bertrand.

Spencer hadn't had to talk to Bertrand. He'd heard her defense right from her own lips.

What other lines of intel did he have?

QuIEK made short work of finding out, and Kayne looked through the list, leaning back in the rickety kitchen chair.

"Gotcha," she said, staring at the screen before flicking a roach off of her arm and fighting the urge to squeal and shiver.

CHAPTER THIRTEEN

Law Offices of Bertrand, Owens & Cromwell | San Francisco, California

Symon signed off on Eckhart's release and accompanied both Eckhart and Bertrand back to the BO&C offices. Bertrand had agreed to let them use the space as their base of operations, though Symon thought it might have been a case of "keep your enemies close."

Regardless, once they had established themselves in the same vacant conference room that Eckhart had been using alongside Alex Kayne, Symon excused himself to find a private space for a video chat.

Mayher answered, her image at a slight upward angle, the background bouncing by as she held her phone while walking. "I hear Kayne is in the wind again," she said.

"Is there ever any different news?" Symon replied.

Mayher scowled and shook her head. "Maybe someday."

"Have you managed to pick up anything new on your end?" Symon asked.

She shook her head again. "No. No one here knows why Eckhart stepped down as CEO. Or they're not talking, if they do know."

"Well, I have the man himself here now," Symon said. "I may be able to get something out of him. For now, I want you to coordinate with the locals and see what you can dig up on Stephen Spencer."

"The head of security?" Mayher asked.

Symon nodded. "He's not shooting straight with us, I think. I can't quite put my finger on it, but something doesn't smell right."

"Got it," Mayher said. "I'll talk to Christian, see if we can use his offices to run a background."

"Christian?" Symon asked, his eyebrows raised.

"*Agent Daniels*," Mayher replied darkly, hinting that she didn't want any guff from Symon.

He let it pass. "Ok, get me what you can. I'm working a couple of different angles here." He thought for a moment. "Can you get me contact information for an engineer named Shai Salide? She's here, in the San Francisco area."

"Person of interest?" Mayher asked.

"Kayne's client," Symon replied. "She had some of her patents stolen by Curie Motors. Eckhart says he didn't know about it, and that he was helping Kayne figure it out."

"So he really was aiding and abetting," Mayher said, sounding mildly disappointed.

"Eckhart's attorneys are going with coercion," Symon said. "I don't buy it, but I'm willing to let it go."

"Why?" Mayher asked. "If he's dirty, we should nail him."

Symon shook his head. "I'm not so sure he is. Call it a hunch. But regardless, he's assisting me in finding her, so I'm willing to cut him some slack. Kayne is the big fish."

Mayher nodded. "Ok, makes sense. I'll keep digging here,

see what we find on Stephen Spencer. And I'll get you something on Shai Salide. Anything else?"

Symon thought for a moment. "Look into Bertrand, Owens & Cromwell."

"Eckhart's lawyers? Why? What am I looking for?"

"Not sure yet. Cross them with the research into Shai Salide and her patents. The firm handled all the acquisitions. See if anything flags."

"Got it," Mayher said.

They wrapped up the call, and Symon returned to the conference room where Eckhart was already intently scanning a laptop.

Symon's first impulse was to come at things a little sideways, to see if he could somehow coax the billionaire into revealing the information he needed. But gauging by the conversations he'd had with Eckhart so far, and by what he'd seen of the man in interviews, he thought maybe a different approach would be effective.

"Why did you step down as CEO of Curie Motors?" Symon asked directly and abruptly.

Eckhart looked up from his work, his expression first mildly startled, then fading into a sort of casual resignation.

"It's a long story," Eckhart said. "And sort of a personal one."

"I've got time," Symon replied.

Eckhart sighed, nodded, and gestured to a chair nearby. Symon took a seat.

"Ok," Eckhart said. "Here's the thing."

Somewhere in San Francisco, California

While it was nowhere near as chilly in San Francisco as it had been in Texas, the wind coming off of the bay still had a bite.

Kayne was bundled against it, having picked up a long, hooded coat from a thrift shop. It was the bulkiest item of clothing she was wearing, and she could shed it in an instant if she needed to make a run for it.

Though she appreciated the coat as an extra barrier against the chilled wind, the hood also served to disguise her as she moved through the city streets. Her large sunglasses also helped. And for good measure, QuIEK was actively scanning for any cameras or surveillance, radio and cellular signals, and any other signs of someone tracking her. Using live masking, the AI smoothly erased her from digital sight as she went. And though it couldn't cloak her from any prying or spying human eyes that might be nearby, it could hide her in other ways.

For a start, as she got closer to the BO&C offices, her smart watch occasionally buzzed, alerting her that she should duck into the nearest doorway or otherwise keep a low profile. This was the signal she'd set up for QuIEK to tell her that police or FBI had been detected nearby. It was a sort of *Spidey-Sense* for law enforcement—the watch was discreet, and the signal was subtle, and it gave her plenty of warning to stay out of sight.

The watch had only vibrated a couple of times during most of her walk, but now that she was within a block of the BO&C offices, she was getting fairly regular pings. Enough so that she was starting to question her plan.

Walking straight back to the scene of the crime, as it were, couldn't really be her best option, could it?

She could have hung back and waited at some locations nearby, maybe a coffee shop, sipping something nice and warm. Or, really, she could have just gone straight to the home address she'd lifted from the BO&C personnel files. But after spending the night in a vermin-infested dump, she was anxious to get out and shake off the heebie-jeebies. She already had half-a-dozen safe houses set up and waiting, a couple of which were nearby.

There truth was, she was feeling guilty.

She wasn't used to it. The idea of feeling any sort of remorse for leaving someone to be picked up by the Feds wasn't really something she thought about. For years now, hers had been the only butt she had to worry about keeping out of prison. She didn't really have "partners."

But in their brief time together, Eckhart had become that to her, in a way.

She wondered now whether her gut instinct, the drive that had forced her to ditch and make a run for it, had been less about any suspicions she had about Eckhart, and might otherwise have been some instinct that things were about to hit the fan. The fact that the FBI turned up just minutes after she'd hit the ground running lent a lot of credibility to that idea. Maybe she'd picked up on some subtle cue, something that not even QuIEK had detected. The human brain was still way more advanced than even the smartest AI. Maybe her subconscious was looking out for her.

Or maybe she'd just gotten lucky.

All of this was swirling around in her head and her guts, making her feel a bit of shame over cutting and running, and leaving Eckhart to face the glare of the FBI. And the fact that the charges against her were effectively aimed at punishing him for helping her—that just made it cut that much deeper.

But then it seemed like things might have taken a turn.

She knew that Eckhart had been released. She knew the charges had been dropped. She also knew that Agent Symon was sitting with Eckhart, even now, inside the BO&C offices, both of them still working on the exact thing Kayne and Eckhart had been working on. *Guilt, guilt, and more guilt.* But also *hope.*

Symon was using all of this as a means of tracking her down, so that he could do his job. But she knew him—now that he was aware of what had happened to Shai Salide, and to others, he would look into that, too. And he would do the right thing.

Effectively, Symon was handling some of Kayne's workload. Though he'd balk at the very suggestion of that, when she eventually teased him about it later.

That was good. That took some pressure off. If Symon and Eckhart could tackle some of the broader issues, it freed Kayne up to deal with some specifics.

And one of those specifics was Julia Faure.

Kayne's sweep of Stephen Spencer's little spy network had revealed that he had an inside man. Or inside woman, rather. And it hadn't taken long to figure out that it was Adele Bertrand's executive assistant.

Julia Faure was a dual-citizen, just like Bertrand. She'd come to the US as part of Bertrand's team, having worked with her for years in the Paris offices. And, Kayne discovered, Bertrand had inherited Julia, more or less, after Bertrand's husband had passed. Julia had been the personal secretary or *Monsieur* Bertrand, serving him since she was barely old enough to work legally.

On the surface of it all, Julia appeared to be as loyal to Adele Bertrand as she'd been to her husband. But as Kayne dug into Julia's digital history, a different tale emerged.

Almost from day one, Julia had been pilfering the firm's coffers.

At first, under Bertrand's late husband, Julia had gotten a regular stipend, outside of her salary. Kayne could speculate all day over what Julia did to earn that bit of side income, but her best guess was that *Monsieur* Bertrand was doing a bit of "outside investing" in the assets of his young and attractive assistant. The money was meant to keep things quiet, given that his wife was a powerful attorney in her own right.

When he died, the money stopped, and Julia found herself answering to his widow.

But slipping back into the role of lowly secretary must not have been part of Julia's plans. According to her banking records, only a few months after the stipend ended, she gained some sort of side income. And over the years, that income had increased exponentially. Julia Faure might not be as wealthy as her employers, but she wasn't far off. She certainly lived in such a way that should have been beyond the means of someone making a receptionist's salary. Either BO&C were incredibly generous, or Julia was skimming.

And she had a partner.

It hadn't taken much digging to discover that Julia and Stephen Spencer were part of a silent partnership in a shell company that, on the surface, appeared to be a holding of BO&C, managing (among other things) IP acquisitions for various big-name clients. One of whom was Ross Eckhart.

Except, Kayne uncovered, BO&C was really only a minor partner in that company. It shared in the profits, but did not actually manage the patents. And, according to the convoluted trail of records that Kayne had managed to untangle the night before, the shell company itself was merely "loaning" the IPs to the various clients who had shelled out money for them. On paper, those patents were owned by Julia Faure and Stephen Spencer.

It was kind of brilliant. Though it had taken a while to trace.

Julia used her position to inject herself into the acquisition process, on paper at least. As filings went to various courts and federal offices, crucial documents would be replicated, altered, and replaced. Things would appear to go smoothly, all around. But in the end, the corporation owned by Julia and Spencer would become the *de facto* owners of the patents, "loaning" rights and profits to Eckhart and any other client, and instead of paying whatever percentage had been negotiated to the original IP owner, they would collect it themselves. And BO&C managed all of it as part of the firm's day-to-day, without even realizing what had happened.

It was fraud on a grand and epic scale. Kayne was actually impressed. The percentages that Julia and Spencer picked up were kind of paltry, in the grand scheme of things. But with thousands of patents folded into the scheme, along with intellectual property across a broad spectrum, the two were actually banking back hundreds of millions, combined. And because they continued to work in their "day jobs," keeping the money in offshore accounts and keeping their lifestyles below the "extravagant" line, there was nothing to really tip anyone off. Who would suspect the secretary of having a nine-figure bank account, even if she drove a Mercedes and lived in a high-rise apartment?

The people that Julia and Spencer ran with were used to extravagance and wealth. Unless these thefts were impacting the bottom line of the firm, they were invisible. And Eckhart had already told Kayne that he was more or less oblivious to the details of these deals, letting BO&C handle everything. He had no reason to suspect anything, because from his perspective everything was running as it should. It wasn't much of a leap to think that other BO&C clients might behave in a similar way.

No one bothered looking for something that was right out in the open, unless it was causing an immediate ruckus.

Basically, Julia Faure and Stephen Spencer were using a tactic that Kayne herself used, all the time: They were hiding in plain sight. But Kayne could see them now. And she was here, edging nearer to the BO&C offices, just to get an even closer look.

Her smartwatch buzzed, and Kayne pulled back, ducking

into the entryway of a drug store across the street from the high-rise office building. She looked through the filthy glass of the store to see Eric Symon stepping out of the building, standing on the sidewalk as he held his mobile phone to his ear.

A private chat, Kayne decided. He wanted to be outside the building for whatever it was.

She felt her gut twist at the thought of what she was about to do, but at this point it was crucial to know as much as she could, to gauge how close he was to catching her. She needed inside information. She hated doing this to someone she considered a friend. Privacy be damned, she needed to know what he was saying, and who he was talking to.

She popped a set of wireless earbuds in her ears, and had QuIEK scan and crack the signal from Symon's phone, dropping in mid-sentence.

"—far she's stayed off the radar. Tracking her digital footprint is pointless. I've circulated photos and video clips we do have, to every agent and officer in the area."

"Think it will be enough?" a male voice asked.

It was familiar, though Kayne had only had a brief interaction with him. She recognized the voice of Agent Roland Denzel, the FBI partner of Dan Kotler. And the current head of a breakout group within Historic Crimes, known by the codename "Outsiders," a pet project from the division's Director, Liz Ludlum. Kayne was a part of that group, technically. She had a sneaky suspicion that Ludlum might have designed it with her and Kotler in mind. *Outsiders*, resources who were useful for taking down bad people and averting bad things in the world, but who were not quite agency material.

"Kayne is the best there is at staying out of handcuffs," Symon replied. "We're casting a wide net, hoping someone sees her. And I think we have a rare opportunity here. This feels like a slip, to me."

"A slip?" Denzel asked. "What do you mean?"

Symon sighed. "Well, usually when we get some lead on her, we show up to find she's plotted ten different ways out and invents four on the fly."

"She got past us this time, too," Denzel replied.

"But it just... feels different," Symon said. "I've talked to Ross Eckhart and his attorney. The way Eckhart describes his interaction with her, it seems like Kayne let her guard down. She got on a private plane with the guy, without knowing exactly where they were going. That doesn't sound like her."

There was a pause. "No, I don't think it does. Not from what I've seen in her files. Or from the experience we had with her in New Mexico. She tends to have her exits mapped out."

"Exactly," Symon said. "And here, she left the building through a door that triggered a fire alarm. She didn't even disable it. She could have."

"So you think she was in a hurry," Denzel replied.

"Yeah," Symon said. "I think she was off her game. Which could be good news. Getting Alex Kayne off her game is the only way we'll ever get our hands on her."

There was another brief pause from Denzel, and then, "Agent Symon... Eric... I know we've talked about this before, briefly. And I know you've had conversations with Director Ludlum about it. But I have to ask—are you certain you are the one who should be pursuing Alex Kayne?"

Kayne quickly glanced out of the drug store window, and saw Symon standing stiffly, his back to the street, his head tilted up to the roofline of the high-rise.

It was a good question, she knew. Because despite Symon's dedication to hunting her over the past few years, the two of them had formed a sort of bond. He'd gotten her involved with Historic Crimes as his CI, which was helping to repair her reputation and maybe give her a way to come in out of the cold.

He'd asked for her help with some of the big and crucial cases being managed by the division. They'd taken down bad guys together. They had a rapport. So even Kayne sometimes wondered if he'd *really* do it—if he'd take her down, as he was sworn to do.

"I'm getting a little tired of answering this question, Agent Denzel. All I can say is, if you or Director Ludlum doubt me on this, then it makes no sense to keep me on."

"And if we reassigned Kayne to a different agent—what would that mean for you?"

Symon laughed. "It would mean I'd leave Historic Crimes and go back to working full time for the Bureau. And if that's out, I'll just leave and find some other line of work. Because either you trust me to stick to the oath I took, or I'm as good as discharged anyway. I spent years fighting to prove I wasn't collaborating with a traitor, and this just feels like more of the same fight."

She heard Denzel sigh from his side of the line. "I see," he said. "Eric, I know you and I have... static. So I feel like I should make something clear. I was the one who requested that you be brought into Historic Crimes. I requested you for the Outsiders, too."

From her vantage point she saw Symon turn, slowly, his gaze dropping back to street level. "You... did?"

"I... thought it might be a way to make up for what happened to you," Denzel said. "In part, anyway. But when Liz... Director Ludlum... came to me to ask for recommendations, you were one of the first people on my list. You're a brilliant profiler. And your ethics are unquestionable, regardless of what all those idiots claimed at the time. I knew you'd suffered a hit, because of Director Crispen. But you're a valuable asset to the Bureau. And to Historic Crimes Division. I wanted you on my team, as soon as I *had* a team."

Kayne could see Symon taking this in.

"I... didn't know that."

"I asked Ludlum not to say anything," Denzel replied. "I didn't want you to assume this was some kind of charity. Because it isn't. I plan to hold you to some pretty high standards. But you tend to prove me right about you, over and over. So if you say you're clear, that your judgment is good on Alex Kayne, then I believe you."

Another pause, and Kayne thought she heard a catch of breath. "Th-thank you." A brief pause. "Sir."

"Listen," Denzel replied, moving brusquely on. "I have some things to deal with on this Derek Conners case. I'm still in Oklahoma at the moment. But I'm signing off on anything you need. I agree with you. This feels like Kayne has made a slip, and I want to push that if we can."

"So do I," Symon replied. "I..."

Kayne had turned away, hiding behind a pillar in the drug store as she listened to the conversation, but she heard the sound of the gunshot in digital echo as it came from outside the store and from her phone a heartbeat later.

She turned, panicked, and saw a black SUV speeding away from the front of the BO&C offices. And when it had cleared away, she spotted a dark shape on the ground.

Her heart pounded.

She rushed through the glass doors of the drug store, dodging through honking traffic and screeching tires. There were curses from drivers who had no idea of what had just happened. Screams from bystanders who had seen the thing happen, or were witnessing the aftermath.

Kayne immediately dropped to the ground when she got to him and found herself kneeling in a spreading puddle of blood.

"Eric!" she shouted, turning him, pressing her hands to the wound. "Eric, *stay with me!*"

"Agent Symon?" Denzel's voice came in her ear. "What's happening? Was that a gunshot?"

She spotted Eric's phone on the ground, a few inches from his hand. She tapped her earbud, signaling QuIEK to allow her to speak over the line.

"Agent Denzel, this is Alex Kayne," she said, holding back a sob. "Eric was just shot. You have an agent down."

CHAPTER FOURTEEN

Zuckerberg San Francisco General Hospital and Trauma
Center | San Francisco, California

The ride to the hospital was a blur.

After giving details to Denzel, Kayne turned her attention
to doing everything she could to keep Symon alive. She had
ripped open his shirt, and was pressing his tie to the wound as
a compress. The shot was in his left pectoral muscle. She had
no idea about the biology involved, whether this was a fatal hit
or not. She just knew that, so far, he was breathing and moaning, which she took as a good sign. But the moaning was
growing quieter, and he'd lost consciousness despite her best
efforts.

She began shouting commands for QuIEK, guiding it to not
only call for an ambulance but to reroute the closest one it
could find that wasn't already occupied or on its way to another
emergency. She had the AI open a path, turning on and off all
traffic lights as needed, pausing the metro rail, even strategi-
cally disabling electric vehicles and other cars that had remote

start capability, using them to form barricades and stop traffic, to keep the roads open.

When the ambulance finally arrived, she refused to let them go without her. Police hadn't been made it to the scene yet, but security from the BO&C building were out on the sidewalk, managing crowd control, communicating with authorities.

Kayne made it clear she was going in the ambulance with Symon, and the paramedics must have decided that saving his life was more important than arguing with her.

Again, once they were on their way Kayne had QuIEK clear a path, and they made it to the ER in record time. Once they screeched to a stop at the ER entrance, and Symon was wheeled out of the ambulance and directly into surgery, Kayne allowed herself to be pulled aside.

"Are you family?" a nurse asked.

"Yes," she replied, without hesitation. "I'm his wife."

The nurse nodded, and after that the conversation was sympathetic, if not entirely informative. They were placating her, trying to keep her calm. She didn't need them for that. She could keep calm in the face of trauma. What she needed was *answers*. And no one was yet in a position to give her those.

It didn't take long for police to arrive. A fact that Kayne was alerted to as her smartwatch began vibrating. If she stayed here, like this, surrounded by these placating nurses and hospital staff, she was as good as caught. And she couldn't let that happen.

She had to stay free, so she could find who did this.

She slipped away, guided by QuIEK through a network of halls and stairwells until she managed to find a relatively empty and quiet space on the fourth floor. She snuck into a vacant room, into the bathroom, and did her best to scrub Eric Symon's blood from her hands and clothes.

She had to abandon the coat. It was camel colored and had become a blood-soaked ruin. There was no way anyone would fail to notice it. But everything under it was dark enough to hide any flecks of blood. And though her hands were still a bit pink, they were less noticeable than her eyes and cheeks. She'd been crying, and it showed.

She rinsed her face, toweled herself dry, and took several deep breaths.

Exiting the bathroom with the coat folded over her arm, she made her way back out into the corridor. She spotted a rolling laundry basket and hid the coat under the soiled sheets. So far, no one had paid much attention to her, and she made her way casually to the stairwell, moving downward as quickly as she dared.

On the second floor she exited the stairwell and wound her way through a set of hallways that resembled an office building more than a hospital. QuIEK was telling her that the ground floor was absolutely riddled with police and FBI agents. One of their own was down, and that was going to put everyone on high alert. She needed to get out of here.

She tried to take a breath, to calm herself. But a sob overtook her anyway, and she found herself crumpling to the floor, gasping as tears streamed down her face.

"Are you alright?" a man asked. He knelt beside her, his face concerned. He reached out, tentatively, and put a hand on her shoulder.

She sniffed, wiped at her eyes, and nodded. "Yes. I'm sorry. It's... it's been a long day."

He studied her. "Do you need anything? Maybe I can find one of the doctors..."

"No," she said, shaking her head. "I'm fine. Thank you."

She got to her feet and moved away, not looking back.

According to QuIEK, there was a sky bridge on this floor

that led to the building across the way. She found it and moved as quickly as she dared. And when she reached the other building, she crossed through to the far side before going to the ground level.

Once she was out on the street, a car pulled up.

"Alex?" the driver asked.

She hesitated, alarmed but not sure yet what to do.

"Who... who's asking?" She couldn't think of a better question.

"I'm Afshar," the driver said. "I'm your Uber."

It took her by surprise. She hadn't set up an Uber. She hadn't even been thinking about it.

QuIEK must have anticipated she'd need a way out of there.

She'd given it that directive, in the simplest terms. *Find the fastest way out of here.* It must have determined that this was the only way she was going to get away from the scene in a hurry, without being spotted. And it had handled details like this for her so often now, it must have defaulted to what it knew —the solution that was easiest to implement.

Or... was it more than that?

She climbed into the backseat. The car pulled out and wove its way into traffic. She checked her phone and saw that the destination was one of her stashes. There would be a change of clothes, among other items. And there was already another car scheduled a few blocks away, an easy walk that kept her in a low profile.

It was a bit baffling, but she couldn't deny it. QuIEK had taken it upon itself to plan not only an escape route, but a waypoint for getting herself back in check, and a second car to get her further away from the scene. All without her input.

She'd have to look into that, later. See what it meant, if anything, in terms of the evolution of her AI software. For the past few years she'd been tinkering under the hood, refining code, adding complexity. She'd taught QuIEK a lot of new tricks, especially around the imperative of keeping her out of the hands of the authorities. Maybe that had paid off in ways that Kayne hadn't anticipated.

For now, though, she put QuIEK to work on a different task. A grimmer purpose.

She was going to find whoever shot Eric Symon.

And she was going to kill them.

CHAPTER FIFTEEN

Zuckerberg San Francisco General Hospital and Trauma
Center | San Francisco, California

Agent Denzel arrived at the hospital less than twelve hours
after Eric Symon was admitted. He abided hospital regulations
patiently, but once he learned that Symon was out of surgery
and in the ICU, he flexed some FBI muscle, to gain admittance
to his room.

"He's in a coma," the surgeon explained. "He lost a lot of
blood, and the bullet nicked his left lung. We were able to
repair that, but he's currently on a chest tube to remove blood
and fluid from around the area. We're mostly concerned that
there is fluid buildup near his heart."

Denzel nodded at this. "When will he regain
consciousness?"

The surgeon shook his head. "There's no way to know for
sure. He went into hemorrhagic shock from the blood loss, and
we've been able to correct it with a transfusion. To be honest, if

his wife hadn't been so quick to staunch blood flow, I'm not sure he would have survived."

"His wife," Denzel said flatly.

"She came in with him, on the ambulance," the surgeon said. "But we haven't been able to locate her since Agent Symon was admitted to the ER. Our staff has contacted the police. We're concerned she may be in shock herself, from the trauma of seeing it happen."

Denzel doubted that Alex Kayne was traumatized, but things regarding her were so sensitive he decided to let all the assumptions run their course. He'd contact local PD to tell them they needn't bother with trying to track down Symon's "wife." He didn't want resources wasted on a fruitless hunt.

He had already gathered every bit of footage that could be found, from the scene of the shooting. Alex Kayne wasn't in any of it. Instead, there was a sort of ghostly gap, as cars and people all reacted to Kayne's sprint through traffic, rushing to Symon's side. That fancy software of hers was doing a good job of keeping her hidden.

It was concerning, to Denzel. Weird. Definitely outside his usual experience.

Regardless, even with Kayne masked out of the video, it was clear she had nothing to do with the shooting. The footage showed a black SUV pull up to the curb near Agent Symon, and the gunman fired from the driver-side window before speeding off. There were plates on the SUV, and Denzel was already running them, but he was pretty sure what he'd find. Either the vehicle or the plates would be stolen. It was effectively untraceable.

There was no clear image of the driver. In fact, there was no way to know exactly how many people were in the SUV, at the time. One, five... no way to know.

The round that hit Symon was already in the chain of

custody, on its way to a local forensics lab, along with two other rounds recovered from the scene. Denzel would check in on those over the next few hours.

Everything was getting a rush, because an FBI agent was down.

"Where is he?" a woman's voice asked from the hall.

Denzel stepped out to see Agent Mayher approaching, her FBI credentials pinned to her blazer and the ebony-toned Historic Crimes Division badge hanging from around her neck. Her face was stern, but worried.

She saw Denzel and headed straight for him. "Is he...?"

"Alive," Denzel said. "But in a coma, in critical condition."

She nodded at this, worry plain on her face. "Can I see him?"

"They've asked us to give them some time," Denzel said. "I was in with him for a few minutes. The doctors are keeping me updated on his progress."

"Has anyone called his family? His aunt?"

Denzel nodded. "It's handled," he said. Then, more gently, "What about you? How are you?"

She looked up at him with a startled expression. "Me? I'm..." she hesitated. "I'm fine. A little rattled."

Again he nodded. "That's understandable. You got here pretty quick."

"I was already waiting for a flight," she said. "We wrapped up in Round Rock, and I was supposed to join Eric... Agent Symon... here in San Francisco, to keep up the hunt for Kayne."

"Any progress? Any idea why Kayne was in Texas?"

Mayher huffed. "Same sort of thing that usually has her poking her head out. She has a client, here in the Bay Area. It's a patent thing. We have some leads. As usual, Kayne's uncovered something we'll need to look into a little deeper."

Denzel nodded at this. "Agent Symon updated me by phone... just before."

She blinked, studying him. "You were on the phone with him. When it happened."

"I was," Denzel said.

"So... are *you* ok?"

He shook his head lightly. "It's fine. I'm more angry that this would happen in broad daylight, with cops and agents all over the place. We were all so hung up on looking for Alex Kayne, we didn't see this coming."

"And Kayne is in the wind again?" Mayher asked.

"She was here," he said, nodding to their surroundings. "She saved his life."

Mayher considered this. "She's... that doesn't surprise me. She doesn't really act like a fugitive, you know?"

"Oh, she acts exactly like a fugitive," Denzel said. "She just doesn't act like a *murderer*. She acts like a human being."

Mayher turned and leaned against the wall, and Denzel stepped closer. The bustle of the ICU went on all around them, and he was becoming conscious of the fact that they might be in the way here. "Let's get out of here," he said. "There's a coffee shop on the ground floor. My treat."

Mayher nodded, and the two of them began walking.

There was a ping from Denzel's phone, and when he checked he saw a message from an unknown number. He opened it.

I found him, it said. *Check your email.*

Denzel shook his head and replied, *Who is this?*

Though he suspected he knew.

Even before he got a reply, he opened the mail app and saw that there was a message marked urgent, from an unknown sender. He opened it and found there were dozens of attachments.

As he and Mayher stepped into the elevator, he started opening each attachment, scanning through. They were mostly financial records and legal documents—a litany of files that were annotated and cross-linked. As he read through, two names appeared again and again:

Stephen Spencer and Julia Faure.

Another ping from his phone.

These two are running a con from within BO&C, the message read. Denzel was now certain it was Alex Kayne.

Eckhart is innocent. You should be able to trace all of this back to these two. I've included bank records, including traces to accounts in the Caymans. Spencer and Faure are joint owners in about a dozen shell companies. It's all cardboard and money.

"What is it?" Mayher asked, noting that Denzel was preoccupied with his phone.

Denzel glanced up, shook his head once, and held up a finger before responding to the text.

Alex, you need to turn yourself in, he typed. Then he paused, realizing something. *You said you found "him." You didn't mean Spencer or Faure, did you? Who did you find?*

He watched as three dots pulsed on screen.

The guy who tried to kill Eric, Kayne replied.

Give me his name, Denzel typed.

Three dots, then it cleared. Denzel waited. Three dots appeared again.

Eric isn't the only target. You're in danger, too. Watch your back.

Denzel's eyebrows went up. *Thanks for the heads up. I can take care of myself. Give me the guy's name and I'll have him locked up in an hour.*

There was another dance of dots. Typing, cleared, typing. Finally, as if she had resolved to just come out with it, Kayne replied.

He's mine, she wrote.

And before Denzel could respond, she added, *Give the files to Mayher. She's going to need something to keep her mind off of Eric.*

Alex, Denzel typed, *don't do this. Leave it to me. To the FBI. This is our job. You shouldn't even be involved.*

He's mine, Kayne replied again. And after that she stopped responding to anything Denzel typed. Eventually he sighed and slid his phone back into his pocket.

"What is it?" Mayher repeated as they exited the elevator and walked toward the coffee shop.

"Trouble," Denzel said.

"Alex Kayne," Mayher said.

And Denzel nodded. "Alex Kayne."

Somewhere in San Francisco

It hadn't taken long at all. Kayne hadn't even exited the second Uber when she'd gotten an alert from QuIEK. The search was over. She had her man.

Or men, as it turned out.

The gunman, who was just some hired jerk from the Dark Web. He was easy. QuIEK had skipped along a trail of cameras—everything from ATMs to traffic cameras to bodegas, anything that had a lens and kept footage on file became QuIEK's eyes—and by extension, Kayne's eyes. She was able to follow the guy to the chop shop where he disposed of the SUV, and then on to the apartment across town that he was using as a safe house.

She had toyed with the idea of going there. Of finding him. Of taking out all the rage she was feeling on this guy's head. But that wasn't going to cut it. He wasn't the trigger man, not the one calling the shots. Taking him down wouldn't be enough.

She sent several anonymous tips, all from disguised numbers and email addresses, to the local FBI. She'd let them take care of the shooter. They could have him.

She had *the* guy.

The man behind layers of anonymity. The man who had reached out through a web of VPNs and masked IP addresses. The man using privacy software purchased from some of the most prominent security experts in the space. The man who thought he was untouchable.

The man who had paid to have Agent Symon killed.

Derrick Conners.

He was the owner of an exotic animal ranch in Oklahoma, and had recently been the target of an FBI raid. His property had been seized, including hundreds of pieces of stolen art. His assets had been frozen. The raid had been solid, and Conners had suffered a pretty big slap in the face.

Conners wasn't one to let a slap in the face go unanswered.

Kayne scanned through the profile QuIEK had built for her and saw that Conner's wealth was spread around all over the planet. His US accounts had been frozen, as a result of the FBI raid, but he still had access to several Swiss and Cayman Islands accounts. Plus, off the books Conners held dozens of US accounts under shell companies and phony identities. This, along with a Midas fortune of liquid assets Conners had stashed here and there meant that the limits of the FBI's grip on him had been solidly reached, and he was in prime shape to skate. He could live the rest of his life in luxury, completely off the radar.

That was one problem. The other was the man himself.

Conners was as shady as they come.

Kayne gave his bio a more thorough and in-depth look once

she was safely in her new home base. This was a time share near the heart of San Francisco's Presidio—a small but upscale rental property that gave her a view of the Golden Gate Bridge, as well as parts of the grounds for Industrial Light and Magic. She would have been thrilled over both of these, any other time. Even when she'd lived in San Francisco, she'd rarely had time to explore the IL&M campus, and had mostly only seen the bridge as she was passing over it.

But at the moment, all of this was just another landscape, just another set of buildings. Something else—some*one* else—had her focus.

She had a shiny new laptop, courtesy of swinging by one of her new resource drops on the way here, and she used this now to do a quick but deep dive into all things Derrick Conners. And the story that unfolded was the stuff of a Netflix documentary series.

Conners had started his dark and oily career as a petty crook, spending time in jail for things like burglary and car theft. He boosted a BMW when he was fourteen, and though that was expunged from his record, he spent a lot of time, these days, bragging about it online. It wasn't even his first crime, he claimed. And from what Kayne could see, it certainly wasn't his last.

He graduated to bigger and better schemes by the time he was seventeen. Using money from an unknown source—Kayne suspected he stole it, but there was no real way to know—Conners bought his first piece of real estate. It was, in fact, the very ranch that would eventually become the focus of the FBI raid. And over the next twenty years, Conners used that piece of property for a dozen different purposes, most of which brought him scads of profit, both illicit and legit.

Eventually, Conners expanded the property by buying out his neighbors. Though, gauging by some of the police reports that went dark and the lawsuits that were inevitably withdrawn, Kayne had a sneaky suspicion that most of his neighbors hadn't actually *wanted* to sell.

Conners also held the deeds on hundreds of other properties around the country and worldwide. Within the state of Oklahoma alone, Conners became one of the biggest landlords around. Though most of his holdings might have qualified him as a slum lord, at best.

From real estate, Conners branched out into venues. He bought several small hotels, conference halls, and other venues, most of which were held through dozens of shell corporations. Even the FBI didn't know about all of them. But, thanks to QuIEK's digging, Kayne now did.

Real estate and events eventually led to investing in a casino, which led to investing in *more* casinos, spread through Vegas, Louisiana, Oklahoma, and Atlantic City. Through these Conners laundered millions of dollars from his various "enterprises," in a trail so widespread and dispersed it was hard for even QuIEK to trace.

Hard... but not impossible.

The next leap in his holdings was a little more murky, but Kayne thought she could guess some of it.

Conners started collecting.

His favorite was to buy exotic animals, especially big cats. He turned his ranch into an open-air zoo, a drive-in safari. It got heavy advertising on billboards all along the highways of Oklahoma, for miles in all directions. Families and individuals could, for just twenty bucks per car, drive through the Oklahoma equivalent of the Sahara and Serengeti, passing through herds of zebra and antelope, packs of fennec foxes and caravans of camels.

It was an eclectic menagerie, and not always region-accurate. Most of the animals Conners collected would never have encountered each other in the wild. They ranged in origin across at least three continents, and across hundreds of regions and climates. It was obviously more important to provide the spectacle than it was to observe the natural habitat of these animals. And Conners had hundreds of species mish-mashed together behind twelve-foot wire fences. Touring the ranch was like running through a dictionary of animals, A to Z.

The big draw to Conner's ranch, however, was the cats.

Lions, tigers, panthers, pumas, cheetahs—if it was feline, he had it. Including some rare breeds, white tigers and Canadian lynx, and dozens of others Kayne had never heard of.

In one respect—and indeed, according to the website—the ranch was helping to keep these animals preserved and protected. Several were on the endangered species list, and Conners actually received stipends from various world governments, for aiding in their preservation.

But Kayne saw through this. In fact, the FBI and several other agencies saw through this as well. Conners didn't care about "preservation." The animals he kept were a source of revenue, and the show of protecting them was a useful deception at best, but could more accurately be described as simply another stream of revenue. If it ever came down to it, if caring for these animals ever tilted away from profit and toward liability, Kayne was sure Conners would host a giant exotic animal barbecue and feel no shame in it.

As she dug deeper, she now came down to the even darker stuff. Conners wasn't just collecting animals, he was into all sorts of things. Some of it on the far, darker end of the legal spectrum.

He had diversified by taking in stolen art, buying pieces on the black market as fast as he could gather them. There was a rumor, in the criminal world, that stolen art could be a bargaining chip, and Conners appeared to be banking on that as a contingency plan. Or maybe he just liked the idea of owning something irreplaceable, that wasn't rightfully his. It could go either way with this guy.

Kayne had the profile that Agent Symon had worked up on Conners, and Symon's impression was that Conners would gladly hold on to something rare and stolen just to keep anyone else from having it. Even if he couldn't sell it, depriving people of it was treasure enough. They guy was a sociopath.

Conners' other collections included an arsenal of weapons that would make an Alt-Right militia blush, as well as caverns of purloined booze with bottling dates spanning centuries, and a metropolitan museum's worth of rare artifacts stolen from collections and cultures worldwide.

And there was more. Hints of things so dark, even Derrick Conners kept no traceable records.

He operated as if he were untouchable, because for such a very long time, he was.

But that time was over. And Conners didn't like it.

When Agents Denzel and Symon brought some real heat down on the guy—the sort of thing that actually forced Conners to retreat—he responded the way someone like Conners always would. He used his reach in the criminal world and put out a hit on the two agents. And in Eric's case, it might turn out to be successful.

Kayne tried not to chastise herself, to be hard on herself. There was no way she could have known someone was out there gunning for Symon. Until today, she hadn't even known about the raid on Conners' ranch, or who Derrick Conners even *was*. She couldn't have predicted or prevented what happened. It had nothing to do with her.

But it hit too close anyway.

She'd seen it happen. She'd knelt beside him, had his blood

on her hands. She'd felt his pulse go thready, seen his eyes flutter closed.

She squeezed her own eyes shut, trying to push the image out of her mind. Her heart was racing. Anxiety was pressing in on her. She needed to get it in check, keep her head, keep her focus.

Kayne had found the second assassin immediately—the one contracted to take out Agent Denzel. She diverted four times the funds the man had been promised, paying him out of Conners' hidden bank accounts, as a "kill fee."

Kill the job, not the man, she ordered. He acknowledged, with enthusiastic gratitude. Though he did question how Conners had managed to track him down. Anonymity was the core of this business. Once the agreement was made, there would be no way to shut it down. That was the way of it. So having Conners somehow reach him, that was a red flag.

The money, however, was enough to keep the guy's alarm and curiosity tamped down. Maybe he'd keep an eye on Conners, maybe he'd eventually come calling. That part didn't bother Kayne at all.

She leaked all the details of the transaction to local and federal authorities, including the description and last known location of the hit man, and a document trail that would implicate Conners in hiring him. It would take a hitman out of commission, which was a significant win, and good work all on its own. It would also help put another nail in Conners' coffin.

But Kayne didn't want Conners nailed into any coffins. Not before he was put in the right state for it.

Helping the FBI build a case against Conners was more about disassembling his empire, so that no one could rise up and take his place on whatever gaudy throne the guy occupied. She was blocking Conners from having a legacy. But Conners' *fate*—that belonged to Alex Kayne.

It took some digging, with QuIEK running backwards through the transactions and payments made to the hit man, tracing a series of IP addresses, ferreting out Conner's real trail from the VPNs he used to mask it. His digital security was good. He'd put a lot of money into it, hiring a string of firms who operated both above and below the table, serving a community of people who paid well to remain anonymous and discreet online and out in the three-dimensional world as well. Conners had invested heavily in staying off all radar, and deep in the shadows. But she eventually found him.

He had stayed in the States, in a compound in Montana. This was a bit surprising—Kayne had thought for sure he'd be in a non-extradition country by now. She'd been prepared to hunt him over oceans. As it turned out, he was only three states over.

She had satellite photos of the place. It was as *middle of nowhere* as anyone could get, along a stretch of the Missouri River, on a patch of land that was mostly scratch and dirt, with jagged fingers of low hills circling the property.

The place was off the books. No records existed to show who owned it. It was just a vast swath of Montana landscape, by all public records, with only a few buildings dotting it. One of those buildings was a fairly large house on a hillside. Not a mansion, by any stretch. And certainly not on the scale of Conners' former ranch home in Oklahoma, or any of his estate-like residences worldwide. It lacked the sophisticated charm of the suites he owned above dozens of casinos, and in hundreds of luxury hotels.

This was a hiding place, with its own airstrip and helicopter pad, with boats docked on the river, with roads blocked end-to-end by massive gates and signs warning that anyone entering the property would be assumed to be trespassing, and all trespassers would be shot.

There was nothing to connect this property to Derrick Conners. He could hide there indefinitely. No one would ever find him.

Perfect, Kayne thought.

She opened a new browser window and got to work.

CHAPTER SIXTEEN

San Francisco, California

Mayher hated to admit it, but she needed the distraction.

She resented everything about this one, though. Because she knew that all the leads she was currently running down had come from Alex Kayne. And Kayne had been there when it happened. Kayne had been the first on the scene. Kayne had been the one kneeling beside Agent Symon, keeping him from bleeding out.

Did she have anything to do with Symon getting shot?

Mayher thought that was likely, at first. But Agent Denzel had pinged her to let her know that they now had a profile on the shooter. It was looking like an outside hit, tied to their case against Derrick Conners—nothing to do with the Eckhart case.

Denzel had been a little sketchy on the particulars, but said he wanted her to know they were circling in on the shooter. Conners was another issue, but Denzel had resources on tracking him down.

Meanwhile, Mayher was told her priority was to get everything settled on the Eckhart case. That was the job. *Do the job.*

She would do the job.

But she wasn't sure if she should *keep* doing the job.

This was something that had been nagging at her for a while now. She had a growing sense that her life—her career—had gotten off track somehow, somewhere along the way. After a pretty good run, working with the FBI and doing some real good in the world, she was finding the work less satisfying than it used to be. She was finding herself thinking more about gray areas, when she'd always seen things as pretty much black and white.

Mayher didn't like gray areas. Alex Kayne represented a pretty wide gray area. A whole spectrum of gray. And, Mayher finally had to admit, so did Eric Symon.

She knew Symon's history. She knew the raw deal he'd gotten, after Director Crispen had been brought down for treason. But she also knew that Symon was *good*. Probably the best.

When she'd been asked to join Symon's team, to help hunt down Alex Kayne and others like her, Symon's tarnished reputation hadn't mattered to her. Mayher wanted to work with the best, to *learn* from the best, and Agent Eric Symon was the best, whether anyone else in the Bureau understood that or not.

So she'd known that working with Symon would come with some challenges. She thought she was prepared for them.

And then came Alex Kayne.

The woman was a running enigma to Mayher. She had skills—that was undeniable. Mayher had been on the receiving end of Kayne's personal combat training, which was formidable. And Kayne had slipped out of Mayher's grasp more than once, sometimes in humiliating ways. Kayne had an infuriating knack for escaping custody, even when there seemed to be no way out.

It was a hard lesson—learning that no matter how good *you* were, no matter how noble your cause, no matter how many resources you had, or even that you had the law on your side, Alex Kayne was going to escape. It was her nature. She was an immutable fact in the universe.

At least, that's how it felt. Mostly because of QuIEK.

Mayher hadn't known about Kayne's "magic software" at first. Symon had kept it pretty confidential. She'd known that it *existed*, of course. The story from on high was that Kayne had tried to cut a deal with the Russians, but had double-crossed them, killing her business partner and going on the run with something that presented a serious threat to national security. Even *world* security. So, Mayher knew the gist.

It wasn't until she and Symon had been asked to join Historic Crimes Division that Mayher had finally learned some of the deeper, scarier details. Kayne had built this thing— QuIEk—supposedly as a way to help keep everyday folks safe and secure online, to preserve privacy, to protect against scams and security breeches and tons of other modern day threats.

It all sounded good on paper.

And Symon had confessed to her that he thought Kayne was actually innocent of the charges against her. He had a theory that Kayne's business partner, Adrian Ballard, had been the one double-dealing with the Russians, and double-crossing the US government. He suspected Ballard had tried to frame Kayne, in advance of making a killing by selling the software to the Russians outright. And when Kayne had disrupted that plan, the Russians had killed Ballard and basically set the whole house on fire. Kayne got framed, and she went on the run, taking QuIEK with her.

And she'd been running ever since.

Mayher knew Symon well enough to trust his judgement. And more, she trusted him as an Agent, to keep his oath. Just because he *believed* Kayne didn't mean he would let her slide. To Mayher, Symon had proven his loyalty to that oath again and again. She believed Symon when he said his primary objective was to bring Kayne in, to put her behind bars, to make her face the charges levied against her.

Easier said than done.

Arresting Alex Kayne was like trying to hold on to a fistful of water. In the end, you just ended up empty handed and all wet.

The real surprise to Mayher, though, was when Kayne was invited to become a confidential informant.

As a CI, Kayne was able to openly share tips and information with Agent Symon, with the FBI, and with HCD. And that information could be used legally in the pursuit and arrest of other criminals.

It was a goodwill play for Kayne, Mayher knew. It might give her some points, to help reduce the penalties, once she was apprehended. *If* she was apprehended. But despite all that "goodwill," Kayne was still a fugitive, and the order was still "arrest on sight." It was a weird, contentious sort of relationship that Mayher struggled to reconcile.

To Mayher, making Kayne a CI was equivalent to endorsing her. It felt like giving her a pass, of sorts. Because, sure, the order to arrest her still stood. But how seriously would anyone really take that, if it meant eliminating one of the HCD's best assets? If they did manage to bring her in, would the HCD be content with losing her as a resource? Or would she just be grafted into service, chipped or tagged or otherwise hobbled, and then sent out to just keep doing what she was doing?

It felt like a conflict of interest to Mayher. And that conflict made her question everything.

Maybe this wasn't the place for her anymore. Not just Historic Crimes, but the FBI. Law enforcement. All of it.

Well, it didn't matter. Not right now. She had a job to do at the moment, and she'd *do* that job, and it would help keep her mind off of the fact that Eric Symon was currently fighting for his life in an ICU across town.

She'd deal with how she felt about that, and other things, later. After. Whatever *after* ended up meaning.

Her phone chirped, and she looked to see that she was getting a call from the Bureau offices in Round Rock.

"Agent Mayher," she answered.

"Mayher," a now-familiar voice said. She could hear the smile from Agent Christian Daniels, on the other side of the line.

She hadn't had a chance to tell him about Symon.

She decided to hold off. A conversation that wasn't focused on whether Symon would live or die was something she really needed right now.

"Agent Daniels," she said, trying to drum up a genuine smile herself. "How's the weather?"

He laughed lightly from his end. "Warmer every minute. I give it a week before everyone down here is back to cargo shorts and T-shirts, and bitchin' about the heat and humidity."

Mayher's smile was genuine now, and she shook her head. "Texas."

"Yeah," Daniels said. "Texas."

Mayher cleared her throat. "Got anything for me?"

"Yes, ma'am," Daniels said, his voice a light and charming drawl. "We have Stephen Spencer in custody here, thanks to the intel you emailed over."

Mayher blinked. She hadn't sent any emails to Daniels or anyone else, regarding the Eckhart case.

"Refresh my memory," she said. "It's been a long twenty-four hours."

"Oh, well, I got an email from you with some links and attachments. Video from the security cameras, enhanced audio, and a bunch of files implicating Mr. Spencer and someone there in San Francisco. A woman named..." He was quiet for a moment, and Mayher imagined he was referencing the emails. "Julia Faure. Says she's a receptionist at Bertrand, Owens and Cromwell."

"Oh, *that* email," Mayher said, rolling her eyes and trying not to sound annoyed.

Kayne. Again.

"I assume you guys are picking up Ms. Faure?"

"Absolutely," Mayher said, but she made a note to check in on that.

"It's a shame," Daniels said.

"What's a shame?" Mayher asked.

"She's got the same first name as you," he said, and sounded for all the world like a dopey, bashful teenage boy making his first pass at trying to flirt.

She smiled again and even felt herself blush. She liked Daniels —he was good looking, in that rugged but cultivated sort of way. He seemed like a guy who would be as comfortable on a ranch as he was in a Bureau field office. Mayher hadn't dated much, over the past few years. The job made it tough to meet anyone who wasn't about to be brought up on charges. And it wasn't a good idea to date your co-workers. Or your partners. Not that there had been any of *that* happening. She'd once thought she and Eric might hook up... but that was off the table. It seemed, anyway.

"Yeah," Mayher said. "We might have to kick her out of the Julia club."

Daniels gave a light laugh from the other end of the phone.

"Well, we have Mr. Spencer in custody, and after showing him all the evidence, he's talking. He says he has a stash of encrypted hard drives in his home, there in the Bay Area. He's willing to give us the passwords for all of it, in exchange for a deal."

Mayher felt her blood pressure spike.

Eric Symon was struggling to say alive. Kayne was in the wind again. Everything felt like it was either up in the air or teetering on a cliff. And Mayher hadn't slept in more than twenty-four hours.

"No deals," she said.

"Oh," Daniels said. "Ok..."

"We're not going to need him to unlock anything," she said. "We have a resource."

If Kayne's going to do my job and send emails on my behalf, I'm going to commit her to some work without asking. It seemed like a fair trade.

"Gotcha," Daniels said. "Well, in that case, I'll let him cool it in a room for a while. His lawyers are all from BO&C, and they made it clear that he's officially dropped as a client. So he's waiting for a public defender. I'm guessing he'll upgrade through whoever that poor soul turns out to be."

"No problem," Mayher said. "I'll make sure Ms. Faure gets a similar set of circumstances. And we'll need to start contacting people who were impacted by this, see if we can resolve the whole stolen patent thing."

"Roger that," Daniels said. "So... I guess we'll be wrapping this up soon. Any... any chance you'll be back this way? Back here in Round Rock?"

Mayher felt her heart thump, and it surprised her. She thought for a moment. She had no real reason to go back. And yet...

"I think so," she said. "I... have some time off coming to me. I hear Austin is a fun town."

"It can be," Daniels said. "If you have the right guide."

She smiled, and after she promised to circle up with him they hung up. She spent several minutes making quick calls to the local Bureau, confirming that they all got the same sorts of emails from "her." They had. Videos, audio, paper trails, all of it. Things were already in progress.

Alex Kayne, cleaning house, tying up loose ends.

Why even bother carrying the badge at all? Mayher thought. When you had an asset like Alex Kayne working for you, the law was just a formality, right?

Mayher shook her head, dismissing that thought and all the emotional baggage that came with it. No need to be petty. Kayne was actually doing the sort of thing that HCD actually *wanted* her for. It was a little shady—posing as an FBI agent, sending emails on Mayher's behalf, accessing evidence using illicit methods. But this was the world Mayher lived in now. Alex Kayne's world.

For now.

She unlocked her phone. Unlike Symon, Mayher didn't have a direct line to Kayne, so she had no real idea how to reach her.

As it turned out, she didn't have to wonder long.

There was a text message, from an unknown sender, waiting for her—just a simple, single emoji. A smiley face with dark sunglasses.

If this is you, Mayher typed, *the security guy has hard drives that are protected by password. I volunteered you to crack them.*

Almost immediately there was a pulsing series of dots, followed by a response.

No problem, the message read. *I already found them, stacked in a secret server that Spencer was keeping in his apart-*

ment Everything is unlocked, and I copied all of it to the FBI servers, under your account.

Mayher nodded. She'd half expected this. But she couldn't resist the twinge of annoyance. Nor could she resist commenting.

You could have asked first.

The three dots returned, then, *Yeah. Sorry. I'm in a hurry. Please keep an eye on Eric.*

Mayher felt another flash, but it faded.

Kayne was worried about Symon, just like Mayher was.

Mayher had a lot of mixed feelings about Alex Kayne, but she knew for a fact that Kayne and Symon had some kind of bond. And Symon—the good man that he was—cared for Kayne, even if he intended to arrest her. It was obvious that Kayne felt the same about him.

How could Mayher hold a grudge against Kayne over petty things? She'd just solved a case that Symon was working on. And, if Mayher knew *anything* about Kayne, the woman was already on the hunt for the person responsible for Symon being shot.

It was suddenly obvious to Mayher.

She raised the phone and typed.

Find them, Mayher typed. *Take them down.*

A pulse from Kayne's end, and then: *I absolutely will.*

CHAPTER SEVENTEEN

Somewhere in Montana

The thing about Montana is it's big. And wide. And empty.

There is a lot of beautiful landscape, and a great expanse of ranches and farms. There are plenty of towns, though most are small. It borders Canada, to its North, making it an attractive place for certain folks to spend their time—especially those who might need to be out of the US in a hurry.

The state is not without its modern amenities, but there are great swathes of it that are virtually untouched by the invisible waves that comprise the digital landscape, over which Alex Kayne was the master.

And that was a problem.

It meant that Kayne was entirely dependent on the satellite smart phone, as she made her way through a patchwork of forests, hills, plains, and river valleys. It was a narrow sort of funnel to find herself in, when she left the large data pipeline of local cellular phone towers and residential and commercial

WiFi, and was reduced to a tiny noodle of broadband running between a satellite above and the small phone she carried in her pocket. Her options became limited, and she was not accustomed to nor a fan of limited options.

This was where things got the most dangerous for her.

She knew, though, that Derrick Conners had a pretty impressive broadband setup in his hideaway. He was using it to keep tabs on the outside world, which Kayne had in turn used to backtrack to his precise location. And his WiFi, as secure and fire walled as it was, was easy enough to crack, and had allowed QuIEK to get a sonar-like scan of the interior of Conners' home. That, along with live satellite imagery of the man's Montana compound, gave Kayne a 3D map she could use for planning her approach, as well as where she needed to go once she'd made it to Conners' compound. She had QuIEK build her a virtual landscape of the place, updated in real time, and she could dwell there virtually. A digital ghost, roaming Conners' compound, unseen, haunting it, waiting.

That was all well and good, and maybe a little creepy to contemplate. But the isolation of the place was going to make any *physical* approach a challenge. Which, of course, was the whole point—the entire reason that Kayne was off-grid and in the wild in the first place.

The problem was that everyone was too wide-open here.

There were miles of open plains between her and Conners. She'd be spotted from miles off, no matter how she tried to get there. QuIEK could hide her from video surveillance—as long as it was networked. But it couldn't hide her from a pair of binoculars, or just someone patrolling in a Jeep or on an ATV.

Infiltrating at night was the obvious solution, but that didn't exactly make it easy. Again—miles of open plains. That meant she couldn't use any lights, which would flag her approach immediately. She'd be forced to stumble through the dark with nothing but moonlight showing her the path. Dangerous, all on its own. There would be any number of pitfalls and obstacles in the dark.

Plus, there was the threat of wild animals. The region was home turf for a surprisingly high number of deadly critters and predators. Hiking her way on foot to Conners' compound, in the dark and possibly even in broad daylight, was out of the question.

If she tried to drive it... well, same issues, really. Just faster. Maybe fewer big cats or bears or rattlesnakes to worry about, but she'd effectively be driving a billboard that said "intruder, shoot me."

That left only two potential options, neither of which fell into the "easy" category.

First, there was the Missouri River. Conners' property butted up against it at one point, and the big house was only a mile or so inland. She could conceivably get a boat from somewhere up or down stream and make her way to a spot nearby, then hoof her way into the compound.

That still left trekking across some fairly rough terrain in the middle of the night. And it was possible that Conners would have someone monitoring the river. They might see her coming. Or hear her—the boat was going to make a lot of noise, and in the relative silence of the night it would pinpoint her location as much as any lights would have. So that option—it wasn't great.

The second option was to drop in from above.

Kayne had no trouble chartering a plane or helicopter, and a pilot to fly her in. There were hundreds of pilots for hire in the region, doing everything from air surveys to crop dusting to dropping hunters in hard-to-reach spots. She could easily have someone fly her over Conners' compound. The trouble was getting to the ground.

She had no experience in skydiving, so that was out. She had no time to train in it, and she honestly wasn't sure how comfortable she was with jumping out of a perfectly good airplane. Even if she *had* already gained experience with it, night jumps were crazy dangerous. She stood as much of a chance of becoming mashed Kayne chow, for the dining pleasure of whatever wild cat or other predators were in the region, as landing safely. This mission was risky enough, thank you.

There was an airstrip and a helicopter landing pad on the property. That presented some possibilities. But she doubted any pilot would be willing to land there, with no questions asked, and without getting clearance from the property owner. Even if they faked an emergency landing, Conners' people might shoot first and ask questions never.

That settled that, then. On paper, coming in by air was the quickest and easiest and maybe even the safest bet. But logistically, it was just impossible. She'd be putting the pilot at risk, even if they decided to help her. And realistically, someone from Conner's camp would definitely spot a plane or helicopter landing at night, less than three miles from the main house. So there was no chance of a stealth approach.

Even her old standbys were out of the question. There was no way she was going to con her way in. It wasn't like Conners would welcome any guests, while he hid out from the FBI.

Again, Kayne didn't like limited options. And right now, her options were as limited as they could get. She needed to find a way to open this up a bit. She needed to think outside of her usual box of tricks.

What if she just called in the authorities?

She had plenty of people to reach out to with the FBI. Her

"teammates" within Historic Crimes would treat any call she made as a tip from one of their confidential informants. They'd be on this in a heartbeat, considering one of their own was in an ICU because of Conners. And they wouldn't have to worry about going in quite as stealthily as Kayne needed to—they'd simply surround the place, cut off all of Conners' exits, and take him down. In theory.

There was always the chance that something would go wrong, and Conners would slip through their fingers. It happened. Kayne was living proof that it happened.

She wasn't sure she wanted to risk that. She also wasn't sure she wanted to be responsible for more FBI and HCD agents being hurt or killed. Maybe it was their job, but she'd be the one pointing them at danger and telling them to run toward it. She was comfortable with that.

But in truth, there was another reason why Kayne was hesitant to bring in the Feds.

She wanted to be the one to bring Conners down. She wanted to *hurt him.*

Seeking revenge was an ego play, she knew. A bad call, really. It meant she was letting her emotions drive her, which was how mistakes were made. It was how someone like her got caught. Or killed. Or both.

That thought made her pause, considering.

Was she running on emotion?

A little. She was at least lucid enough to recognize that fact. But emotion wasn't a deal breaker, just a red flag. It was a sign that she needed to slow down, refuse to rush, and to make a plan.

Making a plan was kind of her thing, right?

She was currently holed up in a dingy little motel on the main highway, about thirty miles from Conners' compound. Those were thirty hard, cold, challenging miles to cross. At the moment it felt like an impassable gulf. And with only two options of approach, both of them terrible, the gulf widened.

By air or by river?

Alone, or call in the Feds?

Stay or go?

She thought about Eric Symon, currently in a coma, recovering from emergency surgery and struggling for his life. Every minute Kayne spent here, in Montana, was one she wouldn't have with Symon. Though, of course, she wouldn't have any moments with Symon anyway. He was under guard, and everyone was on the lookout for her. She'd be arrested on sight, and would likely be blocked from getting within fifty feet of Symon. It was entirely possible that she'd seen him for the last time, kneeling in a pool of his blood.

She shook that thought out of her head.

By air or by river?

Alone, or call in the feds?

Stay? Or go?

It ran like a roulette wheel through her brain. Every bet a bad bet. Every option a gamble she'd never even consider, if it weren't for Eric Symon.

She was sitting on top of the bedspread, pillows behind her back, laptop on her knees. On the nightstand beside her was a styrofoam cup of some of the worst coffee she'd ever tasted, accompanied by a can of Pringles and half a chicken salad sandwich she'd bought at a gas station across the street. Dining options were limited here. Even the motel vending machine was empty.

She stood, setting the laptop aside, and stretched. She fished a plastic bottle of water out of her backpack—the sole luggage she'd brought with her. She was running light. A habit, but also a necessity. At times like this, though, she'd give anything to be back in her old apartment, the high-rise home she'd had in the Bay Area, more than three years ago now. She'd love to be listening to music, making dinner, settling onto her sofa to tinker and unwind with a personal project. Or read a book. Or fall asleep watching Netflix.

The thing that rarely gets talked about, when you hear about someone being a fugitive, living on the run—the life is *exhausting*. Constantly watching every face in the crowd, making sure you can make a run for it at any minute, never having roots or a foundation to return to—it wore on the soul in a way that most people would never understand.

Kayne was luckier than most fugitives. Thanks to QuIEK, a certain level of scrutiny was negated, and a certain level of worry was abated. She could "hide in plain sight" because she had an unseen guardian angel erasing all traces of her in the digital realm. And in the modern landscape, that realm was as much a part of reality as the one we explore with our physical senses.

To erase yourself from that world was to cease to exist, in many ways.

The thing no one realizes, however, is that regardless of how nice or comfortable your hotel or rental house or AirBnB is, it isn't *home*. Those aren't your dishes. That isn't your sofa. These aren't your sheets, or your towels, or your throw blanket. You are a stranger here, passing through. You own nothing, you take nothing with you, you have nothing to return to. The welcome comfort and warmth of home is something that lingers in the back of your mind, a landscape that no longer includes you. It's like having a phantom limb.

You are a stranger in a strange land. Always. And only.

Maybe that was why she'd latched onto Eric Symon and felt oddly close to him. He was her nemesis, in a way. But because of that, he was someone who *knew* her. He was someone who *noticed* her, even when she was invisible.

She would be lying if she said she'd never considered any sort of romantic notions about Symon. About Eric. She had. Of course she had.

But she was infuriatingly pragmatic and practical. It would never work. There would never be that moment where the two of them gazed into each other's eyes and built a bridge of trust that crossed the gulf between them. There was no possibility of a happily ever after. And because that door was closed, Kayne didn't even allow herself the fantasy anymore.

It was more of a Stockholm syndrome thing, anyway. No real romantic feelings, she had long ago decided.

If anything, she'd been more attracted to Ross Eckhart than to Eric Symon, anyway. Physically they were both pretty equal. Intellectually, to. Morally and ethically. They were a lot alike. But Eckhart had an edge over Symon in one key and crucial respect.

She and Eckhart lacked the shared history she had with Symon, but they had some common perspective, common experiences. She'd connected with Eckhart on a more basic level, she thought. More like the sort of thing that happens every day. No extraordinary circumstances muddying the waters. Just connection. Just gut instinct.

No gulfs to bridge.

She shook her head, sipped her water, and turned back to her laptop.

No gulfs to bridge, she thought. Unlike this approach to Conners' compound.

What if she was going about this all wrong?

She'd been thinking about the limitations—all the things that made getting to Conners a huge challenge.

What were the *advantages?*

Her access to this home network, along with the satellite imagery, had allowed her to build a pretty extensive virtual map of both his compound and his home. Was there something there she could use?

She started running through everything QuIEK had found while it scanned and searched Conners' digital presence. She brought up a list of IP addresses—the devices connected to Conners' home WiFi. There was a network of security cameras from outside of the building, covering all angles of the grounds. Nothing inside the home, but she didn't really need that. QuIEK was able to use the signal strength of the WiFi to sense the home's interior. In some ways it produced a better view of the place than any cameras would have.

Of course, there *were* cameras in the home. Laptops, tablets, smartphones—QuIEK could get her video and audio from all of it, adding it to the map, enriching and enhancing that virtual landscape.

Some of the IPs on her list were those devices. But then there were others.

One of the more interesting turn of events in the technical world was the advent of the "internet of things." Basically, the world had embraced the idea of putting nearly every appliance in a home on the internet. The appliances could do things like monitor energy usage, track inventory, alert the user when consumables like soap and detergent were running low. And users could also control certain functions remotely, turning lights on or off, adjusting the temperature, even locking or unlocking doors.

It was clear, from the list of IP addresses, that Conners was a gadget junkie. His entire home was one big network, every appliance, every light switch, even his vehicles, all of it was a part of the internet of things. And there were some IP addresses that were not specifically *on property*. She'd more or less ignored them, since they couldn't contribute to the virtual map that QuIEK had constructed. But now she looked through the, identified what they were and where they were.

She smiled.

No gulfs to bridge, she thought.

The bridge was already there, waiting for someone to cross.

It just didn't have to be Kayne.

CHAPTER EIGHTEEN

Conners Compound, Wyoming

Derrick Conners was a self-made man.

All the magazines and blogs and TV interviews said so. And for good reason—he was telling it to them. That Netflix special alone had been one of the best bits of publicity he'd ever had. Even if it did make him out to be a smuggler and a crime boss, and brought him to the attention of the FBI.

He should never have let them interview him at the ranch. Letting a few million people see some of the art on his walls had opened up this whole can of worms. And things had been going off the rails ever since.

He couldn't rightly blame the Netflix folks. They'd been cool enough, treating him like royalty, asking him questions about stuff that really mattered—about his past and his history, about what he'd built, and how he built it. He didn't regret the interview one bit, even if it did paint him in a bad light. It was his legacy. He'd earned it. By sweat and by blood, he'd earned it.

As a self-made man, Conners didn't owe anything to anybody. That was the whole point. Everything he got, he got by his own efforts. And over time, those efforts got easier. Instead of boosting cars, he got to a point where he was paying other people to boost for him. He had people doing the chop, people doing the inventory, and people doing the selling. He even had other people counting the money, and they knew he was watching them like a hawk. It was amazing how the books came square every time, when the accountants knew the cost for stealing. It only took one shifty bean counter fed to a bunch of wild cats to make the others stay in line.

Not that anyone could ever know for sure that Conners had anything to do with that poor man's tragic accident.

He learned to insulate himself from it all and still have his thumb on all of it. He knew how to use influence from afar, when it was needed, and how to get up close and personal when it was required. Always in ways that he couldn't be implicated. Always with a hedge of protection, from the lawyers and the security guys and the tech guys he paid in mountains of cash. Nobody liked to turn on the guy who paid for their lambos and high-dollar escorts.

In all the years since Conners had started as a scruffy little car thief, he'd learned how to clean up and keep himself clean. He'd learned how to build on what he knew, and how to put down threats. He learned who to trust—which was nobody. And who to put at his heel—which was everyone. He may have started petty, but he graduated to being his own boss, and then the boss of a whole lot of other folks.

And from there, he expanded.

The ranch was one of the first things he'd bought. He didn't have any idea what he'd do with it, at the time, but he knew potential when he saw it. And for a while, all he did with it was run the business there. With so many acres stretching so far, touching so many different roads and highways, it was a good, central place to keep the machine working, keep things in motion, and keep off the radar. He had hidden warehouses there for a while. Garages, run by diesel generators, that kept the operation going day and night. It was like a Ford assembly line in reverse. He was the Henry Ford of chop shops.

Eventually, though a lot of cash handouts and incriminating photos, he had the local PD in his pocket. And for years he never worried about raids on the place. But when he started seeing small aircraft fly over, with no airports in the area, it got him to worrying. That was when he moved the whole business off of a property that could be tied back to him. And he did it in a smart way.

He bought more properties, in more places. He set up corporations that couldn't lead back to him. He made some of his better boys into lieutenants, running things on his behalf. And sure, sometimes they dipped a little too deep for their own pockets, but take a hand off here or an eye out there, and word got around pretty quick that you have to keep yourself in check. Everything in moderation. Don't get greedy.

He didn't just diversify his locations, of course. As he started buying real estate, certain new opportunities arose, and he suddenly found all new ways to bring in the cash. And then to make sure that cash was nice and clean before it was ever associated with him.

The motels, hotels, and eventually the casinos were a gold mine. And cheap to run, in the grand scheme of things. Keep the sheets clean and the buffets open, and money just poured in. And these were the honest, respectable face of his empire. They made good cover for the more lucrative stuff. They made a good filter for the filthy lucre.

Because the lucrative stuff was doing very well.

Drugs, obviously. Idiots just *threw* money at you when you

controlled the drugs. And from there, guns. Guns by the truck-load. There was always a market for them, and it tended to sidle right along with the drug business. Easy money begets easy money.

Conners knew there were rumors he trafficked in humans. And sure, there was some of that. He had prostitutes waiting to help out any high rollers who needed to blow off steam after a night of giving him their money at the craps table. Those girls usually started out poor and hungry, so he considered putting them to work a humanitarian service.

But then there was the more gut-turning stuff. A young girl or boy here and there, mostly to make some of his more loyal clients happy. Mostly for the government types—a little grease to keep them from pointing the Feds at him. He had photos of them all. Truly disgusting stuff. But hey, everyone has their kink. And it wasn't like *he* was the one diddling little boys. If some freak on the Senate couldn't get to it with a real, adult woman, he was going to find his way somewhere. Conners didn't mind profiting off the evil SOBs. He kept the photos to keep them honest. And to keep them on his team.

All of that, disgusting as it was, brought a pretty respectable pile of money into play. And influence. It helped keep the Feds from looking at him too closely, most of the time. And good money was good money, even if getting it did turn your stomach.

But of all things, it was the big cats that really opened up doors for Conners.

Not necessarily the cats themselves—it was more about what the cats *represented*.

They were legal. Legit. And they were a big draw. They gave him a new and legitimate purpose for the ranch, for a start, and a means of getting his face out there on something respectable. They were good camouflage. And yeah, there was a *lot* of money.

When he'd moved all of his operations off of the ranch, it left him with a huge chunk of real estate that wasn't serving any particular purpose. It wasn't like he couldn't afford it, but the waste bugged him. At that stage in his life, everything he owned paid out in some way. Everything except the ranch.

But when one of his buddies asked if he could keep a couple of tigers there, that got Conners' attention.

"You think anybody would pay to see them cats?" he asked.

His buddy—the guy everybody called Old Shay—had smirked, spit on the ground, nodded sagely, and told Conners a tale of money flowing like water.

There were men, right there in Oklahoma, bringing in millions per year just by keeping cats and other exotics around, keeping them fed, keeping them healthy. People came in by the car load to see them, to touch them, to take selfies with them. Then they bought stuff—souvenirs, keepsakes, T-shirts and ball caps, all marked up as much as five-thousand percent.

Crazy money.

Maybe not the level of money Conners saw from some of his real estate deals, or running drugs or guns or whatever else he could. But it was a big draw, with low overhead. And it was legal. It was like stealing from the willing.

Best of all, it put the ranch to use in a profitable way.

By the end of the year, Conners had acquired hundreds of exotic animals, most of which were big cats. He had pens built, put up high fences like a maze winding through the ranch, and hired staff to keep everything fed and cared for and healthy. He built a little museum—more of a tourist center, with pictures and video screens and displays of stuffed, dead critters. And, of course, a gift shop. The only way out was through the gift shop. And that place was a wonderland for little kids, and a devastating blow to the wallets of their parents.

Conners bought billboard space on every road that touched his property, and for hundreds of miles in all directions, throughout Oklahoma and into the surrounding states. He guided people to all those entrances along all those roads, and funneled them to a ticket booth and a road that wound through the whole property. You could go on a safari without leaving your car. You could even download an app that gave you a guided tour, for just $9.99. Proceeds going to the care and feeding and preservation of these amazing animals, *of course*.

The place was a hit. *Disney World of Oklahoma*, some folks said. Mostly Conners said it, and other people ran with it. People in Oklahoma really wanted something on that level—something they didn't have to drive for four days and pay thousands of dollars to see.

With the success of the place, he eventually expanded, buying out everyone around him. Though he sometimes had to have an elbow or a knee bent the wrong way, to convince his neighbors to sell. But eventually he owned one of the largest blocks of land in the state, and he dedicated every square inch of it to those cats and the other animals that people would pay ridiculous money just to see.

Of all the things Conners had running, that ranch soon became his favorite. It became his haven. His home base. All those years he'd worked so hard to get out of Oklahoma, to become a citizen of the world, and now he found himself thinking about that ranch when he was in one of his fancy casino suites, or in his apartments in New York or LA or Paris or wherever. He owned millions of dollars in beautiful houses and apartments, but home was on a ranch in Oklahoma.

He had his house built right in the middle of the property, surrounded by trees and high fences and acres of exotic animals. People who came to see and touch those critters would see his house, too. A symbol of the man himself—out of reach, but standing there in all its glory. Just like Conners.

It was perfect. A comfortable and safe place. A symbol of his wealth and power.

And if he hadn't let the damned Netflix people film him in that house, he'd still be there, right now.

The paintings had sunk him.

Art wasn't really his thing. But owning stuff he could turn into quick cash always was. And rumor had it that if the Feds came knocking, having some famous, stolen art could be a bargaining chip, in a pinch. That turned out to be a load of bull, but Conners had played the *better safe than sorry* card.

And *that* turned out to be all sorry, no safe.

Of course, the paintings were also currency. A lot of them had come his way from those high rollers at the casinos, who found themselves rolling high but living low for a bit. So a Rembrandt here, a Vermeer there—they came in as collateral and stayed as inventory. And if Conners ever wanted to have some untraceable liquid currency for this project or that, he could sell one, no questions asked, usually within a day of putting the word out. They were usually good for a few million, untraceable and under the table.

There's something to be said for five million bucks in your pocket from someone desperate enough to own something, but cautious enough to keep quiet about it.

Things had gone on like that for a long while, and Conners had made the mistake of getting relaxed about some of the precautions he *should* have taken. Like, *Don't have famous stolen art on your walls when someone films you for an international documentary series.*

When the Netflix thing ran, someone watching noticed that Conners had a Degas. Nothing fancy. It was just some women washing their hair in a river or something. Conners hadn't even liked it all that much. But he'd paid a woman six figures to decorate his place, and when she'd found the painting in a stack in Conners' basement, she'd had it framed and put up over the fireplace. Conners didn't bother having it taken down —it looked nice enough up there. And he hadn't snapped to the fact that he was putting a few million dollars in stolen art on full display.

He wouldn't know a Degas from a Dilbert comic, but he did know the paintings were all worth millions on the black market. This particular one, it turned out, rang in at $7.6 million. And it was famous. It had been among some paintings stolen from the Gardner Museum. A heist so famous it had its *own* Netflix special.

After the series ran, the FBI got flooded with calls. And Conners started getting pinged by his buddies in Washington— the ones who turned to him for a fresh supply of young flesh, when the urge hit. The ones who owed him big favors, and were into him for more than they could ever pay. The ones he had photos of, waiting to go out to the media any second, if things went bad.

They let him know they were on it. They would take care of it. They would get the FBI off his back. At most, he'd have to turn over the Degas—a "magnanimous gesture" on his part. "I'm so sorry, everybody, I had *no idea* the painting was stolen when my decorator bought it!" She might go down for it, but he'd come out looking like a poor billionaire who had been tricked into buying stolen property.

Insulated and safe, that was the rule. Give up the painting, and he'd look like a hero. His people in Washington would make sure the FBI were steered in a different direction.

But then he got the knock anyway.

And these were FBI—but for some reason they were out of the reach of his boys and girls in DC. They were part of some new, fancy department. *Historic Crimes Division*. They had a charter that gave them a bit more autonomy, when it came to certain crimes. And they had the authority to look a little deeper into Conners and his business than he or anyone else would like. Or prevent.

And they were not interested in stolen art as "bargaining chips."

Two of those agents in particular had caused all this trouble —Agent Roland Denzel, and Agent Eric Symon. Two smart and smug pricks who both had reputations for being willing to tank their own careers in the name of bringing down the bad guys. Incorruptible. Not the kind of agents that Conners or his DC friends wanted to see anywhere near the ranch.

When they raided his ranch, that was just the first blow. They started digging deeper, finding more, making connections that Conners had thought couldn't be made. But, it turned out, his "buddies" in DC that he had files on—they had some files on him, too. Tit for tat. And as they dug in, Denzel and Symon started uncovering a treasure trove of incriminating evidence that Conners couldn't reach fast enough to cover up. And within a week Conners saw almost everything he'd built, every bit of insulation he'd constructed, the whole damn empire, burn to the ground. Everything.

Almost everything.

He'd gotten wind of the raid on the ranch, and the raids happening at his casinos and other businesses. They'd done their homework, found practically everything. Definitely everything that had any sort of legitimate face, and from there they found quite a bit of the illegitimate stuff, too.

They had him sewn up pretty good. They raided his whole life, warrants in hand, all of them demanding some highly specific access, and yet broad enough that nothing could quite slip through the nets. There were no loopholes that Conners' attorneys could exploit. Everything got caught in the filter.

Conners was toast. Burnt. They wouldn't even bother with butter.

But he did get an early word, at least. And before the Feds could get their hands on him, he got out of there. He lit out by private plane, straight to his Montana ranch, right into the heart of *middle of nowhere.*

This place had always been his safe space. His *secret* space. His hidden home away from home. It was almost as if he'd always known that someday he'd need it. And so he'd kept it off all the books, kept all eyes away from it, kept it registered under names and companies that were unique and distant from everything else he touched.

It was the smartest thing he'd ever done. None of it could possibly be traced back to him. There were threads and paths that circled back on themselves, that led nowhere, or led everywhere. At one point he had a string of shell corporations and phony businesses that owned each other, in a huge circle of legal paperwork and nonsense, with stacks of corporations going six deep and spanning the entire globe.

All that amounted to one fact: This was the safest place on Earth.

Just because he was safe, though, didn't mean he was ready to let the rest of his life fall away in ruin. That hurt, even for him.

He still had reserves of cash. He had anonymous accounts all over the world. He had assets he could liquidate, including more of that stolen art, stashed in warehouses and storage units all over the planet. And sure, he took a bath on some of those pieces. Black market buyers could smell desperation, and his name had been all over the news. But all told, he still pulled in hundreds of millions in on-hand cash. He was going to be alright. He would survive.

But Agents Denzel and Symon wouldn't.

O ver the years, Conners had employed quite a few people who were in the business of putting the hurt on someone. So it was easy enough to reach out to a couple of guns for hire. They didn't need to be the best, they just needed to be competent enough to put a bullet in the head of a nuisance. It didn't even matter if they were stupid enough to get caught. Conners paid big money to the very best security firms to make sure he was completely isolated from all of it. No one could track him. Not ever.

Conners used his anonymous channels to front the hit men part of their fees and promised big bonuses when these two agents were in the ground. The money came from accounts that were owned by some of the shell corporations Conners controlled—the companies that were owned by other companies, in a big, giant circle, until eventually the company owned itself. Money moved in and out of these through secure channels as well. Layers upon layers, and Conners wasn't even under the pile.

He'd rarely ever had to put these things to work in quite this way. Usually, if he needed someone taken care of, there was always someone willing to do the wet work, somewhere in his organization. And that person tended to just disappear quietly, turning up as a suicide or an unfortunate mugging.

But with two FBI agents, things had to be handled with a little more strategy and caution. Feds tended to go hard after whoever took down one of their own. The more layers, the better.

And as far as the Feds were concerned, Conners didn't

even exist anymore. He was so off the grid, he might as well be on a different planet.

He might have to hide out here at the Montana place—maybe for the rest of his life. But he'd do it knowing that worms would turn these two Feds into fertilizer. While Conners drank wine and watched the Super Bowl on a hundred-inch TV, and had girls brought in for a fun weekend, while he caught a tan by the pool or took down a buck from his hunting cabin up river, Agents Denzel and Symon would rot. And that made these new limits on Conners' life feel almost worth it.

Despite the layers, though, Conners wanted to know when the thing was done. That would be tricky. Any contact from the hitters would open up a path that could lead back to Conners. But he had this handled, too. His two guys were instructed to leave ads on Craigslist. Specific ads, with specific wording. Conners could use a VPN to check on those, set up to relay a San Francisco IP address. He didn't even have to look at the ads themselves, he just needed to type in a couple of keywords and they'd show up in a list of hundreds of other results. He'd know them by the headlines, and if anyone was looking he'd just seem like one of millions of people searching for used living room furniture in one of the biggest cities in the world.

He'd been checking every few hours, and eventually he got the message from the first guy.

Orange velvet sofa for sale.

"Orange velvet" was the code for Agent Symon. And it meant that the agent had some fresh, new holes in his body.

Conners did a quick run through area headlines and saw that one of the stories was about a drive-by shooting that had put an FBI agent in critical condition. They didn't name the agent, and police were saying they were following up on leads. Conners didn't bother clicking on the story—the headline told him everything he needed to know.

Symons wasn't dead yet, but it wasn't looking good.

That made Conners smile.

Denzel would be next. His code name was "purple plush chair." Conners would check Craigslist in the morning, to see if that one was done.

And from there, he figured he could start picking off everyone at "Historic Crimes," one by one, as revenue for all this inconvenience they were putting him through. Payback should cut deep.

It was late in the evening. Conners was keyed up. He wasn't used to being so *confined*—though his confinement did consist of a 32,000 square foot home on 600,000 acres of Montana ranch land. He had staff who would bring him literally anything or anyone he ever needed or wanted. If you were going to be confined, this was the way to do it. He could live out the rest of his life in comfort and luxury.

But he was used to being in the thick of it all. He was used to hitting the Vegas strip, going to parties in LA mansions, having $10,000 steak dinners with powerful people in DC. He was used to hopping on a plane and being anywhere he wanted, any time he wanted. Compared to that level of freedom and liberty and autonomy, even this massive space felt claustrophobic to him.

He didn't have any hobbies to help him unwind. Not yet. He figured he'd take up some things. Maybe he'd try painting— that Degas didn't look so hard. And he could afford to fly in teachers and tutors for that kind of thing. He'd have to have them taken care of afterward, of course. You can't leave someone like that lying around, knowing what you look like.

But the hobbies would come later. Right now, he was bored. And anxious. He had nothing to keep his attention, to keep his mind off of his current state.

He'd taken his third shower of the day, and was padding in

bare feet from his master suite to the fourth kitchen—the one closest to his bedroom apartments. This one was stocked with what he thought of as "midnight snacks." Junk food, mostly. He wanted a whiskey and some Cheetos.

As he entered the kitchen, the lights came on automatically. He moved to the large walk-in pantry, a space bigger than the house he grew up in. He picked up a snack bag of chips and then went to the minibar to pour a bourbon.

The lights went out, and suddenly he was thrown into pitch blackness.

"What the..."

He felt his way out of the pantry and emerged into a realm of chaos.

There was the sound of cars honking from outside, and through the kitchen window Conners saw lights flashing in irregular patterns. He leaned over the counter and peered out of the window, and saw that the security floodlights surrounding the house were flicking on and then off, one after another.

Suddenly an alarm screeched all around him—a pulsating, piercing scream. The fire alarm. It yelped into the darkness like an insane coyote, and Conners pressed his palms against his ears, trying to drown it out enough to think.

He let out a flood of curses as he moved out of the kitchen and back to his master suite, fumbling in the nightstand drawer for his phone.

He was used to there being no signal—there were no cellular towers within range of the place, and the terrain blocked out the invisible waves from distant transmitters. But right now he didn't even have WiFi. He couldn't make any outgoing calls. Couldn't even send a text.

He cursed again and went to the wall phone. The compound had its own operator trunk system, and it was hard wired. Outgoing calls funneled through that to get to the outside world. It was separate from the internet systems.

He heard the dial tone and punched in the extension for his head of security.

"What the hell is happening?" he yelled into the phone, after his security chief answered.

He could barely hear the reply over the cacophony of noise coming from both ends of the line.

"Fire alarms are going off in every sector of the main house and in all the outbuildings," the man said. "But that's not all. Basically *everything* is going nuts. We've got breach alerts on every single door and window on the property. All the vehicle alarms are going off. Data is down, and the phone system is acting weird."

Conners shook his head. "What is it? What's causing it?"

"No idea, sir," the man replied. "We're looking into it now. But the alarm systems started calling out for emergency services, and we can't seem to stop the calls."

Conners felt his guts chill like an ice bucket full of beer.

"You're telling me we're calling out for cops and firemen to come here?" he asked.

"Yes sir. That's the default protocol for the system. We changed all that when you got here, but it's reset itself."

"Get the damned thing turned off right now!" Conners shouted.

"We can't sir, I'm sorry. It's too late anyway. The calls have already gone out, and we have no way to reach them to say it's a false alarm!"

Conners slammed the receiver down, then picked it back up and slammed it down several more times. He left it hanging, a ruin of wire and shattered plastic, as he rushed to the walk-in closet. He cursed the air blue as he went.

He shed the robe and pulled on jeans and a shirt as he

shoved clothes and other items into a duffel. He opened the safe hidden behind one of the shelving units and took out all the cash and prepaid credit cards, the burner phones, and his pistol. There was a box of 9mm rounds, and he dumped this into the bag as well.

He rushed from the suite, down the hall to one of the side exits, and was out into the chaos of the night. It was chilly, but he barely noticed. His blood was pumping, and he was practically steaming.

He hadn't called ahead, so he'd have to wait for the pilot to get his act together and get the plane ready. But he figured they could be up in the air in under twenty minutes, maybe faster if Conners pointed the 9mm at him for motivation.

When he arrived at the hangar, though, he knew he needed a plan B.

The hanger was having the same weird issues as the rest of the place. And Conners saw the pilot and one of the mechanics working on the door of the hangar, trying to force it open.

"What's happening?" Conners shouted as he walked forward.

"No idea!" the pilot replied. "The automatic door rolled down when all the noise started. It's working against us. Every time we try to lift it, the motor kicks in to push it back down. We're going to get a ladder to get to it, pull the manual release."

"I need this plane up in the air in ten minutes," Conners growled.

The pilot shook his head. "Not gonna happen, Boss. I'm sorry. She needs to be fueled, and the pumps are shut down. Override isn't working."

"Why wasn't this thing fueled up already?" Conners shouted, outraged.

The pilot looked confused, and said, "Sir... *you* told us to drain it. Got the email this afternoon. Drain it, clear all the lines. Deep maintenance, you said."

"I didn't send any damned email, you idiot!" Conners shouted.

The pilot looked absolutely terrified. "I... but I got..."

Conners cursed him, with some impolite references to what the man could do to his own mother, and then left him there, rushing out into the darkness. There was no time for this. He had to get as far away from here as possible.

The garages were not far, and Conners rushed toward them. He stopped as they came into view.

The doors were all down, and people were working on them, just as they had been at the hangar. From within the garages, a disco of lights flashed. He could hear horns and alarms piercing the night. He grabbed one of his people. "I need a car!"

"They're all going nuts!" the man said. "Computers are all shut down. They're bricked."

"What about the pickup?" Conners said. "The F100? That doesn't have any chips. It's a classic pickup."

The man looked alarmed. "Sir... you... you told us to pull the engine this afternoon."

Conners felt his blood pressure rise, and before he'd even thought about it he backhanded the man. "Somebody is screwing with me," he said, his voice acid.

He didn't wait to hear anything the man said, but instead marched away from the chaos of the garage.

If he couldn't leave by car, and couldn't leave by plane, that left only one option.

The river was a couple of miles from the main house, and thankfully the ATVs weren't having the same issues as everything else. He toyed briefly with the idea of taking one of them overland, getting the hell off the compound and out into the wilderness. He'd take his chances.

But he didn't have any provisions, not even a coat to keep warm. And worse, he had no idea where he could go. His face had been plastered all over the news, and the towns around here were small. It wouldn't take much for someone to recognize him and turn him in. The reward was pretty substantial. He was a living target for anyone who had dreams of getting out of their dust bowl existence, and in this area that was a lot of people.

But there was another way. Another place. A safe haven within his now not-so-safe haven.

The cabin.

If he got on the river he could go upstream, and eventually he'd come to the little hunting cabin he kept further out on the property. He'd have to hike a bit to get there, once he'd left the boat tied off, but it wasn't far. And the cabin was already stocked with food and other provisions. It even had its own phone line. He could lie low until things died down back on the compound, until the police and firemen were told that it was all just a false alarm. And then he could go back. He'd have to deal with some people, make sure everyone was aware of how pissed he was about all the screwups. He'd have to find whoever did this—and it had to be someone on his own team, didn't it? Someone screwing around? Someone trying to play games? He'd find them, and deal with them. But for now, he could tough it out in the cabin.

One night. Two tops.

The more he thought about it, the more he liked it.

He drove the ATV like a man possessed, zipping along the paved path that led toward the river. He slammed on the brakes as he arrived and hopped out, sprinting for the dock. The boat was moored but ready. He pulled the tarp off of it, checked the fuel, and fired it up. In minutes he was racing along the river, lights aimed ahead, GPS guiding him.

With all the bends in the river, it took most of two hours to get to the little pier that served as a landing for the cabin. The place was buried deep in the wilderness for a reason—as far from other humans as he could get. A good thing for hunting. A *great* thing for lying low.

Conners pulled up to the dock, tied off the boat, and hoisted the duffle over his shoulder. He had a flashlight from the boat, and that would help. It would be a slog, but he was in the clear.

He had no way of knowing what was happening back at the compound. He'd left his phone, but it wouldn't have worked here anyway. No cellular, but also no WiFi. Though there would be another hard-wired phone at the cabin. And internet, unless it was down. Either way, he could call and check in once he got to the cabin. And when he did, he wanted *answers*. Somebody screwed up, and he was going to have it out of their hide.

His anger over that fueled him, keeping him warm on the chilled Montana night. Thank God it wasn't winter, he'd have frozen to death. But the cabin had a gas fireplace and full propane tanks. It had a change of clothes, and warm coats. It had whiskey.

He kept his mind on all of that and trudged along the dark trail.

More hours went by. He wasn't even sure how many. He stumbled along in the dark, trying to push himself, hurrying as much as possible. The flashlight was pitiful against the ink blackness of the Montana wilderness, and he found himself gripping it in one hand and the pistol in the other. He wouldn't have much hope in a serious encounter out here, with just a 9mm. He could pop a rattlesnake, though in this chill they weren't likely to be out on the open trail. He was more worried about mountain lions, in this stretch of wilderness. Grey wolves and grizzlies weren't out of the question, either. None of those would be much bothered by flinging lead the size of a lima bean at them.

Never mind. Keep walking. Stay warm. Make noise. Shine the light.

His nerves were shot, his lungs and limbs burned from exertion, but he was getting closer.

He nearly wept when he saw the trail marker and turned. The cabin was at the end of the path.

Hope. Salvation. Warmth. Whiskey.

Finally, after what had felt like a month of stumbling in the darkness, he stepped onto the front porch, reached up above the window frame, and retrieved the key. A moment later he was inside, stomping his feet and rubbing his frozen arms, coughing and sneezing as dust rose from the floor.

He dropped the duffle near the door and huffed in the darkness for a moment. Then he reached and turned on the light for the main room.

The cabin had a solar array and battery power for days. No need for a generator or for fuel, though there was that, too. Just in case.

Battery power was plenty enough, given how little time he spent here. The place was mostly meant to be shelter for Conners and a few of his boys, for a handful of days each year. Most of those days were spent out in the woods, rifles in hand, taking down whatever game he and his boys could find. Which reminded him, there were some hunting rifles locked in a gun safe in the corner. He'd fish one out after he thawed. Should be more than enough ammo in there, too. He relaxed his grip on the 9mm, as if just remembering he had it, then set it down on an end table near his big, plush chair.

That chair was calling him—squared as it was to the fireplace. He'd get the fire going in a minute and relax. He thought he might even have some Cheetos stashed here.

There was a fully stocked bar, at least, and his first duty would be to pour a whiskey, to be followed quickly by another. And probably another.

He moved toward the bar and froze.

On the bar was a laptop. It was open, and the screen was dark.

When had he ever brought a laptop here?

He didn't recognize it.

He took a step back and picked up the 9mm, then slowly glanced around. "Anybody in here?" he asked, his voice low and gruff, menacing.

He wouldn't tolerate squatters. Especially now. Whoever they were, they'd be food for the wolves before morning.

The laptop's screen blinked on, and the glow of it got Conners' attention.

A video started playing. Security footage. And Conners recognized the FBI agent—Symons. He was standing on a sidewalk, outside of an office building. A black SUV suddenly raced forward and slowed. A hand, holding a gun, appeared. Shots were fired. Agent Symon went down.

Conners felt his heart pounding. He turned slowly, the gun pointed and ready. "Whoever you are, you made a big mistake, messing with me. You think what I did to this guy was bad? I'm going to make sure you..."

He was cut short when something smashed into his skull.

He stumbled, the gun still in hand. His vision had gone blurry, but he tried to steady himself. He looked up to see a woman—someone he'd never seen before.

"Who..." he tried to raise his gun, to shoot.

She ended that, raising a full bourbon bottle high into the air and bringing it down hard on his forehead.

Conners fell then, the 9mm clattering off to the side. His vision went from blurred to black. Pain created threads of light —the only thing to pierce that darkness.

And then the last blow came.

CHAPTER NINETEEN

Conners Hunting Cabin, Montana

Kayne huffed and sobbed. She had the bottle ready, gripped in her fist so tight that her fingers ached. She raised it. She intended to do it. The weight of the thing would do most of the work. It would be easy.

She lowered it.

She wasn't a killer.

She'd told herself that a million times. Despite the body count that continued to rise for her. Despite the blood she'd scrubbed from hands and clothes over the years. Despite the faces she still saw when she closed her eyes, the dreams that still shook her awake at night, the constant twisting sense of dread in her guts.

I'm not a killer.

She'd always managed to convince herself, in the daylight hours at least, that the deaths she was responsible for were self defense, and unavoidable.

This one would be different.

She'd *wanted* to kill Derrick Conners. He deserved it. The world would definitely be better without him in it. And she'd waited here, in this cabin, knowing this was where he would run. She'd routed him here, engineering everything that pushed him here, *funneled* him here, knowing this was the only place he could go.

She'd waited and had planned to do it in the most brutal way she could think of. No guns. No knives. She wanted to feel his skull cave in.

What did that make her?

She shivered and stared down at the man at her feet. She could do it.

But she'd never be able to convince herself, ever again, that she was not a killer.

This was vengeance. Plain and simple.

She would have to live with it. And she wasn't sure, yet, what that was going to mean. It was an uncertainty, a cascade of unknown and unforeseeable variables. She had never been comfortable with that level of ambiguity in her choices. She thrived on order in the midst of chaos, on planning and thinking, on being twenty steps ahead of problems that just *might* happen. So this...

She shook, shivering from the thought of what might be more than from the chill of the cabin. She gripped the bottle, weighed it as she tapped it against the side of her thigh. All it would take is to raise it high, one more time, and bring it down on Derrick Conners' head *one more time*.

She sobbed, and she hadn't expected it. She felt stinging tears in her eyes. She wiped them away with her sleeve.

She turned to the bar, and used a paper towel to wipe down the bottle, spilling a bit of the bourbon on it to help break down any oils from fingerprints, and to remove the blood. When it was nice and clean, she replaced it on the shelf where she'd found it.

She closed the laptop and tucked it inside her backpack, slinging the pack onto her shoulders.

She'd come here prepared. More out of habit than planning.

In the pack she had zip ties, which she cinched tight around Conners' wrists and ankles. He groaned a bit, when she moved him, but didn't come awake.

In the pack, she had a syringe filled with ketamine—a pain killer that served as a general anesthetic. It would keep Conners out for a while. Long enough to make sure she got away. Maybe long enough that he'd be asleep when the FBI got there. They were on their way to his ranch. They wouldn't be that far off.

She had alerted them to Conners' location the second she closed the laptop. The cabin had its own WiFi, and she'd set things up in advance, given QuIEK a set of instructions to follow as she cleaned up the crime scene. She had plenty of time. She could be out of here long before the helicopters and boats and SUVs arrived.

She pulled Conners up and into the plush chair. He would have a concussion, for sure. But he should live, despite every impulse Kayne had to make it otherwise.

After making sure he really was ok—minus the head injury —she exited the cabin, leaving it unlocked behind her, and made her way further up the path to where she'd parked a Jeep. It was loaded with provisions—food, fuel, blankets, and other things she might need if she had to hide out in the wilderness for a bit. She didn't think it would be necessary. Just a contingency.

I'm all about contingencies, she thought, bitterly.

She started the drive back up the long mud-and-stone road,

cutting through the darkness with the headlights of the Jeep, retracing her steps to the anemic little paved road she'd come in on. This trip would take all night, she knew, but she'd cross off of Conners' property and onto a proper road near dawn. There was little to no chance that she'd cross paths with the FBI or other law enforcement, on this route. She'd mapped this out in detail.

Once she was on an actual road, she'd stop for gas and food in a little dive of a town nearby, and then she'd be on her way again. Heading West.

Heading back to San Francisco.

She had unfinished business there. She had a friend in need there. Seeing him, one more time, had always been part of the plan, whether there was blood on her hands or not.

And she wasn't sure if this was going to be her last choice of free will—if she'd ultimately find herself finally captured and buried in a cell somewhere. But she had decided that would be fine, if it happened. She'd accept it. Maybe it was time.

But before she went down, she was going to see Eric Symon.

She was going to say goodbye.

CHAPTER TWENTY

Law Offices of Bertrand, Owens & Cromwell | Palo Alto, California

Mayher had two local FBI agents flanking her, and behind her there were two members of the Palo Alto police department. As they stepped from the elevator, they didn't have to go far to find their target. Julia Faure hadn't been given any warning by her employers, who all knew the circumstances. She'd been allowed to come to work, to take her post, and to continue in her day as if everything was fine.

"Julia Faure," Mayher said, raising her Historic Crimes badge. "You're under arrest for corporate espionage, theft of intellectual property, fraud, and... well, this list is long. I'll let your attorneys give you the whole thing."

"Wh—what?" Faure stammered. "What do you..."

Before she could finish her sentence, the uniformed officers had her out of her seat and her hands cuffed in front of her. They were reading her rights to her when Mayher turned to see a smartly dressed woman emerge from the door of one of the executive offices.

Mayher went to her. "Adele Bertrand?"

The woman nodded.

Mayher offered her hand, and Bertrand took it.

"Thank you for your assistance in this," Mayher said.

Bertrand looked a little shaken, but she nodded, and offered a slight smile. "Of course," she said. "Anything to help law enforcement."

"We'll need access to your files," Mayher said.

"You'll need access to *some* of our files," Bertrand replied, a sudden steel coming to her posture and her voice. "I've already been in contact with Agent Denzel, and Bertrand, Owens & Cromwell will cooperate fully. But as I'm sure you understand, we have an obligation to protect our clients. Some of these files contain sensitive information. I've already had members of my team start pulling everything related to IP and patent acquisition."

Mayher could have argued, but decided against it. Bertrand was the head of one of the most powerful law firms on the planet. If anyone knew just how far the boundaries could be pushed, it would be her. As long as BO&C were willing to cooperate on the specifics of this case, it didn't seem like a worthwhile fight to ask for more.

Not yet, anyway.

Mayher nodded, and for the next few minutes she asked Bertrand questions, including how she could contact the other partners, what sort of access Faure had to the firm's files, the number of patents the firm had facilitated, basically anything that might be helpful or pertinent. Faure was already out of the building and on her way to a holding cell by the time Mayher wrapped up and was preparing to leave.

She said her goodbyes to Bertrand and moved toward the

elevator, but paused, turning back. "Is Mr. Eckhart in the building?"

Bertrand's lips tightened. "Mr. Eckhart's whereabouts aren't something I'm compelled to talk about."

Mayher nodded. "Would you ask if he'd be willing to chat? Nothing... nothing on the record. It's not about this case. It's..."

"Alex Kayne," Bertrand said.

Mayher studied her for a moment, then nodded.

"All charges against Mr. Eckhart have been dropped, regarding that matter," Bertrand said.

"I'm aware," Mayher replied.

"So what would you want to talk to him about, off the record?"

"I'd rather keep that private," Mayher said.

Bertrand watched her features, then smiled, laughed lightly, and shook her head. "I know that Ross would tell me to let you talk to him. Maybe I should be in the room."

"If it makes you feel better," Mayher said.

Bertrand nodded and waved for her to follow.

They wound their way through the corridors until they came to the door of a conference room. Inside, Ross Eckhart sat in one of the leather conference chairs, hunched over a laptop. He looked up in mild surprise.

"Mr. Eckhart," Mayher said. Her first reflex was to hold up her badge or ID, but she stifled it. "I'm Agent... I'm Julia Mayher. I'm Eric Symon's partner."

Eckhart stood, and nodded. "Agent Mayher. What can I do for you?"

She hesitated. She'd wanted to speak to Eckhart, but she wasn't entirely sure where she wanted to begin.

No place like right in the middle, she thought.

"You spent some time with Alex Kayne. And you met Agent Symon."

Eckhart nodded.

Bertrand interrupted. "You said this is off the record? Not part of an official investigation?"

Mayher glanced at her. "Can we call it a mix of both? Yes, it's off the record. I'm not here trying to entrap Mr. Eckhart. But my partner is in an ICU, and we don't know if he's going to pull through. And Kayne is in the wind again. Which is... pretty much who she is, really. So I'm just trying to..." she paused, took a breath, shook her head.

"Make some sense of it," Eckhart prompted, gently.

She looked up at him. "Yeah," she said. "We've been hunting Kayne for a couple of years now. She's good at getting away, keeping off the radar. But she made some mistakes, coming here with you. It was like... it seems like she trusted you."

"I think she did," Eckhart said. "To a point."

"More of a point than anyone else, so far. Even more than with Eric."

"Wasn't Agent Symon pretty committed to arresting her?" Bertrand asked.

Mayher laughed. "Absolutely. So, I guess that could put a bit of a kink in your trust of someone."

"Agent Symon is a noble man," Eckhart said. "I don't know if I'd have the integrity to be so committed to arresting someone I liked. It's... admirable."

Mayher started to say something, but instead all she could do was nod. This conversation wasn't going entirely the way she'd thought it would. Though, she had to admit, she hadn't had any real thought about how it *should* go.

"I've been thinking about all of this," she said, her voice subdued. She looked up at each of them, and suddenly the scene shifted for her. She stopped being an FBI agent, or an

216 J. KEVIN TUMLINSON

agent of Historic Crimes. And suddenly she was just Julia Mayher, whose friend was fighting for his life in an ICU.

Julia Mayher, who was starting to question everything about her life, her career, all of it.

She rolled back one of the conference room chairs and slid into it. "I need to sit down," she said.

Bertrand and Eckhart exchanged glances, and Bertrand immediately went to the little station of refreshments in a corner of the room. Eckhart sat in the chair at the end of the table, facing Mayher. "Are you alright?"

Mayher shook her head. "I'm not sure. I'm worried for Eric, I guess."

Bertrand returned with a glass of water, and Mayher took it gratefully. She sipped. The water was cold and refreshing.

"Something else is bothering you," Bertrand said, taking a seat on the opposite side of the table.

Mayher took another breath, letting it out slowly. "It's... nothing important."

"It was important enough to make you lower your guard," Eckhart said.

She looked at him, nodded. Laughed. "Yeah, I guess so."

"It has something to do with Alex Kayne?" Bertrand asked. "That's what you said you need to talk about, with Ross."

"Sort of," Mayher replied. "Like I said... we've been chasing her for a couple of years. And she's always so far ahead of us, all the time. She's just... Well, I hate to admit it, but she's *amazing*. Smart. Capable. Just... *good*. And she and Eric definitely have some kind of bond." Mayher shook her head. "I guess what I wanted to know was, what is it about her? I can't ask Eric, obviously. Not now. And even if I could, I know he'd just downplay it. Be evasive. Maybe he doesn't even know what it is. But you seemed to have a bond with her, too. So, I guess I thought I'd ask you."

Eckhart was watching her face, and he leaned back slightly in his chair, resting his right elbow on the table. He sighed. "The thing that drew me to her was that she's honest, I think. Clever, for sure. But just... honest."

"For a fugitive who routinely deceives her marks," Mayher said, smiling.

"For *that*, yeah," Eckhart smiled. "Don't get me wrong. I know she's perfectly willing to lie and keep secrets. That's not it. I've done some research on her, since this started. I was looking into her when you came in, actually." He nodded to his laptop, now closed. "The thing that strikes me is that she has absolutely no reason to do what she does."

"Running?" Mayher asked. "She'd go to prison for a very long time, if we caught her. That's pretty good motivation."

"No," Eckhart said, shaking his head. "Not the running. The *helping*. You know about her AI, right? QuIEK?"

Mayher nodded. "Don't ask me about the technical bits, but yeah, I'm aware. It's how she keeps ahead of us all the time."

"Ahead of you," Eckhart agreed. "But don't you think that's strange? Why bother keeping *ahead* of you, when she could just disappear? She has it within her power to completely vanish from the face of the Earth. She could craft a new identity—one that's impenetrable. She could amass wealth on a level no one on Earth has ever known, and no one on Earth would even suspect was there. No door is shut to her. She could be literally anywhere in the world, living any way she pleased. But instead, she's running. She's keeping a low profile, but putting herself at risk, over and over, to help people who can't help themselves."

"That's all very noble sounding," Mayher said. "But she's still a fugitive."

"Forget nobility, then," Eckhart replied, shaking his head.

He leaned forward. "Whether you believe she has good intentions or not, the fact is she doesn't have to do it. She could be the single most free person on the planet. Untouchable. She could topple governments, if that's what it took to keep herself safe. But here she is running from place to place, putting herself in danger over and over, just to help some poor woman get her patents back. Just to bring down someone who was hurting someone else, and getting away with it. The kind of thing that happens every day in the world, and that most people don't even think twice about. And those with power and money typically couldn't care any less about of it. So... why does she?"

"You're getting back to the nobility part," Mayher said.

He laughed, nodding. "Yes, in a way. I think it's her nature. I think she sees what's happened to her as being unjust and unfair. But instead of taking on the role of victim, and using her power to bring justice for herself, she's turned all of that into a *responsibility*. She's using her power to help other people, who don't have the advantages that she has. If that isn't noble, then the term has no meaning."

Mayher sighed. "I get that. Eric and I have had this exact conversation, over and over. I get it."

"And yet, here you are, asking me for whatever insight I can give." He thought for a moment, then said, "Actually, I don't think you're here to ask about Alex Kayne at all."

She shook her head. "Then what am I here for?"

He studied her. "You're here to ask about *you*."

Mayher stared at him, then looked to Bertrand, who wasn't saying anything.

She turned back to Eckhart, shaking her head. "No," she said. "No, not... not really."

"You want to know why Alex is so dedicated to helping

people, even if it costs her everything, but you... you're struggling with this, yourself."

Mayher was quiet. Thinking. She felt her chest tighten, her
guts clench. She took a breath and let it out slowly. Then she
stood. "I'm sorry, this wasn't a good idea."

"Why not?" Bertrand asked.

Mayher squared on her. "Because..." she wasn't sure how to
finish.

"Because you're questioning whether you even want to do
this work anymore," Eckhart said.

Mayher turned on him. She was about to say something,
but stifled it. "Thank you for meeting with me," she said, and
turned, opening the conference room door, stepping through
into the hall beyond.

She was moving swiftly through the offices, toward the
elevator. When she got to it she punched the button and
waited.

"Agent Mayher," she heard Eckhart say from behind her.

She turned.

"I understand what that's like," he said. "Not wanting to
stay on the same track. If you... if you ever need to talk..." he
handed her a card. It was blank, except for a phone number.
"Text me," he said. "I'll be here."

She said nothing, and when there was a chime from the
elevator she turned and stepped in. As the doors closed,
Eckhart simply stood, hands in his pockets, watching.

As the elevator descended, she held up the card, rubbing
her thumb over it. She slipped it into her pocket, and rode the
rest of the way to the ground floor with her eyes locked on her
own reflection, in the polished mirror surface of the elevator
doors.

CHAPTER TWENTY-ONE

Zuckerberg San Francisco General Hospital and Trauma Center | San Francisco, California

Kayne had to turn off QuIEK's early warning system. She was in the thick of it now, with cops and FBI all around her, and the constant buzzing of her phone and smartwatch was not only getting on her nerves, it could potentially get her noticed.

Every law enforcement official in this building knew exactly who she was and what she looked like. And they had orders to be on the lookout for her. Agent Denzel knew she'd be here, at some point. Or he suspected it strongly. Either way, he'd given orders to be ready. She'd seen them herself, sniffing around in her backdoor access to the Historic Crimes email servers.

It was nothing personal. She knew that. Denzel was like Symon, in that way. He could be dispassionate about this, just doing the job he was sworn to do. Unlike Symon, Denzel didn't really know Kayne all that well, so maybe there wasn't as much of a personal bond to overcome there. But they'd met, at least.

Worked together. Been in danger together. She'd even saved his life. That had to mean something, right?

Maybe. But probably not.

She was currently sitting in a hospital waiting room full of people, dressed in street clothes. Her hair was tied back in a pony tail, and she was wearing a pair of glasses. Clear lenses, not shades. They weren't even particularly thick frames. They were just meant to help change the shape of her face a little, at a glance.

When she'd checked herself in the mirror, she had decided that she could still pull off looking a little like a teenager. Especially if she used makeup to smooth her complexion, hiding the hints of wrinkles that were starting to form at the corners of her eyes. She wasn't a vain person, but that did smart a little.

Makeup also helped in other ways. She had been studying YouTube tutorials for months, learning how to suggest features and shapes using subtle techniques. It was pretty amazing, actually, how well these things worked. One of the YouTubers she followed could make herself look like anyone from Jack Sparrow to a comic book illustration.

It was a useful skill, and though Kayne was far from a master of it, she'd picked up enough tricks to allow her to severely alter her appearance.

Using coloring wax she was able to change her hair color without dyeing it. Using eyeliner and mascara she was able to change the shape of her eyes. Her eye color stayed the same, but it looked somehow different in contrast to the eye shadow she was using.

And there were more makeup tricks for shaping her nose, her lips, her cheeks, her chin. She could even alter the appearance of her ears.

It took her hours, and it wasn't the most fun thing she'd ever

222 J. KEVIN TUMLINSON

endured—her hands and arms ached from the meticulous application. But it worked. It was transformative.

When she'd looked in that mirror a second time, after all the work, she didn't even recognize herself. To her own eyes, some teenage girl was standing there, wearing the clothes that Alex Kayne had been wearing only a couple of hours before. She looked easily ten years, maybe fifteen years younger.

Now, here she was, in the lion's den, field testing her work in the most dangerous way possible, just to see her friend one more time. Possibly for the last time.

It was worth the risk.

She'd been sitting in this waiting room for more than an hour. There were dozens of other people here, all chatting amongst themselves in hushed, worried tones. Everyone in this room had someone they were worrying over, as they waited. She was just one among many.

To amplify her teenager persona, Kayne had opted to orient position herself as closely to an older couple as she could. Though "older" was a bit relative. The couple she'd landed on seemed to be just about her own age. Maybe even a little younger.

She tried to give off the vibe of "disaffected teenager," keeping her chin down and her phone up, like a shield against the world. This was a handy disguise, as it not only threw off any suspicion, with people hopefully assuming she was the teenage daughter of this couple, but she could freely use her phone, and thus QuIEK, to figure out what to do next.

She was here during the mid-afternoon, which was a peak time. Lots of people in the hospital, moving around, interacting. It was easier to blend in. But the more time that went by, the more the crowd would thin out. People would go home to rest up and recoup before returning to anxiously await news of their loved one's fate. Staff would go off duty, making way for the thinner night shift crowd. Eventually, Kayne's disguise would start making her stand out, rather than blend in. Everyone would eventually wonder why the teenager didn't go home with her parents.

Before the window closed on her, she would need to act.

She'd been using QuIEK to map out every possible exit, and every possible path to Symon's room. She had also mapped and pattern-tracked every police officer and FBI agent in the building, even those who were disguised and undercover.

The bad news: There was absolutely no way to get to Eric Symon without someone stopping her. And that meant she'd be in cuffs and on her way to a cell without even getting the chance to see him. She couldn't even pretend to be a relative, since they had a list of approved visitors. And she wasn't on it.

The good news: Well...

She could always leave.

She'd done enough, hadn't she?

She'd been there for Symon, when he needed her most. She'd knelt in his blood, put pressure on his wounds with her own hands. It was entirely possible that she'd saved his life, keeping him going until the EMTs could arrive. She'd done enough. It should be enough.

But it wasn't.

For all she knew, Symon wouldn't pull out of this. His condition was still listed as critical, and as she'd dipped in and out of his charts throughout the past couple of days, he wasn't showing much improvement. He'd had a transfusion, which helped. His blood pressure was still borderline, though. And he was still intubated, with a damaged lung. They had a tube in his chest to keep fluid from collecting around his heart.

These were not good signs.

And that was why, despite the risks, she *had* to see him.

Even if it meant going to prison for the rest of her life, she owed it to him to say goodbye.

Do I, though?

She'd been thinking about this for the past few hours. Wondering. Trying to figure it out. After a few years of obsessive self-preservation, she was suddenly willing to throw herself in front of the train. Why?

Guilt.

It was the word that kept ringing back around in her brain. *Guilty, guilty, guilty.*

She'd almost killed Derrick Conners. She'd *wanted* to kill him. So much so that instead of using her usual tactics and methods, finding the guy and exposing him, pointing the Feds right to him, she'd gone there personally. She'd wanted to be as hands on as possible. She'd wanted to cave in his skull.

She hadn't. But she'd really, *really* wanted to.

And if she was willing to do that, even for a second, what did that mean? Who did that make her?

And if she was willing to do that for Eric Symon, how could she let him lay in an ICU, drifting toward death, while she just kept running, like it was business as usual?

No.

This was the line.

This was where that line was drawn.

When she'd been framed, when it became clear that there were people who wanted QuIEK for their own purposes, and those purposes were just *evil*, Kayne had lit out. She'd made a run for it. And she'd been running ever since. Until running wasn't something she was doing anymore, it was who she *was*.

Running had become her life. Running had become her identity.

But somewhere in the back of her mind, she'd known that, eventually, the running would have to stop. She'd known that there had to be something that would *make* her stop. A line. And this was it.

She'd gone to Wyoming to kill Derrick Conners. She had stopped herself. This time. But what about next time?

And she'd seen someone she cared about hurt. She'd literally had his blood on her hands.

Her friend. Maybe the only real friend she had left in the world, despite the strange nature of their friendship. This person she cared about, at the very least, was laying there, dying. And by damn, she would see him before it was too late.

Time to move.

She rose from the waiting room chair, stretching, working the kinks out of her shoulders and neck and back. She turned toward the older couple for a moment—maybe that would give the impression that she was talking to them, whispering to them, telling them she was going to go find a bathroom or a snack machine or just take a walk. And then she turned and made her way out of the waiting room and into the corridor.

She passed three undercover FBI agents as she went. Each glanced at her, and their eyes moved on. No sign of recognition. No moves to call for backup. That was one hell of a makeup job.

Kayne's heart was pounding, but she was keeping things in check. She had years of practice at keeping calm despite whatever internal anxiety she was feeling. Her body language said "bored and young" instead of "fugitive about to freak out."

She still had no solid plan about how she was going to see Symon. Even just wandering toward his room in the ICU would be enough to garner suspicion. She'd be arrested before she could even peek in his door.

She had considered disguising herself as a nurse or orderly, but had scrapped that idea right away. They'd be expecting that. Everyone on this floor had been checked and vetted, and the agents and officers on hand all knew who should be here and who shouldn't. A new nurse showing up would immediately cause suspicion, and since she really was the fugitive they were looking for, that would be the end. So, scratch that plan.

Kayne was starting to consider making a sprint for it. She could be down that corridor and in Symon's room in seconds, if she was willing to clobber the two people guarding his door on her way in. And yes, moments after that she'd be pinned to the floor and cuffed before being dragged away to live out her days in a cell somewhere. But she could *see him*. She could touch his arm. She could say goodbye, even if she had to say it with her face mashed to the floor and an agent's knee in her back.

Of course, that might not be the end for her after all. Maybe QuIEK's automated protocols would provide her with some way out of custody. Miracles did happen.

But no, the chances were pretty high that she'd be throwing her freedom away for good. And all for someone who wouldn't even know she was there.

Still... she was short of other options. So... maybe?

She had just convinced herself to give this not-a-plan a go when she stopped short.

From the elevator, down the corridor, Agent Julia Mayher emerged. She showed her ID to one of the uniformed officers sitting at the end of the corridor, and they spoke for a moment. Getting directions, Kayne figured. And then Mayher started walking toward her.

Not really toward *her*, actually. But toward the corridor where Kayne was lingering. The general direction of Symon's room.

Mayher glanced her way once, and Kayne was leaning against a wall, affecting a sullen and bored posture, as if she were tired of waiting for whoever was the reason for her being here. Kayne wasn't looking at Mayher directly, as the agent passed. She was studying her phone, which was displaying an enhanced video from the hospital security cameras. She could see Mayher looking at her, from that other vantage point, and was slightly relieved when the agent passed her by without seeming to recognize or even suspect her.

Kayne slipped the phone into her pocket and pivoted, gaining lock step with Mayher.

Mayher noticed, and as she paused and turned, curious about this strange girl shadowing her, Kayne moved forward, grabbed the agent's elbow and pulled her into the restroom.

It happened so quickly that Mayher had barely reacted by the time Kayne had closed and locked the door. And in the next instant, the agent and the fugitive stood facing each other.

Mayher blinked.

Kayne stood, silent.

"Alex?"

"Julia," Kayne replied.

There was a beat, and Kayne saw tension move like a ripple through Mayher's body. She was waiting to see what Mayher tried. She knew the agent had her weapon holstered on her left-hand side, against her ribs and under her coat. If she went for that, Kayne would have to disarm her.

Mayher could yell for help, but Kayne thought she could probably silence her.

Mayher could spring at Kayne, trying to pin her and arrest her. That would be a tussle, but Kayne figured she could gain the upper hand. Maybe. They'd had their physical scrapes before, though, and Mayher was the type to try to learn from her mistakes and work to shore up any weaknesses. Kayne hadn't really followed Mayher's activities, but she could imagine the agent enrolling in a martial arts class, after learning that Kayne was serious about the *Krav Maga*.

But instead of the things Kayne was mentally preparing for, Mayher simply stood, staring, until finally she shook her head.

"I know you have like forty ways out of here," Mayher said. "So there's no point in me trying to stop you."

Kayne didn't contradict her. She didn't bother saying that she had essentially *zero* ways out of here. But she was more than happy to let her reputation serve her. It could buy her time, at least.

"What do you want?" Mayher asked.

Kayne sighed. "I... want to see Eric," she said.

Mayher shook her head. "The second anyone knows you're here, they're going to lock Eric up tight. Even you can't get to him at that point."

"True," Kayne said. "So... would you help me?"

Mayher looked surprised and even laughed. "Help you? Alex, you're a fugitive. I'm supposed to *arrest* you."

"But you haven't," Kayne said. "Not yet."

"Only because I know your M.O., and I don't want egg on my face."

Kayne watched her, studied her. "That's not it, though, is it? Not all of it."

Mayher was looking right back at her, and eventually shook her head, cursing under her breath. "Kayne... Alex... I just..." She made a frustrated noise. "I just don't know, right now."

Kayne hadn't noticed it before, but now she could see it. Something was *off* with Julia Mayher. "Are... you ok?"

Mayher laughed and shook her head. "Dammit."

"What?" Kayne asked, curious.

"Eckhart," Mayher said.

Now Kayne was confused. "Ross Eckhart? What does he have to do..."

"He was right about you. About your nature. You're... *noble*."

Kayne blinked, laughed a little, shook her head. "I wouldn't call myself..."

"You're the one who takes responsibility for everyone and everything else, even if it costs you. Dammit, Alex, if that isn't noble, nobody knows what the word means. Which is exactly how Eckhart put it." Mayher laughed again, then took a deep breath, letting it out slowly. "Ok, let's go."

"Go?" Kayne asked.

"To see Eric," Mayher said. She looked Kayne up and down. "Christ, I don't even recognize you and I'm standing right in front of you. Is this some new thing QuIEK can do? Is it magic now?"

Kayne smiled. "Not QuIEK. And not magic."

"Whatever it is, I think you can pass as my niece or something. Someone who wouldn't be on the approved list. I think I can get you in."

Kayne considered this. "But... why?"

"Do you really want to ask me that? I'm giving you a gift, here."

Kayne nodded. "Ok. Yeah. Ok. But, wait, if they find out..."

"I'm screwed. I'll probably be in a cell right next to you. So don't make this the one time you got caught, Kayne. Got it?"

"Got it," Kayne replied.

Before they opened the door, Mayher took out her own phone and tapped in a text message.

"Who are you contacting?" Kayne asked, suddenly feeling dread.

"Don't worry about it," Mayher replied. "I'm sure your AI already knows, right? But it's nothing you need to worry about. Just the opposite, actually."

Kayne frowned.

"I know this probably doesn't mean much. And maybe I

haven't earned it," Mayher said, "but maybe you could just trust me."

Kayne considered, then nodded before saying, "Actually, it means more than you think."

Mayher huffed. "Ok, then. Let's go commit a felony."

CHAPTER TWENTY-TWO

Eric Symon's ICU Room | Zuckerberg San Francisco General Hospital and Trauma Center

There were the sounds of monitors beeping and a ventilator whooshing. There was no window, and the lights were dimmed. The smell was a putrid-seeming mix of disinfectants and unidentified aromas that always made Kayne think of foul things she couldn't dwell on.

She hated hospitals.

When her parents had died, she wasn't allowed to see them. Too traumatic for a young girl, maybe. She'd never really gotten an explanation on that. All she'd known was that one day she was a little girl with a mommy and a daddy, and the next day she had only Papa.

When he died, she was older. A decision maker. A caretaker. She was right there with him, the whole time. She saw every needle and every tube that penetrated his flesh. She helped turn him so his sheets could be changed. She emptied his bed pan and held a straw to his lips when he was thirsty.

And eventually she held his hand as the beeps on the monitor slowed, and the lights went out for good.

It had been a peaceful death, but that did nothing to make it hurt her any less. Or to be less frightening. Or to destroy her sense of self and stability. To untether her in the world.

All of that rushed back to her as she saw Eric in that bed. The tubes. The mask. The monitors. The smells.

Déjà vu.

This was not a place she wanted to be. For so many reasons. Seeing Eric like this, knowing what could come next, and aware that at any second she could be recognized and arrested. Or that Mayher could turn on her and use this moment of vulnerability to take her down.

If that was how it turned out, so be it. There were no guarantees in life, Kayne knew. Nothing was certain. Any given outcome was the results of billions of tiny choices, and she wasn't the only one choosing. Her fate was as entwined with the choices made by Eric and Mayher and Denzel, and every soul in this hospital and in this city, as it was with her own choices. All she'd ever done in her life was lean in on the best odds for gaining what she was after, for meeting her goals. But she'd never *controlled* those odds. Even with all her obsessive planning. Even with QuIEK letting her outsource and augment her planning and strategizing and guessing, she was always at the mercy of fate.

All of us are.

She pulled a chair closer to Symon's bed, and as she sat, she took his hand in both of hers. An IV was taped to the backside of that hand, and she was careful not to touch it or the area around it. She just wanted him to feel her.

"Hi Eric," she said quietly, smiling. "I... just want you to know, I got the guy who did this to you. I... he's... he's in custody now. Alive."

She sensed some tension shift in Mayher, though she wasn't sure whether the agent was relieved that Kayne hadn't killed Conners, or if she was disappointed.

"And look at this," Kayne said, squeezing his hand lightly. "You finally got your hands on me." She smiled, laughed lightly. "All that chasing and all you had to do was lay down for a bit and wait. You are a very cunning strategist, Eric Symon. I could never have planned my way out of this trap."

There was no reaction from him. No movement. Nothing to signify that he even knew she was there. She decided, however, that he *did* know. That this *mattered*. That what she *said* mattered.

"I don't have many friends these days," Kayne said. "There's mostly you. And you... you never stop chasing me. It's kind of annoying." She laughed again. "But I think I needed it. I think I've needed it all this time. Not just *someone* chasing me. *You*. So, don't stop, ok? Chase me now. Here I am. You can have me. Take me in. All you have to do..." her voice caught, she stifled a sob. Tears burned down her cheeks. "All you have to do is wake up and tell me I'm under arrest. Got it? You do that, and I'm done. No more running. I'll go sit in whatever cell you want. Ok? Eric? Just wake up and say the word, and I'm yours."

She waited. Hoping.

She meant it. If he'd just open his eyes, right now, she'd happily go to prison for the rest of her life. Because...

Because she loved him.

She wasn't sure what *kind* of love it was. Not entirely. It might have been tinged with romance, but she didn't particularly see wedding bells with Eric Symon. She thought he was attractive, but she wasn't even certain she'd want to sleep with him. She just knew she loved him. Cared for him. Wanted his health and happiness to be above the line, unquestionable. And maybe, someday, if they could ever put this nonsense—her being a fugitive, him being the man hunting her—if they could just put *that* to rest, maybe something might evolve out of this love.

Maybe.

But for now, it was a different kind of love.

It was a love born of respect. A love born of mutual respect and concern. She loved him the way she loved anyone good and honorable and trustworthy.

He reminded her of Papa Kayne.

A good man. Willing to do what good men do, even when the cost could be high. A cost, like the one Eric was facing right now. A cost that, despite having nothing to do with Kayne, was still somehow on her. Still her responsibility.

Love and responsibility were, often, the very same thing.

The monitors continued to beep. The ventilator continued to whoosh. Eric Symon continued to fight a silent battle for his life.

And Alex Kayne stopped running.

She gave his hand a final squeeze, then stood. She wiped the tears from her eyes and turned away from Mayher as she scooted the chair back into place. She didn't want to leave anything in the way, nothing that might interfere with someone who might need to rush in and save Eric's life.

She was always planning a few steps ahead.

But she'd never planned for this.

She turned to face Mayher and took a trembling breath. Then she let it out, a cooling and soothing exhale.

"Ok," she said. "I'm ready."

Mayher had been watching her, quiet. She frowned and shook her head. "Ready for what?"

"Ready to turn myself in," Kayne replied.

Mayher's eyes widened. "Really? Wow. I can't say I was

expecting that. I mean, based on your history, I thought maybe you had a grappling line in the ceiling or something, waiting to zip you out of here."

"You're thinking of Batman," Kayne said, a tiny smile touching her lips. "I'm just me. And I'm done. I can't do this anymore. I can't keep running."

Mayher watched her. "See," she said finally, "the problem is, I don't believe you."

Kayne shook her head. "It's true. I'm done." She held out her arms, palms turned up, wrists exposed. "You can cuff me. Take me in."

"You're wallowing," Mayher said. "I mean, yeah, I think you mean it. Right *now*. But... no. I may not know you as well as Eric does, but I know you. I'd have you in a cell somewhere, and a day later no one would know where you went. Because I know something about you now. Something it took me until now to really figure out."

"What's that?" Kayne asked.

"You don't run because you're afraid of being caught. You run because you're afraid you're the only one looking out for everyone else."

Kayne frowned, shaking her head. She again wiped at a tear bulging at the corner of her eye. "No, I..."

"Alex," Mayher said, her voice stern but soft. "I didn't believe it for a long time. I realize that now. I didn't believe that anyone could have..." she struggled, shrugged. "Pure motives, I guess. But now I do. Because you're here. Because you didn't kill Derrick Conners. Because there was nothing for you to gain by coming to see Eric. And... not just see him... You didn't bother putting any sort of exit plan in place, did you?"

Kayne shook her head. "No."

"Now that, I find really weird. That's not your nature. So something would have to be really big for you to do that, I think. And, you'd have to be a certain kind of person. Ross Eckhart tried to tell me that about you. Eric has tried to tell me, for the past few years. But... I think I get it now."

"Look," Kayne said, "I'm glad you think I'm a good person. But you... you've sworn an oath, right? You have a job to do." She gestured with her wrists. "Do the job."

"Self-flagellation is kind of gross," Mayher said. "It's like you're trying to be a martyr."

"Whatever gets it done," Kayne said.

Mayher nodded. "Well, ok then. You're under arrest. But I'll hold off on the cuffs until your attorney gets here."

Kayne lowered her arms and frowned. "My attorney? I don't have an attorney."

There was a soft knock on the door, and Mayher glanced toward it. "That's probably them, now." She turned to it. "Come in," she said, her voice louder.

The door opened, and in stepped Adele Bertrand. "Agent Mayher," she said, her tone officious but subdued, respectful of their environment. "I'd like a word with my client."

Mayher nodded. "I'll be right outside," she said, and with that she stepped past Bertrand and into the hall, closing the door behind her.

"There are two more agents out there," Bertrand said. "So if you're planning to run..."

"I actually just turned myself in," Kayne said, a little confused by the events transpiring.

"Good," Bertrand said. "That's going to help. Cooperation is always looked on favorably."

"Cooperation in what?" Kayne replied.

"Ms. Kayne... can I call you Alex?"

"Sure," Kayne said.

"Alex, at the behest of Ross Eckhart, my firm has been working overtime to... *untangle* some of your current legal troubles. I have contacts in some powerful circles, including the US government, and believe me, I have been pressing them hard on this. It's taken a few days, but I think we've come to something. Your help as a confidential informant for Historic Crimes has been a very good first step. You've been named as a resource in resolving several threats to national security, including a recent one right here in San Francisco, involving Lee Coben. I spoke with Agent Denzel and with Director Liz Ludlum, and both were eager to write letters of recommendation. As was Mr. Eckhart and his good friend, Ethan Patterson. Who happens to be the head of the Oversight committee for Historic Crimes. You've gained some powerful fans, over the past three years."

"Most of them want to see me locked up for life, but sure," Kayne said.

"There are plenty of people in the halls of government who see you as an asset, and who recognize that you have saved billions of lives."

"Seems like too big of a number," Kayne frowned. "I mostly just help people who can't help themselves."

"People such as Shai Salide. Stevie Reece. Kenneth Hebert. Natalia Rustyovska. Abbey Cooper."

Kayne recognized every name. They were clients. Former clients. She'd kept track of them, after every case. She knew how they were doing. She had QuIEK check in and alert her any time any of them ever had an issue. Anything she might help with, if they really needed it.

They were people she cared for. People who, sometimes, didn't even know she existed.

"There are many more," Bertrand said. "This is just the short list. But there's also everyone who didn't die because of a terrorist attack, thanks to you. And the agents you've helped. The whole world, Alex."

Kayne shook her head. "I just..."

"You're a hero," Bertrand said.

"No," Kayne said flatly, abruptly, sternly. "I'm not."

"Just what a real hero would say," Bertrand smiled.

Kayne glanced toward Symon, laying prone in his bed, strung up with tubes, kept alive by machines.

"Oh, absolutely, he's a hero, too," Bertrand said. "But he knew you for who and what you are, didn't he? Doesn't he?"

"Where's this going?" Kayne asked.

Bertrand smiled. "Well, to a holding cell first. There's still a few things that have to be ironed out. But then, I've booked you a hotel room. A luxury suite, actually. Courtesy of Ross Eckhart."

Kayne blinked. "What..."

"You've gotten a Presidential pardon," Bertrand smiled. "With... some limits. But I think you're going to find them agreeable."

Kayne shook her head. She wasn't sure what was happening, or what she was feeling. She felt slightly dizzy. "A... pardon?" Then, a few blinks later. "From the *President?*"

"Let's go let the nice FBI people arrest you," Bertrand said. "And I'll explain everything."

EPILOGUE

It was Kayne's first time in the offices. Her first time in the presence of so many federal agents and other members of law enforcement—without the worry that someone was going to pull a gun on her at any second, at least.

Well, *mostly* without the worry.

She was dressed for the job. A pant suit and a sensible blouse. Her shoes were stylish, and dressy, but could double as running shoes in a pinch. Old habits died hard.

She had an ID around her neck that called her out as a "consultant." They'd stopped short of giving her one of those cool, black badges. But the ID had the Historic Crimes logo emblazoned on it, and she was told it gave her access to limited areas of the building. Very limited, really.

She wasn't an agent. Just a civilian.

A *free* civilian.

Sort of free, anyway.

She was sitting in a chair across the desk from Director Liz Ludlum.

She liked Liz. A brilliant, capable African American woman who had risen in the ranks, from working as a forensic specialist with the NYPD to heading forensics for a branch of the FBI, to finally taking over as the Director of a brand new branch of US federal law enforcement—who *wouldn't* like her?

But it was Liz's personality that clicked with Kayne. She was pleasant. Open. *Honest*. She didn't tolerate games, but she was ok with a bit of nonsense. Which might explain how she was able to date Dr. Dan Kotler.

"Your movements will be tracked," Ludlum said, peering at her.

Kayne nodded. "Not a fan, but alright."

"It was necessary," Ludlum sighed. "You're kind of the biggest flight risk of all time. There are still a lot of people above me who think you should be locked in a room until we need you, and then only let out if you were physically chained to an agent. I threatened to quit if anything like that happened, and a whole bunch of my team threatened to do the same."

"Thanks for that," Kayne said, nervously.

Ludlum studied her for a moment. "You're still adjusting to this," she said. "Coming in out of the cold."

Kayne nodded. "Yeah. There's that. It's a lot to take in."

"Plus all the new rules," Ludlum said.

"Yeah," Kayne agreed.

There were plenty of rules.

She would be tracked at all times, and if that tracking ever went off line she would immediately go back to the top of the most wanted list.

She had to check in daily, at random times that would be transmitted to her via a special phone she had to keep with her at all times. If she missed check-in, back to the list.

She had to live in an apartment that was within thirty minutes of Historic Crimes. Hudson Valley was home now. And when she wasn't on assignment, she was either in that apartment or in the offices.

She'd have a schedule for shopping. And Ludlum had used her sway to get her some "café time," for one hour per week. But otherwise, her liberties were severely limited.

The list went on. Restrictions. Limitations. Provisos.

It chafed. It made Kayne feel like a prisoner. She didn't like it. But she was determined to try to make it work. Being in out of the cold was better than being constantly on the run.

Right?

But there were other conditions she was less willing to accept.

She would reveal the location of every single module that made up Smokescreen.

She would turn over access to any networks or databases she'd hacked into.

And she would turn over access to QuIEK.

That last one was potentially the deal breaker.

"No one but me will have that access," Ludlum assured her. "Those were the terms."

"Sorry," Kayne said, shaking her head. "But you can understand why I don't trust that."

Ludlum nodded. "I do. There's practically no way to make sure that no one above me has the same access. But... those are the terms. If you don't agree, my only choice is to have you arrested, right here and right now."

Kayne nodded. She knew this. She'd been told this. Bertrand had prepared her well for this.

Of course, Kayne had a contingency plan. In the event of an emergency.

"Ok," Kayne said, nodding again. "I'll set it up. You will have access to QuIEK."

"Full access," Ludlum said.

"Of course," Kayne smiled.

Never. Not in a million years.

She could set something up, to give Ludlum access, along with whoever would secretly piggy back on that. But there would be safeguards.

Restrictions. Limitations. Provisos.

QuIEK was more than capable of running a truncated version of itself, disguising itself so that it *appeared* to be fully functional and playing by their rules. And all the while, it would limit them, even work against them. It would divert them away from things. Set up unexpected roadblocks. Leave out key details. It would *distract* them, while alerting Kayne to any shenanigans.

And if there turned out to be shenanigans, Kayne had decided, the deal would be off.

She'd already made sure that only she would have full access to QuIEK. Ever. And if she died, or if she were betrayed and thrown in prison, QuIEK would self-destruct and take its truncated little clone with it.

Anyone who looked at her code would be befuddled by it. Things would make sense, but nothing would ever add up. The code would evolve and shift. Nothing anyone thought they'd worked out would ever quite be what they determined it to be. And if they started messing around, trying to alter things or dig deeper, QuIEK would retaliate. Any hacker who tried to build their own version of QuIEK, or to take it over, would discover themselves being digitally erased from existence. They'd find themselves in a permanent shadow ban—no access to anything online, ever again. Digital banishment.

It was harsh, but she couldn't risk anyone cracking this.

Attack from orbit, raze the ground and salt the Earth. It was the only way.

Hopefully it never came to that. She really did want to believe Ludlum, and even the people above her. She *wanted* to believe they were on the level.

She just *didn't* believe it.

She also wouldn't share one other *proviso*.

Kayne was only in this for Eric. She wanted to be free to see him, to talk to him, to visit him. Maybe even to work with him, if he woke up.

When he woke up.

He was still recovering, still in a coma. And she wanted to be able to get to him without worrying she was going to be arrested.

But beyond that, she wanted to continue his work.

By being here, being part of Historic Crimes, she was continuing something that was important to him. And so, it was important to her.

And besides, as it turned out, he was going to need a new partner.

The conversation with Ludlum continued for a long while, with paperwork signed and terms explained. Kayne listened, and agreed, and let it all flow over her.

Finally, Ludlum rose from her desk, and Kayne rose from her own chair. Ludlum circled around and extended her hand. "Well, Alex, welcome to Historic Crimes."

Kayne smiled as she shook Ludlum's hand.

And in her pocket, from the agency-issued phone they'd given her—the phone she'd immediately hacked and reprogrammed—QuIEK quietly selected sites where it would be safe to reveal parts of the Smokescreen network, and made an impressive but functionally deficient copy of itself, while also mapping out every possible route of escape that Kayne might need.

Because Mayher had been right. *Dammit, she was right.*

Alex Kayne never stopped running.

Round Rock, Texas

Mayher smiled and sipped a bottle of Shiner Bock as Agent Christian Daniels—off duty, of course—cast another line into the river.

"This was not the date I was expecting," she said.

Christian glanced back at her and smiled, his cheeks dimpling so deep she thought she could fall into them. "I figured you could use some down time. If you want, I can take you out for Tex Mex. Or we can see a movie or something. Whatever you want."

She shook her head. "This is perfect."

He smiled again, spun the reel a couple of turns, and then sank the rod into a PVC tube driven into the river bank.

He dropped down in the camp chair beside her and picked up his own beer. "I told you things were going to warm up."

She laughed and shook her head. "It's hard to believe this whole place was covered in snow a few days ago."

"Texas," Christian grinned.

"Texas," Mayher said, offering her bottle up for a toast.

Christian clinked his against hers and they settled back to watch sunlight sparkle over the surface of the river.

"So, how much PTO do you have?" he asked.

She felt a twinge in her stomach. She hadn't told him yet. Hadn't told *anyone* yet. And their relationship was still too new, wasn't it? This was technically their first date. How much should someone confide in a first date?

"I... resigned," Mayher said, deciding that there was no reason not to be honest. "Yesterday."

"Resigned?" Christian asked, surprised. "That's... I wasn't expecting that."

She shrugged. "I wasn't either, actually. But I just..." she hesitated.

He turned, putting his beer in the webbed holder in the camp chair. Then he turned the chair itself, so that he was oriented on her. "What happened?" he asked.

Mayher said nothing for as second, just looked at him.

If anyone was going to understand, it was going to be another agent, right?

"I... realized that I couldn't... find myself anymore."

His eyebrows arched. "What does that mean?"

She laughed. "It means I found that I was questioning what I was doing. I was doing things that I didn't agree with, I guess. Sort of." She thought, took a swig, then shook her head. "No, that's not right. I agreed with them. I just didn't *want* to agree with them, I think. I don't know. It's confusing."

"What exactly happened?" Christian asked.

She sighed. "I saw someone in a new way, I think. And it made me look at myself and wonder if I really knew who *I* was. And... turns out I didn't. So, here I am."

He laughed. "Are you hoping you're going to find yourself by dropping out and hanging by the river all day?"

"You're the one who brought me to the river," she said. "I thought we were going for pizza or something."

"Pizza? You flew all the way to Texas for a pizza date?"

"Maybe."

He laughed.

She laughed.

"Ok, Julia Mayher," Christian said. "You're officially on a quest to find yourself. What can I do to help?"

She looked past him. The pole was bobbing and bending.

"Reel in that fish," she said. "And after that, we'll see what happens."

Zuckerberg San Francisco General Hospital and Trauma Center | San Francisco, California

The first thing he noticed was pain. Everywhere. But dulled. Distant. It hurt, but he didn't mind. Mostly.

He opened his eyes, and the room was barely lit. He could hear beeping and whooshing. He tried to raise his hand, but it took a lot of effort. And when it finally moved, he reached up to touch his face, only to find that there was something there. A mask.

He was in a hospital.

He tried to speak, but it came out as a mumble, and he choked a bit on something in his throat. He tried to sit up, but no, that was not happening.

In a moment, however, the door opened. A nurse came in, followed soon after by another, and then eventually a doctor.

They were working on him, shifting him, touching him.

"Agent Symon," the doctor said. She leaned over him, smiled. "Eric. It's good to see you back with us. You had a rough time of it."

He tried again to say something, but they quieted him, told him to rest.

He rested.

He slept.

The next time he opened his eyes, the mask was gone. The beeping was still there, but the whooshing had stopped.

His throat hurt. Everything still hurt. And now he cared.

More nurses. Another doctor. Ice chips and pillows.

Days went by like this.

And then, eventually, Denzel showed up.

He had smiled a lot, said how glad he was that Symon was recovering.

He filled him in on everything.

Derrick Conners' arrest.

Spencer and Faure's arrest.

Mayher's resignation.

That one shocked him.

But the news about Alex Kayne was the weirdest.

"She's officially on the team now," Denzel said. "Director Ludlum has arranged a place for her to live. She has some rules, but she's living by them. So far."

"Rules," Symon rasped, shaking his head, laughing. It hurt. His throat was still raw from the intubation. Everything still took so much effort and energy.

"Alex isn't a fan of rules," he finally continued.

"She's going to have to be, if she wants to stay out of prison," Denzel said.

Sounds like she's in prison anyway, Symon thought.

Picturing Kayne that way, hobbled, limited, it just didn't sit well with him. It just wasn't right. It wasn't natural.

But if it was what she wanted...

"She did it for you, by the way," Denzel said.

"What?" Symon asked, his gut suddenly twisting in dread of what Denzel was saying.

"Came in out of the cold. Took the job. Took on all the rules. She did it for you."

This was not what Symon wanted to hear. Not at all.

They continued talking, and after a while a nurse came in to say it was time for Denzel to leave.

"Rest up," Denzel said. "Recover. It's all waiting for you when you're ready. Take your time."

He left, and the nurse brought Symon a dinner of Jello and

apple sauce. He had no appetite for it, but dutifully and mechanically consumed it.

When he was finally alone again, he reached for his phone. They had relented and let him have it, especially after Denzel had vouched for it.

He unlocked it and sent a message to one of the numbers Kayne had given him.

Is it true?

A moment later, there was a reply.

It's true. Rest up. They aren't giving me a day to come see you for another two weeks. So maybe you can come here instead.

He laughed and typed, *Seems unlikely*.

There was a pause, then, *A lot of unlikely things are happening lately*, Kayne replied.

That, he thought, was true.

They wrapped up their conversation. They'd catch up later, both promised. He needed his rest, and she needed time to adjust to her new life.

As he settled back, drowsing from exertion and medication, he thought about Kayne and QuIEK, Mayher and Historic Crimes. And then he thought about the conversation he'd just finished with Kayne, and about all the restrictions Denzel had told him Kayne had agreed to.

One of those restrictions was that she could only use communications that were strictly monitored. All her back-channel communications were forbidden. From now on, it was only supposed to be her Historic Crimes-issued phone. No burners, no VPNs, no secret numbers. Everything she'd had before had to be turned over, and shut down.

And yet, he'd just had a chat with her on a number that still came up as "unknown."

If they thought they had Kayne on a leash, he thought, smiling, they were deluded.

A NOTE AT THE END

This is not the end.

I know it might have read a little like it was. I'm sorry about that. I wasn't trying to scare you.

But no—*spoilers*—this is not the end.

There will be more Alex Kayne stories. I promise.

This is more like the close of a chapter, and the opening of a new one.

And, if I'm being honest with you and with myself, it's kind of symbolic. There's some overlap, metaphorically, between Alex Kayne's life and my own.

For the past two years, Kara and I have been "van lifers." We've traveled and lived full time in a camper van, moving around the US as we explored new places, met new people, and did our work as we went. I wrote at least six books while in that van and gave a solid start to several more. Those will eventually emerge in the world, ready for your reading.

These two years have been amazing. I loved them. During a time when the whole world was locked down in fear, we actually spent our time discovering freedom that few people get to experience in their lives. I'm grateful.

But things end. That is the nature of reality. Bad things, good things, *all* things. And as good as van life was, it's a chapter coming to a close for us.

Mostly. I mean—the other rule of life is "Who can really predict anything?"

In February 2022, Kara and I closed on a brand new house in the Texas Hill Country. In fact, a little over a year of our time on the road was spent waiting for this house to be built. There were delays—some of which we suspect were the result of shenanigans on the part of the builder. The value of the property went up significantly from what we'd signed a contract to pay, and I very strongly suspect that the builder wanted us to walk, so they could mine that extra revenue.

But since we lived in a van and could call anywhere home, and most of the places we called home were beautiful and offered us a lot of opportunities... well, we could wait. We didn't mind. We weren't uncomfortable by any definition.

And so, eventually the people trying to get us to back out of buying the house realized that we weren't going anywhere (or that we were going *everywhere*), and they caved.

It's amazing how fast the house went from dirt to done once they actually started on it.

So now, here I am. I have an office, once again. I have my desk back. I have my little studio space. And I have a view. It's spectacular, and everything I hoped it would be.

The whole home, the neighborhood, the nearby hiking trails, the towns and cities in every direction—it's exactly what we were hoping for, and in a lot of ways more than we were expecting. It's a good home.

So, we've come off the road. But I'll confess, the road isn't done with us.

I can already feel the tug—I'm already anticipating traveling again. This time by air, probably. Back to going to author conferences and speaking and writing from hotels and cafés. Something similar to life prior to 2020. But with maybe a few more restrictions. Rules. Provisos.

The sort of thing I'm likely to chafe and rebel against. It's just who I am.

And that's why this book, in particular, is likely more symbolic than I had intended it to be.

As we come to a close on this particular chapter of Alex Kayne's life, and we start to open a whole new one, the parallels are pretty obvious. Kayne may be coming off the road, but the road isn't done with her.

I can't rightly predict what's coming next for Alex Kayne or Eric Symon or Julia Mayher, or for QuIEK itself, for that matter. But whatever it is, there's sure to be adventure involved.

And the same is true for me.

Today, I paint a wall of my office. In a couple of weeks, someone comes to hang some screens in my windows. I'll buy and build and install some bookcases from IKEA. And in between all that, I'll write books and blog posts, and record podcasts and do livestreams. I'll produce and create work meant to "inform and inspire, educate and entertain," just as my mission statement dictates.

And, when the urge grows too powerful to resist, I'll hit the road again.

Only this time, I'll have a home to return to.

A new chapter. A new era. A new adventure.

I'm happy with all of it.

Thank you for being a part of it.

This is not the end.

Kevin Tumlinson

26 March 2022
Liberty Hill, Texas

HERE'S HOW TO HELP ME REACH MORE READERS

If you loved this book, you can help me reach more readers with just a few easy acts of kindness.

(1) REVIEW THIS BOOK

Leaving a review for this book is a great way to help other readers find it. Just go to the site where you bought the book, search for the title, and leave a review. It really helps, and I really appreciate it.

(2) SUBSCRIBE TO MY EMAIL LIST

I regularly write a special email to the people on my list, just keeping everyone up to date on what I'm working on. When I announce new book releases, giveaways, or anything else, the people on my list hear about it first. Sometimes, there are special deals I'll *only* give to my list, so it's worth being a part of the crowd.

Join the conversation and get a free ebook, just for signing up! Visit https://www.kevintumlinson.com/joinme.

(3) TELL YOUR FRIENDS

Word of mouth is still the best marketing there is, so I would greatly appreciate it if you'd tell your friends and family about this book, and the others I've written.

You can find a comprehensive list of all of my books at http://kevintumlinson.com/books.

Thanks so much for your help. And thanks for reading.

ABOUT THE AUTHOR

J. Kevin Tumlinson, award-winning and bestselling author of fast-paced, hopeful fiction and inspiring nonfiction. He and his wife Kara live in Texas, and she insists they travel the world to  find new perspectives, new stories, and new tantalizing bits of history and thought to share with his readers.

Kevin grew up in Wild Peach, Texas, where he started learning the craft of storytelling at a young age. He began writing the moment he knew how, and never stopped. And, God willing, never will.

Kevin's love of history, archaeology, science, and philosophy has fueled every word of what he's written, and gives him all the excuse he needs to look closer at anything he finds interesting.

Connect with J. Kevin Tumlinson
jkevintumlinson.com
kevintumlinson.substack.com

ALSO BY J. KEVIN TUMLINSON

The Book of Gods and Kings: Dan Kotler, Books 7-9

Quake Runner: Alex Kayne

Shaken

Triggered

Compromised

Aftershock

Historic Crimes Crossovers

The Man Below

The Outsiders Gambit

Evergreen

Evergreen: Book 1

Evergreen: Trace Contact

Citadel

Citadel: First Colony

Citadel: Paths in Darkness

Citadel: Children of Light

Citadel: The Value of War

Colony Girl: A Citadel Universe Story

Sawyer Jackson

Sawyer Jackson and the Long Land

Sawyer Jackson and the Shadow Strait

Sawyer Jackson and the White Room

Think Tank

Karner Blue

Zero Tolerance

Nomad

The Lucid — Co-authored with Nick Thacker

Episode 1

Episode 2

Episode 3

Shorts & Novellas

Getting Gone

Teresa's Monster

The Three Reasons to Avoid Being Punched in the Face

Tin Man

Two Blocks East

Edge

Zero

God Mode

Collections & Anthologies

Citadel: Omnibus

Uncanny Divide — With Nick Thacker & Will Flora

Light Years — The Complete Science Fiction Library

Dead of Winter: A Christmas Anthology — With Nick Thacker, Jim Heskett, David Berens, M.P. MacDougall, R.A. McGee, Dusty Sharp & Steven Moore

YA & Middle Grade

Secret of the Diamond Sword — An Alex Kotler Mystery

Wordslinger (Non-Fiction)

30-Day Author: Develop a Daily Writing Habit and Write Your Book In 30 Days (Or Less)

Watch for more at kevintumlinson.com/books

KEEP THE ADVENTURE GOING!

GET MORE THRILLS FROM AWARD-WINNING AND BESTSELLING AUTHOR, KEVIN TUMLINSON!

★★★★★ "Half way through I was waiting for Harrison Ford to leap out of the pages!"
—Deanne, Review for *The Coelho Medallion*

★★★★★ "Kevin has crashed onto the action-thriller scene

as only an action-thriller author can: with provocative plot lines, unforgettable characters, and enough adrenaline to keep you awake all night."
—Nick Thacker, author of *Mark for Blood*

★★★★★ "Move over Daniel Silva, James Patterson, and Dan Brown."
—Chip Polk, Review for *The Atlantis Riddle*

★★★★★ "Move Over Indiana Jones, there is a New Dr. in Town!"
—Cycletrash, Review for *The Coelho Medallion*

★★★★★ "[Kevin Tumlinson] is what every writer should be—entertaining and thought-provoking."
— Shana Tehan, Press Secretary, U.S. House of Representatives

★★★★★ "I discovered Kevin Tumlinson from The Creative Penn podcast and immediately got his novel, Evergreen. I read it in like 3 seconds. It's the most fast-paced story I've encountered."
—R.D. Holland, Independent Reviewer

★★★★★ "Comparison to Clive Cussler is a natural, though Tumlinson's 'Dan ' is more like Dan Brown's Robert Langdon than Dirk Pitt."
—Amazon Review for *The Coelho Medallion*

FIND YOUR NEXT FAVORITE BOOK AT
KevinTumlinson.com/books